WE PLAYED WITH FIRE

Also by Catherine Barter

Troublemakers

Shortlisted for the Waterstones Children's Book Prize
Nominated for the CILIP Carnegie Medal
Longlisted for the Branford Boase Award

'A sparky and timely coming-of-age tale about
politics, activism & morality'
Katherine Woodfine

'I loved it, so much so that as soon as I finished I started
reading it again. Completely brilliant'
Keren David

'I couldn't put *Troublemakers* down. It's a real page-turner,
with utterly believable characters who are all trying to do
their best. Barter is a fresh, exciting new voice, and
I can't wait to see what she does next'
Susin Nielsen

'A thought-provoking, richly layered YA novel about politics,
love, grief and coming of age'
Guardian

'Wonderfully individual and heartbreakingly real'
Kirkus, starred review

'A touching, truthful depiction of an unconventional family life'
Observer

'A clever, thoughtful novel with a wonderfully
realistic main character'
Irish Independent

'It's refreshing to see a contemporary YA novel that focuses
so much on family and politics'
Irish Times

CATHERINE BARTER

ANDERSEN PRESS

First published in 2021 by
Andersen Press Limited
20 Vauxhall Bridge Road
London SW1V 2SA
www.andersenpress.co.uk

2 4 6 8 10 9 7 5 3 1

British Library Cataloguing in Publication Data available.

ISBN 978 1 83913 006 9

Printed and bound in Great Britain by Clays Ltd, Elcograf S.p.A.

PART
ONE

ONE
HYDESVILLE
MARCH 1848

They weren't allowed in the cellar.

It was dark and earthy, directly below the kitchen, with a dirt floor, and if you stood still down there, ignoring the sounds from the rooms above, you could feel some kind of movement beneath the ground. Their older brother David had said that it was probably water, running below the house.

Maggie and Kate had left the door at the top of the stairs open. It threw a rectangle of natural light on to the floor.

Kate was holding something. She was standing in the middle of the cellar, her skirt trailing on the ground, getting filthy. There was a narrow slit of light between the ceiling and the far wall. It was bitterly cold.

'What's this?' she said.

'Let me see.'

Kate came forward, holding something out, dirty and yellow, the length of her forearm.

Maggie took it for a moment, felt its weight, and then handed it back. 'It's a human bone.'

Kate frowned, turned it over, looked at Maggie and then back at the bone.

Upstairs, Maggie could hear her mother humming softly as she sat sewing in the parlor.

'A what?' Kate said.

'I think it's a leg bone.'

Some girls might have dropped it then, but Kate held it

up in the light and squinted. 'Whose is it?' A typical Katie question, that nobody could possibly know the answer to.

'Where did you find it?'

'Over there.' She pointed to a cluttered corner of the basement. Rotting bits of wood and an old bucket. 'On the ground.'

Maggie had no idea what it was, except that it was a bone for certain. And something about it was suggestive of some part of a human leg, perhaps. She'd seen sketches of the human skeleton before.

'I know whose it could be,' Maggie said. 'There was a woman who was murdered out here. They hanged her from one of the trees in the woods.'

She could see the war in Kate's head, the way her brow creased: her instinct that she was being lied to against her desire to believe it.

'When?'

'A few years ago. Fifty years ago.'

Kate waited.

'They hanged her because they thought she was possessed by the Devil.'

'They didn't.'

'They did. And when she was dead they cut her down, and they cut her body into parts and scattered them all over the woods so that if the Devil tried to bring her back, she'd be in pieces.'

Upstairs, their mother stopped humming. In a few moments she would probably call their names.

'They didn't,' said Kate.

'But they say that the Devil is still searching for all the pieces, and if you find one of the bones, the Devil will find you too.'

4

Kate blinked slowly. 'I don't believe you. And you're not supposed to tell stories like that anymore.'

'It's not a story. It's true.'

'I don't believe you,' Kate said again, but Maggie could see that she did.

It was possible to believe and not believe something at the same time. It was easy.

TWO

David visited on Thursday afternoon, with Calvin. Maggie heard them coming, and waited on the porch. Pale sunlight was scattered through the trees, and the ground was hard, snow cleared on the main paths but lingering in shaded places were the sun hadn't reached. As David and Calvin climbed down from the horses, they were flushed with cold, breath clouding in front of their faces. Calvin gave her a lazy salute as he walked up to the house. Maggie hit his arm gently as he passed her.

They brought a basket of apples that David had picked up from a neighboring farm, and David presented it to their mother with a kiss. Then they gathered in the kitchen while their mother made coffee and their father examined the apples silently.

'We can't stay long,' said David. 'Have to pick up some supplies from the Taylors' before it gets dark.'

'Can I come back with you?' Maggie said.

Kate elbowed in. 'Can *we* come back with you?'

'I'm not sure—' David began.

'Absolutely not,' their mother said. 'I have a hundred things I need help with.'

'Can I help you with anything, Mrs. Fox?' said Calvin. He'd hung his coat over the back of his chair and pushed his shirtsleeves up to his elbows as if it was a summer day.

'You have your work, Calvin,' she said, with an affectionate smile. She gave Maggie a pointed look. 'And my dear *daughters* need to learn their household duties.'

Calvin still called their mother *Mrs. Fox*, although Maggie wondered why he didn't call her Margaret or even Ma by now. He'd lived with them since he was a boy, fourteen or fifteen, since his parents died. Mr. and Mrs. Fox had taken him in so he could help with the farm work, but he was close in age to David and Leah and so he'd gotten mixed in with them, the oldest Fox children. He'd become part of the family, even if his light hair and blue eyes made him different. Maggie and Kate were just little girls then, but Calvin had been their favourite. He was kinder than Leah, and more fun than David.

When their father had eventually abandoned farming for blacksmithing, and they had moved from town to town while he looked for good work, Calvin came with them.

He'd lived with David the last few months, working on the farm, and Maggie was brutally jealous of them – two men, grown, with work to do, proper work, outdoor work, laughing together. If she'd been born a boy she might be out there too by now.

'All come on Saturday,' said David. 'Snow might've cleared by then.'

'There'll be floods if it has,' their father said dourly. He had begun peeling an apple with a knife. 'These are half rotten,' he added.

'If you want apples in March you'll have to take what you can get,' said David.

'They're lovely,' their mother said. 'Thank you, boys.'

'We saw Mary Redfield on our way here,' said David.

'Did you, how nice,' said their mother, without conviction.

'She was asking about the girls.' David looked at Maggie. 'Said she saw them running around the woods yesterday.'

'We weren't running around,' said Maggie.

'We weren't running around,' Kate echoed.

'What were you doing?'

'Picking flowers,' said Maggie, which seemed like the kind of thing Mary Redfield would expect girls to do.

'Find many?' David raised an eyebrow. It had been a brutal winter and spring had not yet stirred any wild flowers out of the dirt.

'Plenty.'

'Oh, why shouldn't they run around in the woods if they want to?' said their mother.

'Maybe they should be careful, is all,' said David. 'You don't know these woods. You could get lost.'

'Somebody was murdered out there,' said Kate. 'Fifty years ago. They thought she was possessed by the Devil so they hanged her from one of the trees. And then they cut her body—'

'Enough of that,' said their father, putting down the apple and the knife.

'– into pieces, so that—' She hesitated, glanced at Maggie. 'So that – if the Devil found her again – something happens. I can't remember.'

'They cut her into pieces so that the Devil couldn't bring her back to life,' Maggie said.

Scarcely before she'd finished the sentence, their father pounded the table with his fist. '*Enough*,' he said.

A short, cool silence. Sunlight dappled the table.

'Well, of course,' said Calvin lightly. 'You would, wouldn't you?'

'And they say the Devil is still looking for all the pieces,' Maggie said, 'so if you find one of the dead woman's bones—'

Their father stood. His chair scraped the floor. He raised

a hand as if to strike somebody, but then pressed it, shaking, to his forehead instead. *'Enough.'* His face was a knot of anger.

Maggie folded her arms, felt her heart fluttering. She had gone too far.

David cleared his throat. 'It's not the Devil you need to be afraid of out here,' he said. 'It's animals. Wild animals. That's what'll tear you to pieces.'

Their father turned away, to the window. 'There's nothing in these woods.'

Nobody replied.

'You shouldn't tell these stories, Maggie,' said their mother quietly.

David and Calvin exchanged a glance. 'I'm passing along the message that Mary Redfield saw the girls running around the woods, is all,' said David. 'She seemed to think you'd want to know.'

'I don't need to be told what my own children are doing, thank you.'

'I'll be sure to let her know next time.'

'I'm not a child,' Maggie said.

She followed David out to the wagon as Calvin said his goodbyes. 'I could come back to the farm with you,' she said. 'I could. I could help with the children—' David and Maria had so many children she could hardly remember them all sometimes. It had been five, but was it six, now? David wasn't yet thirty but already looked permanently exhausted.

'Come on Saturday.' He adjusted a saddle strap as the horse huffed in the cold and stamped a foot. 'You heard what Ma said. There's work for you to do here.' He looked at her. 'And stop telling stories.'

9

She scowled at him, and wrapped her arms around herself, shivering. 'You don't know what it's like here, David.'

'Plenty worse places you could be.'

'I doubt that.'

'Just do as you're told, Maggie,' he said. 'You won't be here long. Just try and – try and be *quiet*.' He bent to remove a branch that was lodged beneath the front wheel of the wagon. Then he broke it in half over his knee. The crack echoed in the quiet and sent a startled bird flying from a tree.

Kate was pale today. She'd said that she'd woken up with a headache. They both got headaches sometimes, sickening ones. When Maggie came back into the kitchen, Kate was leaning into their mother's side, asking if she could go and lie down.

Fragile as a spring flower, Maggie thought. One of those phrases she'd tried to come up with in Rochester when the teacher tried to get her to write poetry, which Maggie was no good at. *Pale as the moon. Cold as* – something else.

As Kate slipped out of the room, Maggie picked up her shawl and started to wind it around her shoulders. But when she went to fasten it, the silver pin was missing. A silver bird pin that David's wife had given her at Christmas.

She searched the kitchen, the front room, the little room downstairs where her parents slept, the bedroom upstairs, furious with herself at the thought of having lost it. She hardly owned anything nice.

And then she was at the door to the cellar. Their father had gone out again, their mother wasn't paying attention, so she crept back down the steps.

The sound and light and smell of the cellar was as abruptly different as entering a church. Cool and damp and dark.

Their mother had been afraid of the cellar ever since they came here.

She couldn't see her bird pin. She couldn't see the leg bone either, or whatever it was.

If you find one of the bones then the Devil will find you too.

The story already had the quality of a memory. She could see it all – the hanging woman, the creak of the tree, a man with an ax. She could imagine it.

Her imagination. Such a dangerous thing, supposedly. A kind of disease.

Perhaps it wasn't a human leg bone, anyway. Perhaps it was from a horse, or something else, a wolf, a cat. Perhaps it had never been there at all.

Down here alone, she felt something different in the air from before, a sense that the shape of the cellar had shifted a little, that something had moved. There was a pressure around her head, a warning that a headache of her own was on its way. A dark shape at the edge of her vision; a feeling like something was knocking on her brain, wanting to be let in.

Maggie wasn't sure how old the house was. It felt old. It felt used and lived-in, and sometimes it felt as though it was full of scratches and whispers, sounds that made their mother jump and press her hand over her heart.

They would all say it was the wind.

The bird pin wasn't there. Perhaps Kate had stolen it, hidden it under the bedclothes. A thoughtless little crime, just to have something to do. Maggie went back up the stairs, closed the door and locked it. She heard a muffled sound on the other side, like footsteps, following her up.

THREE

At night, in bed, was when she most missed Rochester. The silence of the woods was terrible. Then the dark of the house as the lamps were put out. It was a kind of darkness you would never find in a real place, a city. On nights when there was no moon, their bedroom lost all its shape; there were no corners or walls, only darkness. No sound but the howl of wind and the creak of snow on the roof.

In Rochester there was noise all night. Arguments on the sidewalk outside and stagecoaches rumbling by. There were lights that never stopped burning. And the house had been always full of visitors, guests who came from all over New York State and even further. Political meetings in the kitchen, and shared suppers that lasted for hours. Maggie had never seen such mixtures of people talking in one room. Men and women and young and old and black and white, sharing bread and potatoes and corned beef and talking through the night until it got light outside.

The Foxes – John and Margaret – had only been renting the two front rooms upstairs and didn't mean to stay there long. Amy and Isaac Post said they were welcome as long as they wished, but John repeated every day that he had a piece of land in Arcadia near his son, and would soon be building his own house there, and leaving. In the evening he would close his door against the noise and commotion of the Posts' house, and read his Bible privately.

But Kate and Maggie stayed up as late as they could, and Amy was glad to have them there.

Amy. She wore her hair pinned back, with a serious expression, but there were laughter lines around her eyes. When you spoke she gave you her complete attention. She woke before anybody else, and went to bed later, and everyone marveled at her energy, but what Maggie loved was her stillness. The way she listened. The way she stood in a busy room, and let it move around her.

Amy *wanted* them there. She wanted them to learn. Amy and Isaac were Quakers, and Amy invited her to Quaker meetings where all kinds of ideas were discussed, things Maggie had never thought about before. She gave Maggie books and pamphlets and would ask about them a few days later, hoping that she would have read them.

Maggie tried. She read Frederick Douglass's book, that everybody talked about, and other books about ending slavery, and articles and letters that Amy clipped from *The Liberator*, the abolitionist paper. She read pamphlets about women's rights, and the notes Amy was making in preparation for a convention in the summer, where they would talk about the condition of women and whether they ought to be allowed to vote.

Maggie strained her eyes in the candlelight trying to understand it all, until she was exhausted and disappointed in herself for not knowing enough about anything. Then she would sit with Kate in the corner of the kitchen and watch everybody talk. Kate kept falling in love with all the young men who visited, but Maggie was more interested in the women. Which ones spoke and which ones didn't.

There were two sisters, Elizabeth and Della Reid, from one of the most prominent black families in Rochester, and they often visited. Della was twenty-five or twenty-six, but Elizabeth was younger, maybe not much older than Maggie even, but distant and elegant, and Maggie hardly spoke with her. One evening she saw Elizabeth argue with James Crane, the only time she had ever seen a black woman argue with a white man.

James Crane was important in the Rochester antislavery movement, Amy told her, and raised a lot of money, and helped build new schools and spread progressive ideas. But Elizabeth argued with him as if he was no different than anybody, no different than a woman, until he left the house in a rage.

He had organized an abolition meeting at the Unitarian hall, but no black women were allowed to speak; in fact, it was almost all white people, and Elizabeth objected.

'If we have a hundred voices on a hundred issues we won't accomplish anything,' he said. Maggie remembered that. And Elizabeth saying, 'The only voice you want to hear on *any* issue is your own.' And Mr. Crane slamming the door as he left.

'He'd like our race to be free from slavery so long as he doesn't have to talk to any of us,' Elizabeth said afterward, to hesitant laughter. Her voice was perfectly calm and steady, although Maggie could see that she had her hands pressed flat against the table as if to keep them from shaking.

Della left Rochester. She went away and gave lectures, and even went to Europe. But Elizabeth stayed. She was part of a black church a few blocks from Amy and Isaac's house, the African Methodist Church, a new one-story wooden church where they helped shelter runaway slaves. Maggie wasn't supposed to know that.

She found herself writing their names sometimes, when

she was practicing her handwriting. *Elizabeth Reid. Della Reid.*

They were women Maggie thought she could learn from. She could make herself better, braver and more principled. Any day, she thought, she might have something to say herself, and she might find the courage to say it.

That was Rochester. Anyway, it had all been ruined.

It got dark after David and Calvin left. Night crept into the house from the corners. Their father read his Bible and got ready for bed. Their mother sat sewing for a little while, then followed him. It was barely nine o'clock. There was nothing left to do. Maggie sat by the stove for a while, until her father came out of his room to tell her the light was disturbing him, and to go to bed.

She took the candle from the kitchen table up to their room, where Kate was lying across the bed with her head hanging over the edge, her dark hair undone, spooling out on to the floor.

'I can't sleep,' she said.

Maggie set the candle by the bed. 'If you lie like that, all your blood will run up into your brain,' she said, 'and you'll die.'

Upside down, Kate made some sort of face at Maggie, and then bent her arms back over her head, put her hands flat on the floor, and somehow rolled herself off the bed, backward, until she was sitting on the floor, her nightdress tangled around her legs. She looked up, smiling, as if she expected applause.

Kate was twelve. She was strange. She was in a shifting place, like two people in the same body. A sweet child's face turned toward you, and then a few minutes later there would

15

be a turn to her mouth and she was somebody different, somebody Maggie didn't know.

There was a sudden bang on the floor from the room below, and their father's voice— 'Quiet up there!' – which startled them both, and then sent Kate into helpless floods of laughter. She got like this sometimes, at bedtime. Maggie used to laugh with her, but lately she only felt a flat, heavy sensation at night, a desire to be asleep and not have to think anymore.

She dressed for bed in the flickering light, and then got beneath the covers, thrusting her bare feet under the extra blankets that they'd piled on top of the sheets. Kate crawled in next to her and blew out the candle.

She waited until Kate had settled, and then kicked her.

'*Ow.*'

'I can't find my silver bird pin,' Maggie whispered. 'Did you take it?'

'No.'

'Are you sure?'

'I didn't take it.'

'I don't believe you.'

'I didn't.'

'You're a liar.'

'*You're* a liar.' Kate wriggled around on to her side and propped her head up on her hand. 'Maybe the Devil took it when he came to find you.'

Maggie rolled away from her and faced the wall. 'He'll be coming to find *you*, Katie. It was you that found the bone.'

'I'll send him to you.'

'I'll send him back.'

Kate was silent for a moment, then whispered, 'He could be coming up the stairs right now.'

They shouldn't talk like this. Maggie twisted on to her back. 'Katie—'

'If you say the Devil's name in the darkness, he hears you.'

'Then don't say his name,' Maggie said.

'I already did.'

She couldn't help herself. 'Then he'll come for you.'

'I'll send him—'

'I think he's here already.' She made her body rigid, grabbed Kate's arm. '*He's under the bed, he's reaching up—*'

'*No.*' Katie's voice rose to a frantic whisper. She had always been scared of things under the bed. 'That's not fun. Stop it.'

'He's reaching out from underneath right now with his claws—'

'*No!*' Katie scrambled to sit up and shoved Maggie so hard that the bed rocked, and knocked against the table, where Kate had left an apple. It fell to the floor and hit the bare floorboards and rolled.

In the quiet of the house at night they may as well have hit two pans together.

When it finally stopped rolling, the house was silent again for a tiny moment, before they both heard the thud of feet downstairs – somebody getting out of bed – a shuffling, the downstairs bedroom door opening, and somebody thumping upstairs. Maggie half fell from the bed to pick up the apple and shove it under the covers. Katie grabbed Maggie's arm, and Maggie grabbed hers, so that when their father flung open the door they were clinging to each other, eyes wide, ready for the flare of his temper. Their mother was a few steps behind him, holding a lamp.

'It's night-time,' he began, 'and I will not have—'

'It wasn't us,' said Maggie, without thinking, then

regretted it. It would only remind him of her sobbing on the Posts' kitchen floor. *It wasn't me, I didn't do it—*

But Kate obediently echoed, 'It wasn't.'

His face was hard. 'This is my house,' he said.

'John!' said their mother. 'John, the girls! They're terrified. Look at them.'

Given this unexpected cue, they both rearranged their faces into expressions of terror.

In a trembling voice, Katie said, 'We heard it too. It came from the attic.'

Maggie didn't look at her. 'Yes. The attic.'

Even their father, Maggie suspected, was fearful about the attic. They had never lived in a house with an attic before. Nobody had been up there since the day they arrived.

She could see him struggling to understand. 'What's this, now?'

'*Ma,*' Kate said, almost tearful. 'Something was pounding on the ceiling.'

That was too much. Maggie squeezed Kate's arm harder.

'We felt the bed shaking!' said Kate, and Maggie tightened her grip so that she'd almost certainly leave a bruise.

'My God,' said their mother. 'John.'

'I won't have this,' said John. 'I won't – everybody will go to sleep.'

'They're frightened,' said their mother, and he narrowed his eyes and said, 'They're not.'

When their parents had returned to bed, their father's anger left a trace, like smoke, and they waited for it to fade before they spoke again. The wind moaned outside.

Eventually Kate said softly, 'Will you look under the bed?'

'No.'

'Please.'

'Why?'

'I just have a bad feeling.'

'You have a bad feeling from all the lies you've been telling.'

'I heard something.'

'The Devil isn't under the bed,' Maggie said. Then, with daring: 'The Devil isn't real.'

Katie paused, and then whispered, 'Of course he is.'

So Maggie looked. She ought to act like a big sister and be reassuring. She hung her head over the edge of the bed, and let her eyes adjust to the gloom. There was an old wooden trunk, and a pair of shoes, but nothing else, only the dusty surface of the floor and the crooked line where it met the wall.

FOUR

The Devil isn't real.

It wasn't quite what Amy had said. Maggie had been toiling over some dreary bit of writing about sin and temptation, plucking a few scraps from the Bible and throwing in a few half-formed ideas about Satan that she thought her teacher would like.

Amy liked to help her with schoolwork. Not in the dismal, correct-your-spelling way that their father helped. She liked to talk about ideas. She would say things like: 'That's what your teacher thinks. What do *you* think?' Or, more revolutionary: 'That's what the Bible says. What would *you* say?'

She looked at Maggie's essay, smiled, and said, 'Is this how you see the Devil?'

'I suppose.'

'With hooves and a tail?'

'That's what he looks like in pictures.'

'Seducing us into sin?'

'I suppose.'

'I wonder if sin could be a little more complicated than that.'

'Should I change it?'

'When we're thinking about sin, I wonder if we should worry less about a man with a pitchfork, and more about ourselves and the way we choose to live in the world.'

Amy often began sentences like this, with *I wonder*, when she spoke to Maggie. As if she didn't want to tell Maggie what to think – she only wanted to shake an idea gently, to see if it would come loose.

Maggie had begun to change while she was in Rochester. It wasn't just the energy of the city, or the meetings, or Amy's books and pamphlets. It was something inside her. Some kind of movement, some new, dangerous kind of energy in her body.

She would feel it start in her joints, a sparkling, painful feeling, then spread through her body and up her throat. Till she'd press her face to the pillow at night sometimes, wanting to scream, or she'd bite the back of her hand, or she'd feel that she could throw a chair across the room, and she'd feel it rising in her, the strength to do it. *I hate you*, she'd think, about nobody in particular, just an all-over sensation, rising up and then pouring out of her.

Then she'd think: *I am a bad person*. And turn the hate back in on herself. She'd stand out on the porch of Amy and Isaac's house till her father dragged her back inside.

And sometimes she'd think she might cry, at the sight of a bird, or the sound of rain on leaves, or with a sudden powerful love for her mother, sitting at the table with a book of some kind, one of Amy's. And then she tipped over into fury again, at all of them, for being themselves, for not knowing her, but imagining they did. And then calm; she'd lean into her mother's side, look at whatever she was reading, hold a candle closer to the page so her mother could see it.

And then Amy would ask her: 'Is this how you see the Devil?'

Not a man with a pitchfork, perhaps, but she couldn't help feeling he was a man of some kind, or that he took a man's form. Perhaps just an ordinary man, a thin white man, wearing a suit. That was how she began to think of him. She drew a picture, in the corner of her writing book, a man in formal clothes with a long face and flat, glinting eyes like coins. Then the picture frightened her, and she scribbled it out.

The next day, her father was nailing a board across the cellar door. Maggie halted at the kitchen table. His spine was bent as he held the board in place with his shoulder, hit a nail cleanly five times into the top left corner. He held another nail in his mouth, took it out and started carefully on the lower corner.

'What are you doing?'

He straightened up, rapped his knuckles against the board as if to test its stability, and gave her a brief look that suggested he thought this was a foolish question.

Maggie revised it. 'Why are you doing that?'

'Your mother,' he said.

'She's down there?'

'She's hearing things. Thinks there's an animal. Something coming up the stairs.'

'There's nothing down there. We were both down—' She stopped herself. 'I mean – *is* there anything down there?'

He frowned. 'If there is then it's not getting out.'

She felt a thrum of anxiety at the thought of the door being sealed permanently. What if her bird pin was still down there? She might have missed it last time.

And besides, it was a forbidden place. A shame to lose it.

'But if something gets trapped, won't it die?'

'It will.'

This fact clearly meant little to him, so Maggie said tentatively, 'Won't it smell?'

'It'll likely freeze in this temperature.'

'But when it gets warm.'

'We'll be leaving when it gets warm.'

'Oh.'

'Not too long now, I expect.'

He smiled at her. He was happy when he thought about the house they were building, out near David's farm. Kept promising he'd be back to work on it within weeks, they'd be moving before summer. It would be the first house they lived in that was their own.

He looked back at the door. 'In the meantime, that should put a stop to it.'

Maggie looked at the sealed-off door. The board was scratched and dented, a piece of wood he had salvaged from somewhere. 'I hear things too,' she said. 'Down there. And Katie too. This house—'

'None of that.' He turned away and bent down to place his hammer back in the bag of tools at his feet. 'This is a fine house.'

He didn't want to be here anymore than the rest of them, she knew, but it had been his decision to come, and he was determined to defend it. Defend it with blunt tools and planks of wood, if necessary.

'Won't the next family who live here be angry that you've boarded up the cellar?'

'That's up to them.'

'Couldn't you have asked us what *we* thought?'

The kitchen door rattled slightly at a gust of wind. Outside, Maggie could hear the door to the small barn swinging back and forth, slamming shut and creaking open again. It was built on the north corner of the house where the wind was the worst.

23

'What who thought?'

'Me. Katie.'

'Your thoughts aren't required. On this or any other matter.'

That sparkling feeling in her joints was back: it sent tingles to her hands, made them shake. 'We live here too,' she said.

'You live with me, under my roof. You all do.'

'But—'

'That's enough, Margaretta.' He didn't look at her, but began wrapping a leather cord back around his tool bag. 'I won't have every decision I make questioned. Do you understand?'

There was a faint tremor in the air, as there always was when he gave a command: a moment of doubt as to whether it would be obeyed.

Kate was still in bed. She claimed to have another headache. Maggie came into the room, sat next to her and placed a hand on her forehead. Kate pushed her away. She was very pale, and blue under the eyes. But she often looked that way. They were all pale, the Fox sisters, Kate, Maggie and Leah too. Sickly-looking. Amazing they had all survived. Some women's faces reddened as they got older, with sun or exertion, but Leah was over thirty now and pale as ever.

'Go away,' Kate said.

Maggie looked out of the small window at a gray sky and the sharp branches of the tree nearest the house. It was an old birch that had been nearly torn from its roots during a storm and now leaned sideways. It was surely, their mother said, going to fall and kill one of them soon.

'He's boarded up the cellar,' she said.

Kate scrunched her face. 'Why?'

'He said Mother was hearing things down there.'

'There is something down there.'

Something prickled across Maggie's skin. Kate's eyes were blank and glassy, like the surface of dark water. 'There's not.'

'There is. We shouldn't have gone down there.'

'Well, we did,' said Maggie.

'We shouldn't have.'

'But we did.'

'I don't want to go down there again.'

'Just as well, because now you can't.'

With a lot of effort, Kate wriggled her way out of a tangle of bedsheets and sat up. 'What did she hear?'

'She thought something was coming up the stairs.'

'Did he believe her?'

'Of course he didn't. He thinks we're all just silly women. Silly girls. Hearing things.'

Kate blinked. Her braids had come loose and hair curled at her forehead.

Kate was easily turned against their father. His lack of interest in Maggie's opinions was nothing compared to his lack of interest in Kate's. She may as well have been garbling nonsense for all the attention their father ever paid to her. In Rochester, her tearful proclamations that Maggie was telling the truth, she had to be – they hadn't even warranted their father's anger. He simply ignored her.

'He doesn't know anything,' Kate said.

Maggie stood up and went to the window, pressed her forehead against the glass. She felt a passing urge to pick up a lamp or a candlestick or something, and smash it, and then smash all the windows in the house and run out into the forest screaming. That would give Mary Redfield something to talk about.

'I'm so tired of him,' Kate said.

Tired. Yes, there was something exhausting about him – talking to him was like throwing yourself against a wall over and over, hoping it would break. But tiredness had its own strange energy. When they were little girls they used to try and stay up all night together, just to see what it was like. Deep into the night, long past midnight, they'd tip out of exhaustion into a wild, stupid wakefulness.

They had played all kinds of games, as children, as if they found trouble irresistible. Hiding under the bed. Impressions of their teachers. Moving their father's tools so that he couldn't find them. It was satisfying and thrilling and frightening to break his silence into anger, to see what he might do.

Maggie scuffed her foot against one of the uneven wooden floorboards. They were all uneven, she saw, when she looked carefully, and the floor sloped downwards to the east corner, where a tiny gap between the floor and the wall showed a sliver of light from the kitchen. It must be all the crooked floors and loose boards that filled the house with those strange sounds, creaks and bangs that came from nowhere.

What would it take to scare him?

What would it take? What would he look like, if he was afraid? What would he look like if he believed her?

She heard him cough, downstairs, and a chair scrape the kitchen floor. He would sit and look at the cellar door now, considering his work.

Why stop at the cellar? Why not board up the windows, their bedrooms, the front door? A closed-up space could be controlled.

26

She thought of that apple, hitting the floor and rolling. Such a simple thing.

'We could play a game,' she said. 'Which one of us can make him think there's a ghost in the house.'

'That would be fun.' Kate lifted her head. A little color came back to her cheeks. 'Let's do that.'

Their voices were lowered. She couldn't hear him, downstairs, but she could sense him there, sitting at the table, breathing.

'Whichever one of us can do it—'

'No,' said Kate. 'I want to do it together. I don't want to do it on my own.'

She didn't want to get caught on her own, get in trouble on her own.

'Fine.'

'Oh, good,' said Kate, smiling. 'Fun.'

'Good.' Maggie looked back out at the jagged outlines of the branches against the sky. 'I have some ideas.'

If she could make him only *doubt* himself for a moment.

Their mother went to bed first that night, and they lay upstairs together in the dark waiting for their father to leave the kitchen, where he sat, as always, reading his Bible.

When they heard him go to the bedroom, they waited until he would be in bed. They waited until the dark and quiet had settled completely.

Then Kate darted barefoot across the floor to the other side of the room and struck a candlestick five times against a loose floorboard. They'd tried it earlier, while nobody was paying attention. A strike on this particular floorboard produced a strange effect, a hollow sound that seemed to come from the kitchen.

27

At Kate's fifth strike, Maggie leaned over the bed and tapped on a floorboard beneath it with a candlestick of her own. Another five taps: and when she finished, Kate had already flown back across the room and into bed.

Neither of their parents could have been asleep, because the thud of footsteps and murmur of voices downstairs was almost instant. They both closed their eyes, leveled out their breathing, and when they heard the door open and their father whisper back downstairs, 'They're both asleep', they didn't move. Maggie could feel him still standing there, his body in the doorway, the dark shape of him. She could imagine his expression, the set of his jaw.

When he went back downstairs, Kate pressed her hand over her mouth to stop herself laughing, and then whispered, 'Let's do it again,' but Maggie told her no. Not yet. It was worth a little patience.

Downstairs, their parents' voices rose and fell, in and out of earshot.

'– kind of *bird* could possibly—'

'– an old house, plenty of ways—'

'– the girls are only—'

'– the girls might even have—'

'– the girls' room, we should—'

The girls, the girls, the girls.

The next day their father came into their room with his tools, prized up floorboards, moved their bed, knocked on the walls with a hammer. They pretended to have heard nothing.

'You should sleep downstairs with us tonight,' their mother told them, fretting, but enjoying herself a little too. 'It was pounding on the walls. *Pounding.*'

'Pounding is hardly the word I'd use,' said their father.

'You ought to look in the attic.'

Their father paused, inspected the hammer he was holding. 'I will, then.'

'You ought to.'

'I said I will.'

'I'm going to ask the Weekmans about this,' said their mother.

'Perhaps if the Weekmans had done a few repairs from time to time on this place,' he said, 'we might be able to have a peaceful night's sleep.'

Their mother tutted. 'Oh, James Weekman can't tell a hammer from his own—'

'Enough,' said their father. 'There's no need to talk to anybody about a few noises in an old house.'

'I'll talk to whomever I please.'

John looked at his wife, and then his daughters. Maggie met his eye and held it. 'Let's not get the girls excited,' he said.

The next night, they tried ten strikes each, hitting the floorboards harder this time. The following night, a door slammed and a chair knocked over. Early in the morning, a slower, softer tap on the floor, with a piece of wood they'd found in the forest.

The following night, they lay in bed and wondered whether to do it again, the candlesticks perhaps.

'Just three knocks,' Kate said. 'That's all. I'll do three knocks on the corner floorboard, just before they go to sleep, and then I'll come to bed and they'll never—'

'I don't know.' Maggie rolled over on her side, looked at the outline of Kate's face in the moonlight. 'If we just do the same thing over and over it gets dull. An actual ghost wouldn't do the same thing over and over, would it?'

'It would. That's what ghosts *do*. They walk the same path over and over, in the house where they died or something.'

The room was cold. Maggie had been in bed long enough that her body was warm, beneath the piles of sheets and blankets, but her head was cold, her scalp, the tip of her nose. It was tempting to go downstairs and stoke the fire, sit in front of it for a while. 'Who told you that?' she said to Kate.

'I don't know. I thought everybody knew. You should know, after you saw—'

'No.' Maggie rolled on to her back and looked at the ceiling, where she could see the shifting shadows of the trees outside. 'Not tonight. It gets dull.'

Kate complained a bit but it had never taken much for her to fall asleep once she closed her eyes, and soon Maggie was listening to the slow, even sound of her breathing.

She was half asleep herself when she heard, or thought she heard, three gentle taps in the corner of the room, and she mumbled, 'Katie, stop,' before she reached out and found her sister's body, still and warm and sleeping. Something was wrong, she thought, something didn't make sense, but her mind was already closing and she couldn't hold on to the thought, until it came back to her when she woke in the morning and her eyes fell on the empty corner. She had woken earlier than anybody else, and the house was silent. Kate was asleep. But she did not feel alone.

'Hello?' she whispered into the quiet room, but of course there was no reply.

She slipped out of bed, the cold floor painful against her bare feet, and stood at the top of the stairs. Nobody awake. The house was all hers. She tapped her fingers gently against the door frame, and then pressed her ear to the wood, half expecting a response.

It was like holding a seashell to your ear, but instead of hearing the sea, she heard the house: creaks and groans deep in the frame, cold timbers rattling in the wind. The weight of the snow and the tiny creatures in the earth beneath them.

It occurred to her that it had always felt alive, this house, or something close to alive. Felt as if it was listening to them. She tapped her fingers again, then heard footsteps downstairs, coughing. Her father was awake.

He had taken to roaming the house each morning, pressing his own ear to the walls and looking beneath Maggie and Kate's bed. Behind their closet. He was quiet, listening to Maggie and Kate and their mother catalog each strange noise and movement excitedly. Quiet with the anger of a man for whom something had slipped beyond his control.

FIVE

There was a history in their family that was mostly unspoken.

John Fox was a religious man. A serious man. The head of their family.

But not always.

For a time before Maggie and Kate were born, their father was a different sort of man.

Maggie had learned this in scraps, in whispers, in muttered remarks and the scornful look on her older siblings' faces whenever their father lectured them about morality.

Leah, the eldest, told Maggie that drink had made John angry, then sad, then reckless, then angry again. When he was sad he would sometimes cry in the street, wander aimlessly until somebody brought him home. When he was angry, he would find his wife or one of his children and try to draw them into his anger so that he would have an excuse to rage at them. He didn't hit Leah, but David, from time to time, did something to deserve it.

When he was reckless he would gamble.

Their mother left. She took the children and went to her sister's.

When John sought them out, a decade later, he had found God. His eyes were clear, his clothes clean, his voice serious. He was out of the wilderness.

She took him back. They moved north. Maggie was born soon after.

And it was true that Maggie had never seen him drink, never known him to gamble, never known him to stay away all night. His anger, still easily stoked, now turned quickly into a hard silence; he'd never raised his fists. He read his Bible every day, wire spectacles resting on the end of his nose.

But she knew these things had happened.

She sometimes thought about him leaving again.

It was easy to imagine his absence. He was so often silent. But the money he brought home, they depended on that. It was hard to imagine that David could support all of them. Leah earned money in Rochester by teaching piano, but not enough. Not enough to support even her own daughter, who was nearly seventeen now. Lizzie had gone to live with her father in New York City, months ago, and Leah was living alone.

Maggie was almost old enough to find work of some kind – but she doubted she could teach, and it wasn't clear to her what else she might do. Her sewing was bad. She could hire herself for some other sort of housework but she had no aptitude for any of it. Factory work filled her with dread. Anyway, she knew from the way people spoke about Leah that it would be considered a failure for her to have to work. She ought to find a husband and set herself to work making cakes and stews and keeping the house warm for him.

Although Leah had tried that, and look what happened. He'd left one weekend for a business trip and never returned. Left Leah, aged sixteen, with baby Lizzie and not much else. There was some doubt as to whether they had even divorced, though Leah claimed they had. So.

What Maggie really wanted was to go back to the city, and to explain to everybody that she was not wicked. She was not what they thought she was. Back in December, when they'd first arrived in Hydesville, Maggie had lain in bed day after day, looking at the blank walls, the lonely, mismatched pieces of furniture – a chair, a closet, a small table. She had placed her own things, the few things she cared about, in a small box in the corner: the Bible she'd had since she was a little girl, her silver pin, some pamphlets that Amy had given to her.

She was supposed to be sick, that's what everybody had been told. That she had been fevered, delirious, that she had not known what she was seeing or saying. They were taking her to the country to recover.

They made it true, somehow. She *was* sick. When they arrived in Hydesville she felt weak and her throat was sore. It took too much energy to talk. Her mother piled extra bedclothes on top of her and her father left her alone. Headaches came and went, and shadows crowded at the edge of her vision, black spots crawled across the walls. Sometimes when she closed her eyes she saw a bright slash of yellow on a dark road. A little girl with twisted arms.

She might have lain in bed for weeks, except that Calvin visited her, as serious and anxious as if he'd been told that she was dying. Perhaps he thought she was. He'd brought her some chocolates that he must have traveled out of his way to buy. And Calvin knew about sickness. He had lost his parents. So she felt ashamed. She got out of bed, and brushed her hair, and told everybody that she was better.

And for a while, Maggie had tried to be good. Tried to be quiet, and pleasant, and well-behaved. She would not apologize, she refused, but she tried not to make up stories, the way she used to for fun. She tried to be the kind of young woman who would be allowed, any minute, to go back to

Rochester and resume the life she had been just on the brink of living. But Christmas came and went, and then a bitter, dark January, and February when the snow never stopped, and now March, with the wind so cold it felt as if it could break bones, and here they were, still.

SIX

They should stop, they told each other. They didn't stop.

The sound of an apple hitting the floor was surprisingly loud and, in the middle of the night, strange. But apples got soft. A chair scraping suddenly across the floor, when everybody was supposed to be asleep, was effective. A spoon hit against the side of a lamp was eerie if their bedroom door was open. Sometimes they did nothing, but in the morning they would tell their parents that their room had been filled with strange creaks and moans all night.

And sometimes their mother would say, *Yes, I heard it too.*

The stories they made up dropped seeds, sprung up saplings of their own.

'The girls are very sensitive to it,' she heard her mother tell Mary Redfield. 'If there's something in the house, it's the girls that it's drawn to.' Then she'd tell Mary Redfield about her grandmother, who supposedly had had visions. 'The girls might have the gift,' she said. 'They say it passes down the female line.' She took a sip of coffee. 'A blessing and a burden.'

Maggie waited, breathless, at the bottom of the stairs, hoping she would say more, but Mary changed the subject to the strange behavior of one of her horses and Maggie couldn't bring herself to ask her mother if it was true, about the grandmother with the gift, if her mother believed it, and if she believed that, then why couldn't she believe her about Rochester.

*

They could both crack their joints, since they were little girls, and it was their father who told them back then that other people did not find this as entertaining as they did.

Like many facts about his daughters, Maggie knew he'd already forgotten.

It was Kate's idea, on a Friday morning, that they ought to be able to scare their parents when they were actually in the same room. Kate's idea that there might finally be a use for their bone-cracking talent.

She practiced, pressing her feet against the end of the bed. 'Can you tell what I'm doing?' she said, as the short, sharp cracks sounded.

'No.' Katie's feet didn't appear to be moving, which made it unclear where the sound was coming from. Even looking at her bare feet, Maggie couldn't really tell that it was her sister's own bones making that sound.

'Can you do this?' Kate sat up properly, cracked her knuckles to punctuate the question.

'You know I can.'

'As well as I can?'

Maggie gave her a tired look. 'Yes.'

Kate swung her legs around to the edge of the bed and put her feet on the floor. She did it again: three sharp, rapid cracks.

'You'll hurt yourself,' Maggie said.

'I don't think so. You try it.'

Maggie hesitated, not wanting to do something because her baby sister had told her to, but not wanting to suggest that she couldn't do it.

'Fine.' She didn't bother to sit down. She cracked her knuckles – that was easy – and then stretched up on tiptoes, trying to feel those places in her feet where the bones were loose and could snap back and forth in place.

She came down again on her heels, cracked each of the toes on her left foot in succession. It was louder, better, than Kate had done it.

Some people were beautiful, some people were intelligent: Maggie and Kate could crack their own bones. You had to make the best of what you were given.

Kate was smiling. 'It's horrible.'

Irritating that Kate had the idea and not her, but Maggie couldn't deny it had potential.

'They wouldn't know it was us,' Kate said. 'Not even in the same room. I don't think they would. Do you think they would?'

It had the virtue of not sounding like a noise the human body ought to be able to make. Bones were not supposed to be heard, unless they were breaking.

Their mother was coming up the stairs. She opened their door, peered at them. 'What are you both doing?' she said. And then, 'It's freezing up here.'

'There's a crack in the window,' Maggie said.

'How did that happen?'

'I don't know.'

Maggie had only noticed the crack that morning – thin as a human hair, crossing the top corner of the window in a straight line. Perhaps a bird had flown into the window.

She was reluctant to tell her father, who would probably nail a board over it.

A sound, like feet crunching on ice. Their mother's eyes went wide. 'What was that?' she said.

Kate was silent.

'I don't know,' said Maggie, and improvised: 'We heard it before. It sounds like something in the floor.'

'Dear Lord,' she said. 'This house—'

38

'It's as if something's trying to talk, Mama,' said Katie.

Maggie wanted to laugh at her sister's little-girl voice.

'You come downstairs, both of you,' their mother said. 'My sweet girls, freezing to death in their own room.'

She turned and went downstairs again. Before they followed, Maggie nudged her sister. 'Why did you do that?'

'Why did *you*?' said Kate.

Kate never quite knew when to stop, that was the problem with the whole enterprise. Maggie wanted to control the game and its boundaries, but Kate got too excited.

'That's enough for today,' Maggie said, and Kate gave her a petulant look, cracked her knuckles pointedly.

SEVEN

The smell of snow was in the air but for the moment the sky was low and white and still. Her mother had tried stuffing all of their shoes with straw to make them warmer, but Maggie's feet were still cold, and now they itched. She had been sent, alone, to the small post office on the main street where her mother thought there might be a letter from her cousins in Buffalo, or from Leah. She'd borrowed her mother's thick gray shawl and wrapped it twice around her shoulders, and halfway across her face, then fastened her black wool cloak over it. The cloak had been Leah's once, and was wearing thin, and above the shawl her eyes were dry and raw in the bitter air. Still, it was good to be away from the house, and on her own, feeling her heart beat faster as she followed the upward slope of the road to the center of Hydesville.

It was hardly even a village, much less a town. The main street was still scattered with trees, and bounded by forest. None of the buildings – a grocer, a tavern, the post office and the blacksmith's where her father had found work – looked permanent.

A boy her own age worked at the post office, Stephen Whitaker. She liked his sharp cheekbones and the way his mouth curved, but he was nervous and awkward, and she associated him with disappointment: each visit, she hoped desperately that there would be a letter for her, with a Rochester postmark, and there never was. She understood that Amy couldn't have written to her at first – they had left the city so quickly, and Amy had been in the middle of all kinds of activity, organizing the convention and gathering signatures for a petition. But now time had passed—

There was no other explanation but that Amy had not forgiven her. She believed James Crane. She believed that Maggie was a wicked girl who invented ghost stories to cover up her own sins.

The street was almost empty, and when Maggie went into the post office, for a moment she thought that it was empty too, until Stephen stood up from behind the counter, brushing his hands against his shirt. He blinked at her, startled. 'Thought I saw a rat down there,' he said.

Instinctively, Maggie took a step back, casting her eyes across the floor.

'You're not scared of rats, are you?' he said.

'Of course not.'

'I didn't think so. You must see them all the time in your house, with the creek so close.'

She was vaguely insulted. 'No.' She had never seen rats around the house, in fact, which was itself strange.

'You must hear them, then. That's why the Weekmans moved out of your place. They said they were hearing things.' He smiled at her, as if he was sharing a secret. 'They thought it was haunted. Did you hear that story?'

She blinked, thinking for a moment that she had misheard. Her heart began to beat a little faster, as if she'd been caught in a lie, which was silly. She rubbed her hands together for warmth and tried to look uninterested. 'No. Haunted by what?'

'I don't know. They just said they heard strange sounds. But it's just – I mean, it's rats, isn't it?'

For a moment she wondered if he was making fun of her. If he'd heard what happened in Rochester and wanted to laugh at her, the ghost-girl. But she wasn't sure he had the wits for something like that.

Questions rose in her mind: who else had heard this story? Could their father have heard it? What *kind* of sounds?

But somebody else came in behind her, a man she didn't recognize, and she didn't want to ask any more in front of him.

'Are there any letters for us?' she said faintly, and Stephen glanced backward at the stack of mail, but she already knew the answer was no.

Perhaps she should run home and tell everybody what Stephen had told her – *listen, it's true, it isn't only us* – but she was confused, as if the story had been stolen from her somehow. Weren't they only pretending? It left her with an uneasy, cold feeling.

She took a route home that cut through the small Hydesville graveyard, on a sloping, scrabbly patch of land in sight of the church but surely a little too far, she had always thought, to really be hallowed ground. Not that it was her place to say so. It was a quiet place where she liked to walk, even if it reminded her sometimes of the cemetery behind the schoolhouse in Rochester.

Wandering the graveyard, she looked for familiar names. There were some Whitakers – Jeremiah, Patience: Stephen's family had been here a long time. A lot of the graves were very old, with names worn away by the weather and hardly readable. The first inhabitants of Hydesville.

They would've been pioneers then, just like the ones buried behind the school. Staking out a new town in the forest, the ground fertile and space abundant. Americans, proudly pushing back the wilderness, bringing order and community and progress.

She'd read stories about things like this as a girl. When New York State was a wilderness. Even as a child, she'd sensed there was something not quite honest about those stories, but it was hard to name what it was. And nobody liked children to question truths that were held sacred.

EIGHT

Something was happening at the house.

Mary Redfield was standing outside, with Kate and their mother. They were all looking up at the window of the upstairs bedroom. Their mother had her arm around Kate, who leaned into her side, and Mary Redfield was twisting a handkerchief in her hands.

Maggie approached them. She looked up at the window, but there was nothing to see, just the small dark square of glass. Katie turned her head away, pressed her face against her mother's coat like a child.

'Where have you been?' her mother said. 'It's no more than a ten-minute walk to the post office, Maggie.'

'Why are you all standing out here?'

'I was just visiting—' Mary Redfield began.

'We were in the kitchen,' said her mother. 'Katie was helping me with the shirts.'

'We were all in the kitchen,' said Mary. 'All of us.'

'I thought he was upstairs,' said their mother. 'Your father. I thought he was upstairs. He'd promised to look in the attic.'

Maggie suddenly felt something wet on her face. She looked up. The sky was gray. It had started to snow again.

'I was just visiting,' Mary said again. Her face was drawn. Her lips were chapped with cold.

'Can we go inside?' said Maggie.

Kate drew her face away from their mother's coat and

44

looked at Maggie. She looked small, pale, fragile, but there was something flinty in her voice when she said, 'No.'

'It's starting to snow.'

'We were all in the kitchen,' her mother went on, 'and your father called down from your bedroom – he said, *Where's Maggie gone?*'

For a moment, the story stopped there, and Maggie wrapped her arms around herself, and said, 'Why don't we all—'

'It wasn't him,' said Mary. 'It wasn't your father who was upstairs.'

'Your father came in the kitchen door.' Maggie's mother's eyes were wide. 'We thought he was upstairs, I could hear him upstairs, and then he came in the kitchen door.'

'A man asked where you had gone,' said Mary. 'A man's voice *called down*.'

Tiny snowflakes began to gather on her mother's dark hair. Kate turned her face away again.

'Mercy on us,' Mary whispered to herself.

The front door swung open, creaking on its hinges, and John came out. He was holding a hammer. He coughed. 'There's nothing,' he said. 'No one up there.'

'The attic,' her mother said.

'No one in the attic.'

'Did you look?'

'I looked.'

'John—'

'Margaret, I looked,' he said, gentle but firm.

'A man's voice.' Mary was twisting the edge of her shawl in her hand. 'A man's voice.'

'I looked,' said John. 'I looked.'

*

'How did you do it?' said Maggie.

On a makeshift bed in Mary Redfield's front room, Maggie took Kate's hand. It had been hours since it happened; she'd had to wait until the others left them alone. It was dark outside now, and Mary was still moving from room to room, lighting lamps. Mr Redfield had not yet returned from work.

Kate took her hand back, and tucked herself against the wall, a blanket up to her chin.

'How did you do it?'

'I didn't,' said Kate.

'Katie—'

'I didn't. How could I?'

'You don't lie to me. We don't lie to each other.'

'I didn't do anything.'

'Did somebody help you?'

'No.'

'I won't tell anybody.'

'It wasn't *me*.'

'Then who was it?'

The Redfields' cat had jumped on to the window sill next to the bed and sat looking at them. Kate reached to stroke it but it ducked its head away.

'Was there somebody upstairs?'

'Yes,' Kate whispered.

'Who?'

Kate didn't answer.

Maggie wanted to grab and shake her. 'Katie, this is all just a game, remember? This isn't real.'

'I promise,' she said. 'It wasn't me.'

'I don't believe you.'

In the flickering light Maggie saw Kate's expression harden.

'You *know*,' Kate said. 'You already know.'

'I don't know anything. I want you to tell me.'

'There was somebody upstairs.'

'A man?'

'Yes.'

'Katie—'

'Yes, a man.' Kate screwed her eyes shut for a moment, and when she opened them she leaned forward and grabbed Maggie's hand. 'I think when we were playing games – I think we woke him up.' Her nails dug into Maggie's palm and her voice was soft and urgent, but there was a spark of something bright and hopeful in her eyes.

They heard a knock at the front door, and both jumped. Murmured voices in the hall. Their father was back: he had ridden out to David's farm to ask him to come and stay the night in the house.

He came into the room, bringing cold air and a coat dusted with snow. He looked at the girls. 'David couldn't come,' he said. 'Calvin's here.'

Calvin appeared behind him, flushed and bright-eyed.

Maggie stood up. 'You've come all this way at night?'

Calvin said, 'It's not so late.'

'I'll stay with you and Father,' said Maggie. 'I'll go back to the house.'

'No.' Her father shook his head. 'You all stay here.'

'That's probably best,' said Calvin, although Maggie could tell he didn't quite understand why he'd been brought.

'Calvin and I – we'll sleep in the house tonight,' their father continued. He looked at Calvin. 'You'll take the room downstairs.'

'Fine,' said Calvin.

'Put your mother's mind at ease.' He was still looking at Calvin, although of course Margaret wasn't Calvin's mother.

47

'Good,' said Calvin. 'Happy to.' He looked at Maggie. 'You're alright?'

'I wasn't there,' she said. *This isn't real*, she wanted to say. *We've tricked you*. But she could feel Kate behind her, watching.

'And if we hear anything,' said John, 'you'll be our witness, Calvin.'

'Sure,' said Calvin. 'Good. Happy to.'

'There are witnesses,' said Kate. 'We've all heard things. Me and Maggie and Mother, and now Mary Redfield too.'

'A proper witness,' their father said.

'Oh,' said Kate. 'I see.'

'Yes.' Maggie met Calvin's eye. 'I see.'

Calvin looked at the floor and scratched the back of his head. 'Well, I'll do my best.'

'We'll take some tea before we go.' John looked about the room as if expecting it to appear, before his gaze fell on Maggie. 'Some tea,' he said again.

'I don't live here,' Maggie said.

'Your mother and Mrs. Redfield are resting. They won't mind—'

They could all hear Mary and their mother talking upstairs, where they'd taken a whiskey bottle and two glasses, for their nerves.

'I don't mind making—' Calvin began.

'I'll make it,' said Maggie. 'Fine.'

Calvin followed her into the kitchen. He closed the door behind him.

They both looked around the unfamiliar room. It was cluttered and lively, another cat sleeping on a chair in the corner.

'Have to admit that I'm not altogether sure why it is I'm here,' said Calvin.

48

'Well, you're our *witness*.'

'So I gather.' He looked at the cat for a moment, and then went over to it, scratched its head. It didn't open its eyes but began to purr. 'We used to have a cat like this,' he said, almost to himself. Then looked back at Maggie. 'Your father says you've all been scared by noises in the house.'

'There are noises in the house,' said Maggie, 'but I'm not scared.'

'I didn't think you were.'

'You know Mother always feels better when you're around, though.'

'Well, that's nice. I like to be around. Not too sure how I'm going to help, but—'

'But here you are. You're kind.' He was always kind, so much that Maggie wondered it didn't exhaust him sometimes. *Calvin is secretly terrified that he's going to be sent away,* Leah had told her once, privately. *He was scared of it when he was a boy, and he can't shake it now.*

'So you didn't hear this mysterious voice?' His face was serious enough but Maggie could see the light in his eyes.

Maggie picked up a teaspoon from the table. It was warm from lying next to a lamp. She looked at it for a moment. 'Not today.'

'Where were you?'

'I was visiting town.' She paused. Tried to think of a way to make her life sound more interesting, but nothing came.

'And your father says there's been noises.'

'Yes.'

'Because,' he said, 'it's easy to get ideas. Long winter, old house, dark nights.' He paused for a moment. 'You're shaken up by what happened back in Rochester.'

Maggie's throat was tight.

'The accident,' Calvin added softly. That had always been the word he used. Her father preferred *the incident*, if he spoke of it at all, but for Calvin it was only ever *the accident*, an unfortunate event that was nobody's fault.

'People say in town that the house is haunted. The last family left because of it.'

He studied her. 'Like I said. It's easy to get ideas, but Maggie—'

She braced herself for it, her lesson.

'– there's no such thing as ghosts. There's nothing to be scared of. I'll stay in the house and all, but—'

'I told you that I wasn't scared.'

'Good. Because dead is dead and that's that. What's dead is gone.'

Maggie tilted her head. 'Gone to heaven?'

'If you like.'

Maggie turned away from him and bent to stir up the fire in the stove. There was already water in the copper pot on the kitchen table, so she lifted it on to the stove and looked around for cups.

It would be easy to confess to Calvin, the games they'd been playing. He would laugh. He wouldn't tell anybody.

But she didn't know how to explain a man's voice at the top of the stairs. So what would she be confessing?

'Well, I'm sleeping there tonight,' he said. 'So I suppose I'll find out.'

'I suppose you will,' she said.

NINE

Maggie woke earlier than her sister. The house was cold, and she scrambled to make up the fire, trying to be quiet. The Redfields and her mother must still be asleep upstairs.

A strange white light through the house told her that the snow had settled, even before she opened the curtains. It wasn't deep, but lay bright and unbroken across the ground. The sky was a hard blue, and the snow was sparkling in bright sunlight.

Pulling on yesterday's clothes and as many layers as she could find, she slipped quietly through the front door, let it click softly shut behind her.

The walk back to her own house was short. Birds were chattering in the trees. She ought to put some food out for them, she thought, they were probably starving, trying to peck for worms and insects in the frozen ground. She didn't know what she hoped to find at the house, but her thoughts were stuck on men, all men, and their certainty. How nice it would be to shake it loose, make them doubt themselves for once. Make them see that there were more things in the world than they were capable of explaining.

When she arrived, Calvin was sitting on the steps in front of the kitchen door, with a cup of coffee and his coat buttoned up to his chin. He was gazing at some distant, invisible spot on the landscape, sunlight catching the ends of his hair, and didn't notice Maggie at first.

'Calvin,' she said, as she got close, and he jumped, splashed his coffee.

'Scared me,' he said, but he was smiling.

'I wasn't trying to. You're outside in this cold?'

'It's warm enough in the sun, and who knows how long that'll last.' He got to his feet, stretched out his shoulders. 'I needed some air.'

He had shadows under his eyes, Maggie saw, and a sleepy, heavy-lidded look.

'Is my father—'

'Still asleep, as far as I know.'

'Well?' She tilted her head. 'Catch any spirits?'

He gave her a long, curious look. 'Are you doing it, somehow?'

Although they were outside, they were both talking quietly, as if they might wake the town.

'Am I doing what?'

'Or you and Katie. I won't tell.'

Maggie glanced at the house. The windows were dark but none of the curtains had been drawn. She shivered. She said honestly: 'I'm not sure what you mean.'

'I'm not sure what I mean either.'

'Did you hear something? Did something happen?'

Calvin looked back at the invisible spot in the distance. 'It's a strange house,' he said. 'I slept downstairs. You were right, it makes all kinds of sounds. Kept thinking there was somebody knocking at the door. I almost thought to open it, thought somebody was playing a trick on me.' He gave her a pointed look and Maggie almost laughed.

'You can't possibly think that we would go sneaking around outside in the middle of the night, Calvin. On our own? Just to scare you?'

'Of course not.' He clearly wasn't sure. 'But then I could've sworn—' He paused. 'I must have been dreaming. I could've sworn I woke up and there was somebody in the room.' He looked at her, smiled a little. 'It's you girls, filling all our heads with ideas. You've got me hearing things.'

There was that pressure on her brain again. An urge to lie down.

It was hard to believe they'd filled his head with anything. Calvin was sensible, practical. He only believed in what he could see. He didn't even believe in God. He'd never admitted it straight out but Maggie knew that he didn't.

There was something in his face – not fear, but uncertainty. She ought to feel satisfied.

Except she hadn't done anything. She hadn't *been* there.

'Is this all because of—' He broke off. She could see him trying to form the question. 'Maggie, is this about Rochester, somehow? Are you still – angry, at us?'

Yes, yes, yes, of course I am. She didn't answer.

'I wouldn't blame you. I *don't* blame you. You know that?'

'I don't want to talk about it.'

'You were sick. And anyway, she might have only slipped. I know that you wouldn't—'

'I said I don't want to talk about it.'

He nodded, and they were silent for a moment. 'Want to go inside?' he said, then, 'Coffee's still warm. I have to get back to the farm soon.'

'Yes,' said Maggie. 'Let's.' And she went to follow him through the door. She hesitated, briefly, at the threshold. For a moment, she didn't want to go in.

Their father said that he'd heard nothing, seen nothing. When Calvin told his story, John looked at him reproachfully.

'It's a creaky old house, all I'm saying,' said Calvin. 'There's nothing bad here.'

'That's right.'

He did look tired, though, her father. Tired and old. He'd been handsome, once, her mother had told her, but he'd ruined himself with drink. Alcohol changed a person's face over time. Distorted it somehow. Clean living and prayer wouldn't undo the damage. That's what her mother said. Trying to warn them.

'I have to get back,' said Calvin. 'I'll go and talk to Katie and Mrs. Fox on my way. Tell them it's alright.'

'Good,' said John. 'Perhaps they'll listen to you.'

'I could come with you to the farm,' said Maggie. 'I'd like to see David and the children.'

'No. You'll stay here. You just heard the boy. Nothing bad here.'

'I just thought—'

'No,' said John. 'Nobody's going anywhere.'

TEN

She tried to remember, in the months afterward, exactly how it had happened: the sequence of events on that last day in March, that led to the rest of it – the newspaper articles, and the pamphlet by the reporter, Mr. Lewis, that told all about it. How that day began and how each moment collapsed into the next until the evening came and changed everything.

It started at lunch. They were all in silence, eating soup, when the table gave a sudden jerk. Maggie thought Kate had done it; she looked at her, but Kate's expression was startled.

Their father pushed back his chair, got to his knees to look under the table. Stood back up and stayed standing, for a moment, as if he had something to say. But they were all very quiet: just four bodies breathing, waiting for something else.

The moment he sat back down, two sharp cracks came from under the table on Kate's side.

'Something's here,' her mother whispered, a spoonful of hot soup held halfway between the bowl and her mouth. 'Listen.'

And they did, obediently, all listen.

And then two sharp cracks from the ceiling above their heads.

Something ran cold through Maggie's blood. Pumped straight from her heart to the ends of her fingertips.

Kate's face was turned up, toward the ceiling, attentive and alert, a shimmer of something around her, like dust caught in the sunlight. 'Hello?' she said, and the two sharp cracks sounded again. Their mother dropped her spoon and pushed her own chair back.

Maggie didn't move.

A man's voice said, *Here you are.* But he said it inside Maggie's own head, and nobody else heard. *Here you are.*

Kate, very slowly, as if pulled by an invisible string, was rising from her chair.

Are you doing this? Maggie thought, and tried to send the thought direct to Kate's mind. And perhaps she did, because Kate flicked her dark eyes in Maggie's direction, gave her a knowing look that Maggie didn't understand, and then looked back at the ceiling.

'We're listening,' said Kate, but her father grabbed her arm roughly and pulled her back down to her chair.

'You stop that,' he said. 'You stop that.'

'*John,*' said their mother, reaching a hand toward him, and John pulled away from Kate and held his arms up, and Maggie wondered if he had been about to hit her, his youngest daughter.

He turned away from them, and went up the stairs, and they heard his footsteps, heavy and creaking, cross their bedroom floor, turn and walk back again, and then stop.

And after lunch, when their father went back into town and their mother went to visit with neighbors, Maggie found Kate with her nose pressed against their bedroom window, looking out at the sky and the snow-capped trees. Maggie sat on the bed, waited a few moments, and said: 'What's happening?'

Kate took a while to answer. She turned, eventually, and came and sat at the other end of the bed. She bit her lip and twisted one of her braids around her hand.

There was a shifting sound above them, from the roof, but it was only snow, breaking apart and sliding down.

Maggie knew a man when they'd lived upstate who'd been killed by snow falling from his roof. She thought about him sometimes.

'He's trying to talk to us,' Kate said.

And when their father came home he shouted for the girls, because his tool bag had been opened, and his tools were lying all over the kitchen.

'It wasn't us,' Kate said.

The sky was low and white and threatening more snow, and cold air had followed their father into the house. Maggie looked at her sister, in case she could see any of the dirt or grease from their father's tools smeared on Katie's hands or her clothes. She couldn't.

And when both their mother and their father were home, mid-afternoon and the light dwindling, a steady tapping sound began, that seemed to move around the walls, through the bones of the house.

They followed the sound to the upstairs bedroom, Kate and Maggie and their mother holding hands. John walked ahead. He touched the walls, pressed his ear against them, and then jerked back as if he'd been stung. The tapping came from all the walls at once. They looked at each other helplessly.

And then Kate knelt up on the bed. 'Are you talking to us?' she said. John looked at her, fearful and silent.

The tapping stopped.

'Are you talking to us?' Kate said again.

'How could it answer?' Maggie hissed. Kate looked at her, composed, and then up at the ceiling.

'Spirit,' she said. 'Do as I do.' And she clapped her hands three times.

Maggie heard the answer in her own brain before she heard it in the walls. Three knocks.

Kate clapped twice. Two knocks.

Silence. 'Try again,' their mother whispered.

Four claps. Four knocks.

All at once, Kate began to cry.

'I won't have this,' John said, and Maggie saw him try to set his face against it. He murmured, almost to himself, 'It's an animal, in the walls.'

The women looked at him.

'I'm going for David and Calvin,' he said, a shaking hand rubbing up and down his jaw. 'That's what I'll do. They need to hear this.'

Of course, thought Maggie. More men had to be fetched. Who could know what was real or not, without a few men to say for certain?

He left. From the window, through the silently spinning snow, she saw her father make his way across the gently accumulating drifts to the stable, stumbling, led on by the small, warm glow of the lamp. A tiny figure, dark against the white background. Maggie swept her eyes across the landscape, the trees and the covered road, small points of light in the distance from other houses, half expecting to see a gathering of human figures looking toward them, more spirits summoned up out of the cold.

*

When David and Calvin arrived, it was late in the evening, a low white sky, and the light was gone. The house had fallen silent and the men made inspections – went up to the attic, and stood outside, walking around the house in circles. They came inside again, traded glances, tried to reassure.

And Maggie built the fire again in the stove, so they could have coffee, and then a sound like the shattering of ice across a hard floor came from the attic, and the taps started again, a flurry of sound, and then stopped. Started again.

'Do it again, Katie,' their mother said. 'What you did before.'

When it answered Katie's claps again, David and Calvin raised their eyebrows and looked at her with unreadable expressions.

The knock at the door made them all jump.

John went to answer it. It was Mr. Duesler, come to return some tools he'd borrowed. John said hoarsely, 'Will you come inside? Will you listen to something?'

And so he was the first of the neighbors. First Mr. Duesler, who ran to fetch the Redfields. Then Mrs. Duesler, then the Faulkners, the snow outside the house churned up by people dashing back and forth to all the nearby houses. *You must hear this.*

As they began to gather in the kitchen, murmuring feverishly, Maggie took Kate's hand.

'Who is it?' she whispered. She hated to have to ask her little sister questions.

Kate looked at her solemnly. 'He hasn't told us yet,' she said. And smiled.

'Katie. All these people—'

'There's a man out there!' Mrs. Faulkner cried suddenly, pointing at the window. There was a rush toward the door, and a crowd gathered to peer out.

'There's nobody,' their father said, but they all stayed where they were, trying to see something.

'They want to hear him,' Kate said. 'We shouldn't disappoint them.'

Maggie looked at the group in the doorway. Their excitement sparked in the air like a source of natural energy.

'There's nobody there,' she heard David say. And they all turned back, to where the girls were standing. Above them, from the empty bedroom, a floorboard creaked.

And then they were all upstairs.

Kate's eyes were very bright. They were wide, fixed on some invisible mark in the center of the room. She clapped her hands three times.

Everybody fell silent, and looked expectantly at the girls, excited by this new turn in the performance. Maggie heard it first, the sound inside her brain, knocking: then it came from the walls. Three sharp knocks.

Kate clapped twice. The sound came back. Two knocks. Mary Redfield's candle flickered, and went out. There was a short, high gasp from a corner of the room, quickly muted by the thick, dead air. So many people in one room, in heavy clothes still damp from the snow, lamps throwing out pockets of shifting light. A man coughed.

Kate did it again, six claps in a row. The pause was longer this time – and the answering raps came from below, from the kitchen.

'She's doing it, somehow,' said Mr. Redfield. 'Somebody look downstairs.' There was a shuffle of movement at the door, the creak of heavy footsteps on the stairs.

Calvin and David both looked uneasy; David's eyes were scanning the walls and ceiling, Calvin shaking his head slowly.

Kate's hands fell to her sides, and she looked at Maggie. The bright look was gone from her eyes, and Maggie could see that she didn't know what to do next. It was her little sister again, looking to her for a cue. Maggie cracked her toes, each one in turn, so quickly that nobody had time to register where the sound came from; it landed dead in the thick air and was immediately lost in a flurry of voices— 'It was there, in the corner,' 'No, there,' 'I heard something upstairs.' Kate answered with the cracking of her own toes. There was another shriek, and Maggie felt the two of them, her and Kate, charged with a fierce and unexpected power.

And something else. A weight building like the approach of lightning.

'Ask it a question,' said Mr. Redfield, the challenge in his voice undercut by a note of fear. 'Go on, then. Ask it a question.' He was looking at Kate.

'How will she do that?' said David.

A pause, and Mr. Redfield said, 'One rap for yes, two raps for no.'

'Mercy on us,' their mother said weakly, from the corner.

'This is nonsense,' said David.

'Who are we speaking to?' asked Mr. Redfield. 'Answer me.'

Maggie grabbed her sister's hand. 'Are you a spirit?' she said.

'Are you a spirit?' Kate echoed.

The short, sharp rap made both of them jerk backward. Her sister's hand felt cold and clammy.

'Are you the spirit of somebody who has died?' said Kate.

A rap. It was hard to place the sound. Maggie could have believed it was from the walls or from downstairs. She could have believed it was from an apple dropped against the floor. She felt giddy, as if she might laugh.

'Who is it?' somebody hissed.

'Did you die in this house?' said Kate.

A rap.

'A long time ago?' asked Mary Redfield.

'This is becoming—' David began, and someone *ssh*-ed him.

Two raps.

'How old is this place, anyway?' somebody whispered, and was *ssh*-ed themselves.

'When did you die?' said Kate. 'Was it – a long time ago?'

Two hard pounds on the floor sent a reverberation through the room, followed by sharp gasps and the sound of a woman's sob.

'How long is a long time?' said one of the men.

'Ten years ago?' said Kate, and then, 'Five?'

One sharp rap on the floor.

The stairs creaked, followed by thumping footsteps, and there was a fearful murmur in the room, before Mr. Faulkner came back in.

'Nobody down there,' he said.

Kate laughed. Maggie turned to her in shock. Kate let go of her hand and crossed the room, took hold of the back of a chair. It was the chair they had dragged back and forth across the floor to scare their parents.

Kate moved the chair into the center of the room and stood, holding the back of it. 'Are you an injured spirit?' she said.

The group had parted where the chair had been, and Maggie saw her father again, watching from behind the Dueslers, his brow low. He had taken off his spectacles, and his face had lost its shape. His mouth was open as if fixed on the edge of saying something.

The next knock was from beneath the chair and Maggie saw a flash of movement: she could see Kate's hands were tense, gripping the chair so that her knuckles were white. Their eyes met for a moment.

'Were you murdered?' said Kate, and the rap came before she had even finished speaking.

'In this house?'

The next rap was lost as somebody – Mrs. Faulkner – suddenly said, in a steady, clear voice: 'There's somebody standing behind you, Maggie.'

Kate jerked backward, still holding the chair, so that it clattered on the ground, and Mrs. Faulkner sank to the floor, caught quickly by Calvin, who was standing near her. 'I'm sorry,' she said. 'I'm sorry. I felt faint. I don't know what I'm saying.'

When Mrs. Faulkner was on her feet, Calvin bent to pick up the chair. Kate grabbed it from him, and he stepped away from her.

'Were you murdered?' Kate asked again. She turned the chair so it faced the window, but then she knelt on it, backward, facing the door. The door seemed to tremble, for a moment, and then a soft knock came from beyond it, from the top stair.

Then a moment of perfect silence.

Then three or four soft raps came from the walls, and a frantic murmur rose among the group, heads turning, arms clutching one another.

'Ask another question,' said one of them, a man.

A candle flickered and went out, left a trace of bitter smoke in the air.

'*Oh,*' somebody whispered.

Kate placed her elbows on the back of the chair and clasped her hands together. She closed her eyes, as if she was praying, but Maggie could still see the dart of her eyes behind the lids.

The group had formed a loose circle now, with Kate on the chair at the center, and Maggie on the edge. Their father stood beyond the circle, in the corner of the room. He was in shadow, his face hollow, and collapsing in doubt, a weakness that Maggie had never seen before, so that she could imagine, suddenly, how he might have looked drunk and sad and wandering in the street.

On the opposite side were Calvin and David.

Their faces were all turned toward the sisters, whites of their eyes catching the candlelight, waiting for them to say what would happen next. Kate didn't move.

Maggie had the sense, unsettling but not unpleasurable, that something had been set in motion, that could not now be stopped. They were waiting for her to speak.

She stepped forward into the circle.

'You must tell us your name,' she said.

They called out each letter and waited for an answering rap. *C – H – A –*

His name was Charles.

And with every letter and every knock, the room fell further into silent, stunned belief. They continued. More questions were called. More answers sounded from the walls:

He was a peddler who had visited the house, before the Fox family had lived there.

He had been murdered, his money stolen, and his trunk full of goods.

He was buried in the cellar.

'In the cellar?' somebody said. 'Where in the cellar? We'll go and look. We'll look tonight, we'll dig—'

'We will *not*,' said the girls' father. He had barely spoken and his voice was choked and trembling. 'We will *not*.'

Maggie's head had begun to pound. She felt weak, exhausted. The room was hot, full of bodies and breath, and she began to feel too warm and too cold in quick succession. Their neighbors' expressions blurred, and for brief moments Maggie imagined that parts of their faces were missing, a mouth or an eye turning to an empty black space.

They had to end this, Maggie thought. Or something terrible would happen.

'Katie—' Maggie whispered, but Kate held up a hand.

'And if we spell out his name,' Kate said, 'will you tell us who murdered you?'

A hush fell, and then a rap came. A thrilled murmur.

Kate seemed to be waiting for her, and so Maggie softly began to speak.

'*A*—'

'*B*—'

No one had expected the rap so quickly, and they all jumped.

'*B*,' Kate said. 'Now start again.'

Maggie began again.

She heard her own voice start to fail as the letters arranged themselves into a name. *B-E-L-L*.

A wayward breeze passed through the room, as if a window had been flung open.

Maggie saw recognition sparking on the faces around them.

'Mr. Bell,' said Mrs. Faulkner. 'John Bell. He lived here – he lived in this house. He did – for just a few months, he lived—'

'Yes,' said Mrs. Redfield. 'I know John Bell. He moved out of town but I remember—'

'I know him,' said Mrs. Duesler. Her voice was scarcely a whisper, high-pitched and tense. 'He lives in Red Creek now, but this was his house.'

Somebody real, they had named *somebody real*, but they couldn't have, they couldn't know, she had never *heard* of John Bell – Maggie's heart raced, a sickness turned her stomach – but his name had been spelled and they all believed it. Everybody here believed it. Maggie looked around the room. The open, frightened faces. They had accused a man of murder and all of the neighbors believed it.

Not us, she thought, it isn't us, we haven't accused anybody, it's the peddler, but she could see her own alarm mirrored in Kate's expression.

Their father was shaking. In the dark, Maggie could feel his fury as if it was something burning.

ELEVEN

It had to end, of course, and it did: they all had to sleep, and
their damp breath had filled the air and people were dizzy
and sweating in their winter clothes. Mrs. Faulkner had
come over faint again and there had been a commotion
trying to help her, and the mood broke apart, and the spirit –
the thing, the storm in the air, the sounds – disappeared.
Kate, suddenly, was pale and tearful, and Maggie found
herself pushing people away from her, standing in-between
her sister and all the frightened, demanding faces.

The guests were ushered out, and their mother insisted
that Maggie and Kate sleep in the downstairs bedroom,
while David and Calvin slept upstairs. And there was scarcely
any more conversation between them. Maggie slept as if she
were dead, and didn't dream.

When she woke, her parents were gone from the room,
and Kate was looking down at her. Kate's loose hair was wild
and wavy and there were purple shadows beneath her eyes.
Snow was thick outside and the sound inside the house was
muffled. Through the window, the sky was a hard, bright
blue and the air was still and cold as ice. Maggie could see
her own breath, and her feet – even beneath a pile of
blankets – were painful with cold.

It was the first of April, and winter should be over, but it
felt colder than any day Maggie could remember.

It was the first of April, so were they all – the neighbors, everybody – waking now, and thinking that this was all an April Fool?

She sat up, and she and Kate looked at each other, as if they'd both just woken from the same cold dream.

In the kitchen, their mother sat with a plate of bread and a small butter dish, and a cup of hot tea which she turned in her hands slowly. She looked sick with tiredness, and when they came into the room – they hadn't dressed, only wrapped blankets around themselves – she looked briefly as if she didn't recognize them.

'My girls,' she said, as if she wasn't sure.

'Yes, Mother,' said Kate, and circled the table to wrap her arms around her and kiss the top of her head.

Their mother had gotten thinner this winter, Maggie noticed, and there was a sunken look to her cheeks. Maggie sat down at the table and reached for her hand, which was warm from the tea.

'It's alright,' she said. 'It's going to be alright.'

Her mother's eyes were watery. 'Last night,' she said. 'I hardly know if I dreamed it.'

Maggie squeezed her hand. 'It's alright,' she said again. 'It wasn't a dream but don't be scared.'

'Mr. Bell. Those things that were said. If he hears about it – what will he think?'

'He'll feel ashamed,' Maggie said, with a shaky confidence that had come to her overnight. She couldn't think of Mr. Bell as a real person, not yet. 'Because he knows what he did.'

'My grandmother had visions. We all laughed, it only seemed like fun, but she was always very serious.' With her free hand, her mother wiped at her eyes, and then gave

Maggie a shaking, hopeful smile. 'And I did believe,' she said.

Everyone had believed, last night. How could they not? It surged through Maggie like water breaking a dam. She hadn't been alone. They had all *believed*. And so how could they not look back, her family, not look back to what had happened in Rochester—

'My girls,' their mother said again, and Maggie glanced up and met Kate's eyes, which were very serious and years older than they had been yesterday.

Their father had gone to work. David and Calvin had gone back to the farm, but they planned to return that night to keep watch.

'They should be here,' their mother said. 'In case anything happens.' And she gave them both an uncertain, half-hopeful look.

Their bedroom, where David and Calvin had slept, was disordered and unfamiliar. One of them had slept on the floor and left a tangle of sheets, and the bed had been moved. It was cold as ever but smelled different, smelled like men, but perhaps it was partly all the people who had been here the night before. There was a dropped handkerchief on the floor, and marks and scuffs on the boards that Maggie was certain were new. Kate picked at the sheets, making a face, and then went to the window to peer out. Pale sun lit the room; it was hard to remember how it had felt in the dark.

Maggie sat down on the bed. The springs creaked. She ran her thumb along the edge of the frame.

Kate turned back. 'There's nothing here. Listen. Doesn't it feel different? He's gone.'

Maggie closed her eyes. Tried to open her mind somehow,

concentrate on the flow of her blood and the sound and texture of the air.

She felt nothing. It was only a room.

'Come here.' She reached out a hand toward Kate, and pulled her on to the bed. 'We have to try and talk to him again.'

'I don't think he's here.'

'He has to be.'

'Maggie—'

'Sit with me. How did it start?'

'When?'

'Yesterday. I don't know. Ever. When did he start talking to us?'

Kate frowned, and rubbed her eyes. 'We started talking to *him*. And he—'

'– and he answered.'

'Yes.'

Maggie grabbed both of Kate's hands, and held them tight. 'You know it's real now, don't you?'

'Of course I do.'

'Then we have to try and talk to him again.'

'He's not here.'

'Of course he's here, Katie. Where would he go?'

She shrugged. 'He's not here *now*.'

'The neighbors are going to come back. And David and Calvin and Father and all of them.'

Kate blinked at her as if she didn't understand what point Maggie was making.

'And if nothing happens,' Maggie said. 'If everything is quiet . . .'

Slowly, Kate caught up with her. 'They won't believe it anymore.'

'They won't. They'll think we tricked them.'

In the distance, outside, Maggie could hear the beat of hooves through the snow, somebody approaching the house.

'Katie.' She had a headache. Or was it only cold. Shadows lurked in the corners of her eyes. She was still holding Kate's hands and she thought if she let go she might fall to pieces. 'Let's try and talk to him now. Just to see if we can.'

'He's not here. It feels different.'

'I know. That's why we have to try. Let's try now. They're all going to come *back*, Katie.'

Real belief came through repetition, Maggie thought, a thing repeated over and over until it had the quality of truth. It wasn't enough for it to have happened once. It would have to happen again, and again, and whenever people wanted it, or everybody would think they were liars. Worse: everyone would think they had accused somebody of a terrible crime, all for a game.

Kate said quietly, 'I don't know how to start.'

Neither did Maggie. Her mind raced back through it all, looking for the start. The cellar. But it was boarded up now.

A headache. She pulled her hands away and pressed them over her eyes. Think. Try and think.

Voices outside, deadened by snow. There was no wind. The timbers of the house rested. Sharp icicles glistened above the window. Their mother moved in the kitchen.

Maggie grabbed for the single candlestick that stood by the bed, held it for a moment as if it would fly away, and then rapped it hard three times on the wall. Then she held her breath. *Please*, she thought. *Answer us.*

Footsteps crunching up to the door. Maggie didn't know how to explain the panic that was gripping her. Only that she saw all of their faces, everyone in Rochester, standing around her and thinking *liar*.

She wasn't. She could not let them think she was.

Answer me, she thought, but the room gave no answer. It was silent and bright as snow.

She didn't instruct Kate, didn't force her to do anything. Kate didn't mind. Kate agreed with her. A few more games, a few tricks: they had no choice. It was only to make people see the truth. They came downstairs, and slowly, as the day unspooled itself, and the men returned, and curious neighbors crept back, Kate snapped her toes and whispered to the walls and gazed wide-eyed at the ceiling, blew out a candle and knocked a cup from the table, and then flushed with pleasure as the guests gasped and chattered excitedly.

Maggie could hardly concentrate; she was tense with nerves and couldn't seem to time anything correctly. Dread and hope were mixed up in her like some kind of strange poison. Whatever they did was met with astonishment and fearful delight.

The neighbors came back the next day, and the next, and brought others with them. Mr. Bell's name was mentioned only in whispers, as if nobody else wanted to be implicated in the accusation, but they all wanted to go into the cellar, of course. And down there the ghost took care of itself. Eight or nine people crowded into that tiny, dark and creaking space, with water running beneath them. Their fear and expectation fired their imaginations and they heard whatever they wanted to. Then they found the leg bone – Maggie had almost forgotten about it – and brought it upstairs with them, laying it on the kitchen table like some sort of prize, while their mother looked on aghast. Maggie and Kate pretended never to have seen it before, as the excitement rose again, more fervent than ever.

The real peddler was silent. Maggie wondered if he was angry.

The reporter, Edward Lewis, arrived on April fourth. He'd traveled a long way, he told them all, although it wasn't too clear where he'd traveled *from*. He had heard what happened, and would they please do him the honor of allowing him to write about it?

He'd begun his interviews immediately, carefully transcribing every story the neighbors had to tell. Maggie never saw him without his notebook.

He was handsome. Younger than her brother, but older than Stephen Whitaker, with wiry curls and the trace of an accent Maggie couldn't place. And he wrote for newspapers. Everybody wanted to speak to him.

I heard the spirit speaking. I saw the closet move. The youngest girl, her eyes went black. Edward Lewis nodded, wrote it all down. 'Extraordinary,' he would murmur. 'Go on.'

Their mother spoke to Mr. Lewis for hours, their father too. Maggie saw that he was impressed by Mr. Lewis, somehow, and took him seriously.

Maggie listened to them through the floorboards of the bedroom, John's flat, deep voice admitting yes, he had heard the sounds. No, he said. He couldn't explain it. Maggie could feel his distress, in admitting it.

She was ready to talk to Mr. Lewis. She ran through versions in her mind. Perhaps he was saving the sisters for last. When he saw them he would smile, and sometimes wink. Maggie chose to believe that the wink was a promise, that at the end of the week Edward Lewis would sit down with her and say, *Now, Miss Fox, tell me what really happened.* And she was ready. She had practiced her story. She waited.

On the third day of his visit, he arrived at the house with a bundle of papers tied with string. It was evening, turning dark, and Maggie had lit a few candles to help her mother see the shirt she was mending. Their father had only just returned from work and stood wiping down his tools with an old rag.

Kate came downstairs when she heard Mr. Lewis's voice, and stood shyly in the corner, twisting her hair.

'Mr. Fox, Mrs. Fox.' Mr. Lewis pushed an errant curl back from his forehead, and gave Maggie a quick, knowing smile. 'You'll be happy to hear I've almost finished my interviews.'

Her mother had risen to her feet and fussed over him, trying to take his coat.

'I've collected enough statements for ten volumes, but a single pamphlet will have to be enough for now. I believe I can tell the story well.'

John was looking at him, still holding the rag in his hand.

'I'm sure you'll tell it wonderfully, Mr. Lewis,' said their mother. 'Will anybody really be interested?'

'I believe they will be.' Again he glanced at Maggie. 'In fact—' He dropped his bundle of papers on the table with a flourish. 'Mr. Fox. Do you know Lucretia Pulver? She's nineteen. She lives a mile north of here now, but a few years ago she lived right here for one winter, in this house.'

John's face was blank. 'I don't know her.'

Maggie didn't know Lucretia Pulver either, but she felt a beat of alarm that whoever she was, she was about to push into the center of Maggie's story.

'She lived here,' Mr. Lewis said, 'for one winter. She was hired by Mr. and Mrs. John Bell.'

A short silence. 'Oh,' Kate whispered from the corner.

Her father cleared his throat and said stiffly: 'Was she?'

'Just a girl herself at the time, of course, but what she told me—' He gestured at his papers. 'She told me she remembered a peddler who visited. She didn't have any money that day, and he said he'd return the following morning. But he never did. She never saw him again.'

Mr. Lewis paused, candlelight playing over his face. He was entertained, Maggie saw: enjoying himself as if he was in a play. He was a storyteller, delighted to have an audience.

'But in the weeks afterward, Miss Pulver started finding trinkets, thimbles and ribbons and vials of essence that she was sure had come from the peddler. Only Mrs. Bell denied she'd ever seen him.'

Maggie's mother put her hand to her mouth. Her father's face was rigid.

'And,' said Mr. Lewis. 'And she claims after all this that she heard strange noises as well. She slept in the room upstairs and heard knocking under the foot of the bed.'

Kate crossed the room to Maggie's side, and took her hand. Her palm was cold. Maggie was light-headed all of a sudden. She thought she might faint. She wrapped her free hand around the back of a chair to steady herself.

'What does that mean?' said Maggie's father.

'It's not my place to give these stories meaning, Mr. Fox. I only record them.'

'You'll print it?' said Maggie. 'What she said?'

'I believe I've a responsibility to share it all. The full story. Don't you think?'

None of them spoke. Perhaps he'd expected a different

response. He rubbed his face and pulled out a chair from the table, sat down. 'I would think you'd be pleased. All these pieces, fitting together. It only gives credence to what all of you have said.'

'Mr. Bell,' said Maggie. 'Does he know about it?'

She did not know what Mr. Bell looked like, and so he was a fractured image in her mind, made up of broken pieces of other men's faces. She was frightened of him, more than of the peddler.

'He knows and I'd say he's furious, but he won't speak to anybody. Certainly not me. Quite a thing to happen to a man's reputation, a murder accusation. I may score out his name in the pamphlet, of course. I don't have time for legal trouble.'

'A murder accusation,' said their mother, as if grasping the fact for the first time. 'Could they – the police—'

'I made some enquiries in that direction, but I'm told they're not very interested in murders without bodies. Or ghost stories, for that matter. I doubt they'll be knocking at your door. Don't alarm yourself, Mrs. Fox.'

'There *should* be an investigation,' said Kate, in a small voice. 'He won't be at peace until the truth is out.'

Mr. Lewis raised an eyebrow. 'The peddler?'

'Yes.'

'Well, find yourself a body, Miss Fox,' he said, smiling. 'And there's sure to be an investigation. And don't forget to write and tell me when you do, so I can start the second volume right away.'

He did not ask Maggie for her story.

When she came downstairs the following day, her mother told her he had sent a note to say that his interviews were

76

finished, that he had returned home to write his pamphlet, and that he would send some copies to them in a week or two when it was done.

She wondered if her father had taken Mr. Lewis aside and told him that his daughters weren't to be spoken to, or if Mr. Lewis simply thought they were too young or too stupid to be worth bothering with. Either way, when he published his pamphlet – *A Report of the Mysterious Noises Heard in the House of Mr. John D. Fox* – they hadn't contributed anything to it.

He sent them several copies. She read his introduction. He did not mention their names. *This mystery*, he called it. *This strange affair. These noises.* The murder parts came later, in the statements.

She turned through the neatly printed sheets. Pages and pages of statements, but she couldn't find her own name. *The girls*, they were called. *The youngest girl. The other girl.* Even their own mother's statement didn't use their names.

Had Mr. Lewis wanted to protect them? Had he taken their names out? Anybody reading could find out who they were – John Fox's youngest daughters. Everybody knew. Surely Mr. Bell knew.

Mr. Bell's name was scored out, in the main part, but he was mentioned at the end. A list of people had signed their names to a statement: *Mr. John C. Bell is a man of honest and upright character, incapable of committing crime.*

It was not convincing, she thought, included at the end like that. It seemed like an afterthought.

She took a copy to bed with her to try and read again by candlelight, but she fell asleep still holding it.

She dreamed she was on a wagon, but the reins had slipped her hands and she was thundering toward the edge of a cliff, with no way to stop, horses gone wild, the wagon beginning to splinter and the wheels coming loose. The wind on her face, a feeling of weightlessness. When she woke, the room was full of sunlight, and she was hungry. Sitting up, she found that she was lying on top of the pamphlet. The pages were bent and the ink had smudged her nightdress. She swung her legs out of the bed and put her feet on the cold floor. She tried to press the pamphlet flat against her knees, with her palm. And then she started reading again, still looking for her name, still finding only *the girls*, *the oldest girl*. They were the center of the story, but they had no names.

Kate was sleeping behind her. Maggie turned and brushed a hand over her forehead, and Kate scrunched up her face and rolled on to her side.

She turned back to the pamphlet. She'd thought it would only be a few pages, but it was thick, with small lettering. Thousands and thousands of words, all saying what had happened.

All saying what they had done.

She found Lucretia Pulver's page, and read it again.

They had not known, could not have known, that a man named Bell had ever lived here, much less that a peddler had ever visited, and then disappeared.

It was all in here in print. They had not made those sounds themselves.

If any embers of doubt had still lingered in her mind, they were extinguished.

She felt wide awake, and strong.

She had to do something.

She reached for a pencil that was lying on the table by the bed, and wrote her name on the front, next to Mr. Lewis's. She wrote her sister's beneath it. Then she turned the pages and wrote both names again, carefully, in the margins, in each place where they were mentioned.

Later, she took a clean copy of the pamphlet to send to Leah, and wrote a letter to go with it. She began the letter several times over.

Dearest Sister.
You may be surprised to read what it is we have been doing in Hydesville. Some very strange events have occurred and even our father cannot explain them.

She wrote slowly, concentrating on her spelling. Leah had always been able to write well.

All of the neighbors have been visiting the house, and they are all amazed. As you can see, a well-known journalist has written about it all. He says if it is not a haunting then it is impossible to explain what it is.

As she wrote, she could already imagine Leah's irritation at not being a part of the story.

I miss you very much, she wrote, *and I hope soon we will be together so I can tell you even more about it. I would like you to share the pamphlet with some of our friends in Rochester, such as Amy Post, to see what they might think about it.*
If a haunting can happen in Hydesville, they must see that it can also happen in Rochester.

Leah wouldn't for a moment believe that Maggie missed her, but it seemed a useful thing to say. She almost ended the letter there, but there was still space at the bottom of the paper, and she decided that perhaps it wouldn't hurt to state things more plainly.

I miss Rochester and would like to return, she wrote. *I am different now and there are many things I would like to do in the city.*

Maggie waited a week, but Leah didn't reply. It was David, eventually, who decided things had gone too far. He arrived one afternoon and found that downstairs, in the cellar, two men and their father were digging in the dirt, looking for bones.

His wagon was outside and he had one of the children with him, Charlie, who'd wanted to come because of all the excitement, and who was now hiding behind his leg and staring at Kate as if she'd grown another head. Kate – she had a headache – was looking back at him blankly, her eyes large and dark, circled with shadows.

'Mother,' David said. 'Mother, this is becoming absurd. What's next? Are you going to dismantle the whole house?'

'No,' said their mother mildly. She was sorting through buttons on the table, looking for three that would match the pale yellow material she was using for a summer dress.

The men's voices, arguing, rose up through the kitchen floor.

'This isn't good for the girls,' said David.

Maggie sighed theatrically, and scowled at him.

'If the wind changes, your face'll stay like that,' he said.

Charlie found this expression funny. 'The wind changes you'll stay like that!' he said. 'Wind changes you'll stay like that!'

'Kate ought to be having lessons,' he said, trying a different approach. 'Maggie ought to be—'

'What?' Maggie said. 'Getting married? Finding work? Sweeping the floor?'

She *should* be sweeping the floor. It was one of the chores that was supposed to be hers, and all the visitors had endlessly tracked dirt and snow throughout the house. They'd all become distracted from housework.

'– ought to be helping with' – he gestured vaguely – 'with things.'

'I am,' she said.

'This business has gone to all of your heads. And this so-called journalist—'

'Mr. Lewis was a very decent man,' said their mother. 'Very kind.'

'He spotted an opportunity to make some easy money.'

'How unusual, in this country.' She found a polished ivory button and held it out to Maggie. 'What do you think?'

'It's pretty,' said Maggie.

'I'm not sure I have two more. We could use it for the collar, I suppose. Or we could make a trip into town.'

'Or perhaps a peddler will visit,' said David.

'David—'

'Excuse me, I forget. There's already one buried in the cellar.'

From below, somebody cursed.

'Mother, I came to say, all of this isn't good for the girls. Kate looks exhausted. You *all* look exhausted.'

Maggie bit her lip. She *was* exhausted, some of the time, but she was more than that. She was lit up like fire. She felt strong, as if she could break tables and smash glass. When she had written to Leah she thought the letters might burn through the paper.

'You could all come out to the farm,' David said.

Maggie sat up straight.

'Or.' He paused. 'Leah wrote to me. She's got hold of this pamphlet somehow. I dare say she could take the girls back for a while. Or I could take you all there. Until the new house is finished, at least.'

There was silence, briefly, below and above the kitchen.

This was typical Leah. Trying to take control and pretending Maggie had nothing to do with it, suggesting they visit Rochester as if it were her idea.

But it would do. It was enough.

'Perhaps the farm would be better, David,' their mother said.

'James Crane has gone away.' David looked at Maggie, and then over at Charlie, who was edging curiously toward the stove. David grabbed the collar of his little shirt and pulled him away. 'He's gone back to New York City, according to Leah. He's taken Hannah. So you wouldn't see him.'

Nobody had said James Crane's name in all the months since they left. They were silent. Maggie felt heat rising in her face. Something turning over in her stomach. There it was, *James Crane*, like something that had been buried lurching out of its grave.

'People do forget,' said David. 'They do sometimes. They move on to other things.'

'I'm not sure,' their mother said softly. Maggie stayed quiet, in case they all looked at her and saw the thoughts that were in her mind.

The men emerged from the cellar then, dirt on their shoes, sweating slightly.

'What's wrong?' said David.

'Can't dig any further,' said one of them. 'We hit water.'

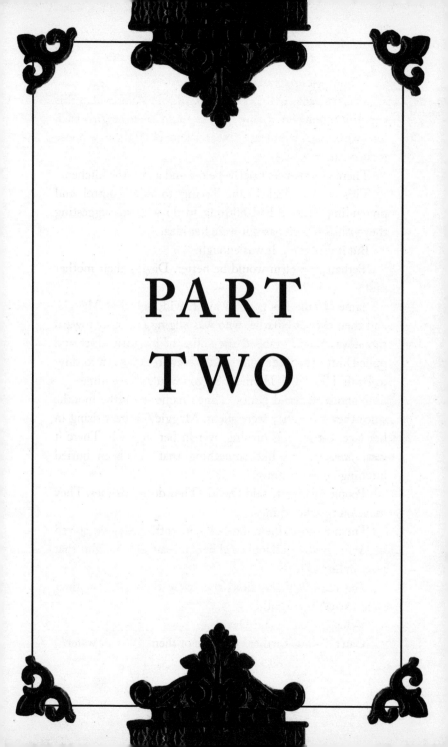

PART
TWO

TWELVE
ROCHESTER
NOVEMBER 1847

In the year before they moved to Hydesville, Maggie and Kate took lessons at the schoolhouse a few blocks from Amy and Isaac's house. There had been an old pioneer cemetery lying directly behind it, but in the summer of 1847 it had been dug up. Three men had come and done it, removed the gravestones and leveled out the ground the best they could. They were clearing space for a new school building.

It was James Crane's idea, and partly his money. He was rich; he made his money in imports of some kind, but people said he was generous with it. He formed a small committee of men, local business owners, who had plans to build schools all over Rochester.

The existing schoolhouse consisted only of one long hall, with high windows and a sagging roof, and a small room and kitchen to the side for teachers. Children of all ages were taught together. There was not enough space to separate them.

And the cemetery was overgrown, a dense tangle of weeds and small headstones all crooked and weathered, with names that could no longer be read. It had to be cleared.

They'd moved some of the stones inside the schoolhouse while they worked, and the weathered slabs were propped against the wall at the back of the hall all summer and into fall. One of them split clean in half when it was moved. One was dropped at the doorway, and cracked the floorboards. The men laid the broken pieces of stone next to one another.

There had been some trouble over it, disturbing the graves. But the space was needed, and somebody wrote in the local paper that if it was not allowed to build on land where people were buried, then America was done growing, because all the land was taken. So the stones were moved and the foundations laid. By October the new building was half finished: a timber frame, with sharp corners, strong and brittle as a skeleton.

Nobody said much about the bodies themselves. They were more concerned with the stones. Her teacher, Miss Kelly, told her the bodies had been buried so long, a hundred years or more, that their coffins would have rotted and the bones dispersed through the ground. Bones did not stay where they were buried, she said. It was something to do with water, and animals, and the natural turning of the earth. So it was best not to worry about the bodies.

The stones were there all through the hot, dry end to the summer, when the schoolhouse had sweltered, and they had been there as September began to cool everything, and they had been there into a sharp, crisp October. And then into a strange November, where cold days were broken up with times of unsettling warmth, dark evenings where it was too mild for a shawl, mornings where the sun burned over the fallen leaves.

'The seasons are disturbed,' Miss Kelly said to Maggie one day as she handed back a piece of work. 'The gods must be unhappy with us. *Hoary-headed frosts fall in the fresh lap of the crimson rose.*'

Maggie looked at her blankly, and Miss Kelly gave a passing smile. 'Shakespeare,' she said.

Miss Kelly had very thick, long dark hair that she let hang loose as if daring anyone to call her mad, and her eyes were a bright, clear blue. She wore what Maggie was sure was a man's coat over her blouses and skirts, and she quoted poetry and Shakespeare in a strange accent, a blur of Irish and American. She was not married, though Maggie thought she must be nearly thirty, and she had heard people say, unkindly, that no man would have her.

This was most likely true. She was a good enough teacher, but some people thought she should not be teaching because she had fits and convulsions. She had once sat down on the floor during a lesson and then had fallen sideways, her eyes half open, and made a soft choking sound as her body jerked. Maggie burned with shame for her. Another day, she had stopped speaking in the middle of a sentence, and grasped the back of a chair, and turned very white. She didn't fall, but it was as if she had gone somewhere else, left her body. Her mouth pressed down and her eyes were vacant. 'I'm sorry,' she had said again. 'It will pass.'

It did, and she went back to the lesson. But everybody, Maggie too, whispered about her and laughed. The children would do impressions of her falling over, and say she was possessed with evil spirits, a witch. To make fun of Miss Kelly was to protect yourself from her.

And they began to say, unkindly, that Miss Kelly was responsible for the strange things that happened that fall. A window cracked, suddenly, when nobody was near it. One of the timber pillars from the new building collapsed, destroying part of the new roof and leaving a splintered mess everywhere. Doors swung open, when there was no breeze. A shelf full of Bibles were found lying on the floor just after lunch, and everybody swore they had not been near them. One morning, a scrawled word was written on the chalkboard, untidy looping letters that had not been there the day before. Miss Kelly wiped it away without comment, but it fixed itself in Maggie's mind. She thought the word was *leave*, although it was hard to read. *Miss Kelly*, the children said. *Writing things in a trance. The Devil guides her hand.*

And the fire. One evening, as the children were gathering their things to go, a little boy suddenly shrieked and pointed, and they all spun around to see a shattered lamp, and flames beginning to lick the wooden frame of the back door. The flames were put out soon enough, with a rug thrown over them and pitchers of water fetched from the kitchen. But the scorch marks remained and everybody knew, everybody swore, in the weeks afterward, that the lamp had not even been lit, so how could it have caused a fire?

Maggie felt, sometimes, that she even saw things the others did not. Shadows in the corner of her eye, at the windows. Fluttering movement, shifting objects. She slept badly. She had liked school, before, but as she turned fifteen it began to fill her with a sense of doom. She wondered if she was too old for it, and would be asked to leave.

The hall, with its gloom and chalk-dust air, induced a pressure in her brain. Her headaches were worse. So were Kate's.

Then that day in November. Wet and dark, rain snapping at the windows.

She had argued with her father in the morning, and her mother had taken his side. It had left a heavy feeling she carried all day. The feeling built and built as she watched the clock move closer to three o'clock, when she had to go home. All she had wanted was to go to a lecture with Amy, and his refusal had been immediate, with no explanation. She shouldn't have shouted, but she couldn't help herself sometimes. It was a wonder he didn't beat her.

When the children all left at three o'clock, Maggie stayed at her desk. Kate lingered beside her, anxious to leave.

'I have to finish.' Maggie showed Kate her workbook, the unfinished Bible passage she was copying. 'Walk home with Sarah. Tell Mother I'll be home soon.'

Kate did not need persuading. She wouldn't stay in the schoolhouse any longer than needed.

Maggie stayed where she was, as Miss Kelly walked among the desks, collecting the writing books. Little Hannah Crane, Mr. Crane's daughter, was still there too.

Miss Kelly stopped at Maggie's desk. She looked tired. 'You're staying to finish your work?'

'Yes.' Maggie looked past Miss Kelly, over her shoulder. Nobody liked to be alone with her.

'Hannah has to wait for her father. He can't be here until half past three. Will you wait with her? I have some errands to run before the evening class.'

An excuse to give to her mother for not coming straight home. 'Yes, Miss Kelly,' she said. 'Of course.'

They were left alone. Maggie looked at her writing book. She couldn't concentrate on what she was copying, what the words meant. Something from Matthew. *But if it is by the Spirit of God that I cast out demons, then the kingdom of God has come to you.*

Wind rattled the roof timbers. The lamps which hung from hooks on the walls trembled with the rocking walls. They had not been lit. It was too early. But a rainstorm was building, and it had plunged the hall into early darkness.

The gentle scratch of Hannah's pencil across her workbook disturbed Maggie's thoughts. She looked at the little girl, bent over her work with a protective arm, her legs swinging beneath the desk, feet barely touching the floor.

She wore a yellow dress, and her hair was tied with two yellow ribbons. Maggie wasn't sure if she was six or seven. She was the youngest child who took lessons here.

The clock showed ten past three.

She shouldn't have stayed. Her parents would be angry that Kate had walked home without her. If only she could leave and not go home, walk and walk, into the forest, be free somewhere.

She thought she heard the sound of something wet and heavy being dragged along the ground, just outside, beyond the door that opened on to the land behind and the new building. She turned, and saw something pass the window: the shape of a man's shoulder, a dark coat and hat.

The back door was open. It had not been, a few moments ago, she was sure, but now it stood open, shaking on its stiff, creaking hinges, and a sharp cold draft cut through the room.

She looked behind her. Hannah had put down her pencil. Her gaze followed Maggie's.

The dragging sound had stopped. Maggie pushed back her chair, and went to the door to close it. Beyond the door, where the frame of the new building stood starkly outlined against the sky, Maggie saw a man and a woman. They stood behind the new building, where the trees began.

The man leaned on a rake. He wore a black hat, tilted back and showing a gaunt, weathered face. A white man with sunken cheeks half obscured by an untidy black beard. He wore a black coat and boots, farmer's clothes, but cut in a way nobody wore anymore. She could see sickness on him, hunger, a raw red cast to his eyes.

The woman's hands were clasped, her face sharp and angular, her eyes deep and dark. She wore a heavy skirt and a white cap.

Rain scattered around them. The air smelled of turned earth. Cold drops sliced against Maggie's face, and she wiped at them with her hand, but the man and woman did not move.

Dread sank through her body like mud.

The flat beams that propped up the skeletal roof creaked. A ladder had been left, tied to one of the timber pillars, and it trembled in the wind. It caught her attention for a moment, and when she looked again, the man and woman were gone.

This is a dream, she thought. Sometimes, before a headache started, the world became dreamlike, bent and bright and distorted. It must be that.

The click of little footsteps, and Hannah appeared at her side in the doorway, and took hold of Maggie's skirt. 'What is it?' she said softly.

Maggie searched for her voice. It was trapped in her throat. She should not have stayed. She was not wanted here.

They must leave.

'I don't know.' She forced out the words. She wiped at her face again, and when her hand fell, she saw movement. She turned. The dark shape that she had thought was an old tree at the east edge of the building was now the bearded man, much closer. He was looking at Hannah.

Hannah whispered, 'Who's that?'

Move. Maggie tried to send the message to her legs, and eventually they obeyed. 'Come with me.' She took Hannah's arm and pulled her back. Hannah stumbled a little in her smart shoes, still looking over her shoulder. A shadow passed the window, the man moving to the door. Maggie's grip tightened and she began to run down the hall, between the desks. She was dragging Hannah now, although her own body was still cold and heavy and she felt as if she was running through water. She would not look behind her, but she felt that he was there, at their heels. The main door was close. In just a second they would be out on the main street.

She reached it, flung it open and felt a squall of rain sting her face. The nine white steps that led up to the schoolhouse were sharp and slick with rain and she almost slipped, stumbling forward, the ground lurching. She caught herself, and she did turn then, and she saw a dark shape almost upon them.

She was holding Hannah's arm, and then she wasn't.

Everything was silent, as if suddenly submerged in water. Hannah's yellow dress was vivid against the dark sky, a slash of color flying through the air, and then falling very fast to the ground.

The sound her two little arms made as they broke – Maggie would never forget it. Hannah's scream a few seconds later was terrible, but it was the clean *snap, snap* that made a permanent place in her mind. The sound of a foot stepping on a tender branch and breaking it in two, then two again.

Hannah, on the wet road, her arms bent and her bright dress ruined, screaming; then her father, suddenly, on the road and running toward them, shouting something Maggie couldn't understand; she felt hot breath on the back of her neck, but when she spun around there was nobody there. She looked back down the hall; the far door was still open, and she had a clear line of sight all the way to the frame of the new building, where she thought she saw the woman with her hands over her face.

When she turned back Mr. Crane had gathered Hannah up in his arms but he was looking over her head, straight at Maggie, his face rigid with shock and fury.

*

It was several hours before Mr. Crane accused her, and fully dark by then. At first, amidst Hannah's screams and tears, they helped each other. Maggie ran for the doctor while he stayed with Hannah. He had thanked her when she returned. 'He threw me,' Hannah had begun to say, as her tears dried and her face went pinched and white with pain and shock. 'He threw me.' But Mr. Crane only shushed her.

Maggie was at home, in the kitchen with Leah and her mother, when somebody pounded on the door. Her father had only just returned from work, had not yet removed his shoes or hat, so he answered. It was near seven o'clock.

'I am here to tell you, Mr. Fox,' came a voice from the hall, thin and furious, 'that your daughter is a wicked and sinning girl.'

John Fox might have wondered, for a moment, which daughter he meant. But Mr. Crane continued, 'For what evil reason I cannot possibly imagine, she *threw* my child down the schoolhouse steps, and I saw it with my own eyes. I hope you never hear your own child's bones break, Mr. Fox.'

Maggie should have denied it, and told everybody that Hannah had slipped on the steps. It all would have been so much easier.

Instead, she tried to tell the truth. She came into the hallway, tears in her eyes. 'Mr. Crane.' She stood behind her father. 'Mr. Crane, I didn't throw her, I would never – how could you—'

Her father's head snapped around to look at her.

'Mr. Crane, there was somebody else in the schoolhouse. Ask Hannah, she'll tell you.'

'She doesn't know what she's saying. She's delirious with pain.'

'It was a man – or not a man, something else, I think—'
She swallowed, panic surging, a lump in her throat so that
her next words came out a hoarse whisper. 'Mr. Crane, I
think the school is haunted.'

Later, she would think back to that moment. Over and
over. The mixture of contempt and anger she saw cross both
their faces. How her cheeks burned when she heard Leah
and her mother come into the hallway and turned to see their
aghast expressions. *Haunted*.

They might believe that Hannah had slipped, but who
would believe this? To have spoken such nonsense was as
good as a confession.

Mr. Crane turned back to her father. 'Mr. Fox,' he hissed.
'The girl is deprived of her mind. She is demented.'

But she had said it once, so Maggie persisted. She had a
purpose now, more than her own defense: the school wasn't
safe. Something had been disturbed. The new building
should be abandoned. The gravestones should be put back.
She was sure of it, or somebody else would be hurt. Over
and over, she said it. Each time, her father's disgust grew
deeper.

She did not return to school, and there were whispers the
police would be told. Mr. Crane wrote Amy and Isaac a
private letter Maggie wasn't to know about, but she was sure
it said that the Foxes should be put out of their house.

Hannah was very sick, they were told. The shock had
made her sick. Both her arms were splinted and she wept all
day.

'A man and a woman,' Maggie said. 'I know I saw them.
They were angry. And the man had a kind of force. I can't
explain it but I *know*. I can still feel him, it's as if he's stuck
to me—'

Her mother told her, tearfully, that she was mistaken, and surely it had been an accident.

He *was* stuck to her, his fury lingering on her skin like some sort of residue that could not be washed away.

Calvin was summoned from the farm. And he told her, gently, that under certain conditions it was possible for the mind to conjure phantoms and delusions, and that whatever had happened, it was certainly an accident.

Amy listened to her protestations, and looked at her for a long time.

'Do you believe me?' Maggie said.

Amy said, 'Do you believe yourself?'

And Maggie couldn't bring herself to answer, because she did and didn't, at the same time.

What Leah said was: 'You have to stop this. Just say that she slipped, Maggie, or you don't know how it happened, but stop with this story of the ghosts. It doesn't *matter* what you think the truth is. I don't *care*. Blaming ghosts only makes you look as wicked as Mr. Crane says you are. Stop.'

She couldn't stop. Over and over again, till her voice was hoarse, and still nobody apart from Kate would say they believed her. Amy and Isaac withdrew, working all day and eating supper separately, and said they were praying for the child's recovery. Maggie tried to speak to Amy again but she was kept away.

She knew her mother didn't believe her, but somehow it mattered less than Amy. Her mother loved her. Maggie never doubted it. Her mother would love her if she committed a terrible crime, if she lied or stole or murdered somebody. But she was gentle, too gentle, and mild, and always deferred to the loudest voice in a room. She was not one to argue, or to stand up for things. Even if she *did* believe her, Maggie knew she couldn't withstand the force of John Fox and James Crane and Leah and Calvin, all saying that it couldn't be true. She was better at soothing than arguing.

But Amy. Amy's opinions were her own; they were carefully formed, and correct, and they mattered. Amy had taken so much time to talk to her, to give her things to read and to ask her difficult questions – she had seen potential in Maggie, a quality that Maggie wasn't sure she could see in herself. Amy respected her. Her mother's love was constant, it hardly mattered what Maggie did, but Amy's respect had to be *earned*, and to have lost it was as painful, she was almost sure, as a broken bone.

She was told to stay in her room, and then one afternoon a few days after it happened, Leah put a hand on her forehead and said, 'You're fevered, Maggie. I think you're very sick.' And then looked at their mother and said pointedly, 'She may have been sick for days. She hasn't known what she's saying.'

A fever. Leah and their mother could hardly keep from repeating it over and over, as they helped her into a nightdress, fetched water and a damp cloth which they placed on her forehead, drew a sheet around her. Back and forth, still whispering to each other. The lamps were turned down low.

Kate lingered in the doorway and then tried to help. She fetched a bundle of dried herbs and held them over a candle till they lit. Then she blew out the flame and left them smoldering in a small bowl.

She sat on the end of Maggie's bed and looked at her sister. 'Are you really sick?' she whispered.

Maggie said, 'I don't know.'

Just outside the bedroom door, Leah was saying, 'She couldn't have known what she was doing. A fever, her mind – she'd lost her senses. She can't be blamed.'

'Because it doesn't make any sense,' her mother whispered. 'That she would have done this.'

'Of course it doesn't make any sense, Mother.' Leah was very firm. 'A *fever.*'

'Then – a doctor—'

'No. No doctor. Mr. Crane knows every doctor in Rochester. You're her *mother.* You know better than anyone when your own daughter is sick. Don't you?'

'But Leah – I don't—'

'The girl has a terrible fever. You know it, I know it. That's all there is to say.'

And then, in the dark room with the sharp smell of burning sage and sweetgrass, Maggie began to feel that she *was* sick. Terribly sick. A headache beat like a drum in her skull and her sight was blurred. Perhaps the man's anger had poisoned her. Yes, she thought, I am sick, now.

A meeting of the men was called.

Maggie sat against the pillows, watching a candle by the bed begin to gutter and smoke, while below her in the drawing room, they gathered to talk about her. Kate crouched on the stairs to watch, and with each arrival she ran back to report to Maggie. James Crane had come, and the local doctor, and Calvin, and their father, and Isaac, as it was his house, after all.

When the drawing-room door had been closed, Kate darted down to the small cloakroom next to it, where you could press your ear to the wall and hear everything. And when it was over, Kate came back and repeated all of it.

The police would do no good, Calvin had said. The Fox family would help to pay for the little girl's care, he would pay himself if he had to, but Maggie was sick, anybody could see that: she had a fever that day, no one knew she had it but she did and couldn't have known what she was doing. It was a terrible accident.

Kate did impressions as she narrated the conversation. Narrowed eyes and a deep voice for James Crane. The softly spoken doctor. Calvin, nervous.

James Crane: *I saw it with my own eyes. The girl is evil.*

The doctor: *We shouldn't use words like that. She has some sort of malady, certainly. A disturbance of the mind—*

It's an ordinary sickness, that's all, Calvin said. *A fever. It will pass.* He said, *The schoolhouse steps are too steep.* He said, *We'll pay for Hannah's care.*

James Crane: *That isn't the issue. I have plenty of money. Who are you*, he said to Calvin, *who are you anyway?*

Some sort of intervention, the doctor said. *A – kind of hysteria, she ought to be taken to a quiet place—*

I am telling each of you – James Crane, his voice rising – *I saw the girl push my daughter* – throw *my daughter* – *she hit the ground with a greater force than a slip could ever cause—*

Finally, her father spoke, but not to defend her. *We'll take her away. We'll leave, as soon as possible. We'll pay and we'll leave. Will that settle it?*

The police should be called, said James Crane.

She's only fifteen, Calvin said. *The police, it wouldn't be right—*

She's no longer a child, James Crane said. *There ought to be consequences.*

There'll be consequences, John Fox said. *There will be.*

Lying in bed, her eyes stung. Kate drifted in and out of view. She was very hot. She thought: I am sick, now.

THIRTEEN
ROCHESTER
APRIL 1848

An iron smell came up from the river. Maggie leaned against the stone wall of the bridge, went up on her toes to peer over the edge, and took a deep breath. Iron mingled with the grassy, wet smell of spring. Her body was confused: it had been winter when they left Hydesville, but somehow it was spring here.

They had arrived late the previous night, and fallen exhausted into their beds, hardly stopping to talk to Leah or look at her house. Maggie had woken first, and found Leah waiting for her in the kitchen. She had suggested a walk to the market.

Maggie looked north downriver. They had been gone from Rochester for nearly five months, and there were new buildings everywhere, the bank crowded with more flour mills and houses and shipping offices than she remembered, and more people to go with them.

She knew that thousands of people flooded through the city on their way west, but thousands of them stopped here too. Her father used to complain about all the men – the Irish especially, he never trusted the Irish – who'd come to build the canal and had stayed, building taverns and gambling dens and worse to entertain themselves, but a city had to be built somehow, didn't it?

People came up from the South too, running from slavery, following the Genesee up to where it emptied into Lake

Ontario. All those people, all in motion. Her heart beat faster with the thought of it.

She turned to Leah. 'Well?' she said. 'Are you going to tell me what you think?'

'What I think?'

'Of the pamphlet. I know you've read it.'

Leah was watching the progress of a small packet-boat as it cut a line through the water. She was wearing a black dress. She always did, hoping that people would think she was a widow. A black dress with a modest lace collar, almost certainly too heavy and warm for the day. There were traces of sweat at her brow.

Leah wasn't beautiful, but she was arresting: people looked at her.

'I have read it,' she said. 'Yes.'

Maggie had placed her own copy of the pamphlet, with her name written on every page, in the small drawer by the bed when they had arrived, to keep it safe. It was already smudged, with pages coming loose. She planned to take it to Amy as soon as possible, to show her: printed words, written by a man. Her father's name on the front. Its authority was undeniable.

'And?' said Maggie.

'You must be very pleased with it.'

What did that mean? It was so frustrating to talk to Leah. It was as if she talked in code, everything she said layered with some hidden implication.

'I'm not pleased with it. I'm not anything. It's just the truth.'

'You're hoping that people will read this and think again about your schoolhouse story. If this was real, perhaps that was too.'

It stung. Maggie took a deep breath, let the smell of the water into her body. 'It *was* real, Leah. No one can doubt it now.' She forced confidence into her voice. 'I'd like to see Amy. She should know what's happened. Everybody should know. They should read all those statements. The witnesses.'

Leah didn't seem to be listening. 'I found it strange, the pamphlet – that nobody seems to have asked you and Katie for your own accounts. Nobody seems to have been interested in what you thought.'

'Nobody ever is,' Maggie snapped.

'Well, on this occasion I *am*, Maggie. I'm very interested. And if this was all a scheme of yours to make people believe you—'

Maggie began shaking her head.

'– then it's been a spectacular success, and I'm extremely impressed.'

'No. Leah, no. That isn't it. There were sounds in the house that we couldn't explain. And everybody heard them. We asked questions, and somebody answered.'

'But, Maggie—' She saw Leah falter, looking for the words. She placed her basket on the ground and reached for Maggie's arm. 'Maggie, didn't this spirit need a little *help*? To communicate? All these raps and knocks and so on.'

Maggie shook off her arm. Her stomach twisted itself into a knot. 'Because I'm so very deceitful?' she said. 'That's right. I made this up too, so I could throw Katie down the stairs and blame the ghosts, only I never got around to it.'

'Maggie.'

'You should be careful in case I throw you into the river. I'm very strong.'

'Maggie.'

'It was real.'

'Of course it was. A spirit, absolutely. But there would have been no harm in adding a few effects of your own, would there? I know you and Katie, and the games you used to play, the tricks on our father – I'm not suggesting that you're *liars*, only that the two of you were always good performers—'

'We weren't performing.'

'But if you *were* – listen, Maggie. If you were, I wouldn't object. Do you understand?'

Maggie tried to make sense of this. She had known that Leah would be angry to have missed all the excitement, that she would want to make herself a part of it somehow. But she had the sense that Leah was somewhere else, two steps ahead of her, waiting for her to catch up.

'You wouldn't object.'

'I wouldn't.'

'Why not? After the schoolhouse you told me never to tell those sorts of stories again.'

'This is different. Something different has happened here. I read the pamphlet three times through, Maggie. It's extraordinary. I've been thinking about it. I've thought about it every day, and what it means. What it *might* mean. And I've shown it to a few friends, and they were very interested. I think they'd like to meet you, now that you're here.'

The thought of anybody wanting to meet her was strange, and powerful.

'Whatever you tell me, Maggie,' said Leah quietly, 'you can trust me to support you.'

'Support me? The way you did with Mr. Crane?'

Leah's expression changed. 'Yes. That's right.'

They were silent, looking at each other in the clear morning light. A group of boys passed them on the bridge, whistling, on their way to work, and Leah had to step aside.

'I've noticed, lately,' said Leah. She lowered her voice, and Maggie had to lean in to hear her over the blur of city sounds around them, steamboats in the water and horses and passing conversation. 'I've noticed that people have become more interested in spiritual communication.' Leah's expression was perfectly serious. 'I believe that's why the pamphlet is such a success. All those copies sold. It arrived at just the right moment.'

Maggie didn't like the way she spoke. As if she were talking of a new invention, a new kind of stove or steam-hammer.

'I'm sure you've noticed that these are times of change. Times of upheaval and excitement. Everybody is very interested in the *new*.'

'Spirits aren't new,' Maggie said softly.

'No.'

'Then what do you mean?'

'This thing, these events in the house. You called out questions and the spirit answered. A conversation, a kind of direct communication, using code, using the alphabet. It's almost scientific. It's not so different from the telegraph, is it? Voices through the wires. If humans can send messages across great distances, why not spirits?'

She ought to have stayed in bed, Maggie thought. She should have let Leah fetch the breakfast things on her own. The journey had been long; she hadn't yet summoned up the strength to talk like this. You had to be alert when you talked to Leah, you couldn't drift off, or she would have trapped you in some way.

'It's nothing like the telegraph,' she said.

'It's a lot like it. It's something nobody would have imagined possible, and now here it is. These ideas are in the

103

air, Maggie, they're in the water. There's a man who's written all about this very recently, the spirit world. He says he wrote his book in a trance, and sold quite a few copies, from what I hear. We're living in a *moment*.'

'You didn't say any of this in November. You didn't say we were living in a moment. You told everybody I was delirious.'

'I've done a lot of thinking since then.'

'Leah, it isn't something new.' It came back to her, despite the warm morning and the sound of birds. The memory of their dark bedroom, the pressure that built in her brain and the raps from the walls. 'It's something old.'

Leah didn't seem to be listening. 'It occurred to me that it must have been difficult in that house, after that night, in Hydesville. All the excitement, and then the neighbors coming back wanting to hear more.'

Maggie was thirsty. She hadn't drunk anything since she'd woken up. She turned and began to walk away from Leah, back across the bridge in the direction of home. Thinking she must get home and have a glass of water.

Leah picked up the basket and hurried after her, falling into step beside her. 'Because the first time they hear something, they're amazed. But if they don't hear it again, they start to doubt themselves. Unless there's another demonstration, they start to look back and wonder if they were deceived. Is that right?'

Leah knew what they had done. She *knew*. Maggie was gripped by something like panic. Soon everyone might guess it. She began to walk faster, but Leah took her arm.

'Maggie. Stop.' Maggie spun around, braced for some sort of accusation, but instead Leah spoke in a soft voice. 'I know what you want. I know why you wanted to come back here. You want people to listen to you. And they will, but you'll need to do more. The pamphlet's forgotten soon enough, or it becomes something to laugh at. There will have to be *more*.'

Another crowd passed, a group of older men with tools slung over their shoulders, and Maggie was almost pushed aside. Leah kept her grip on her arm.

'You know that as soon as our father has finished building the house you'll be expected to go back there, you and Kate. And before long you'll be married off as a farmer's wife, or worse, or you'll need to find work of some kind, and you won't like it.' She paused. 'So I'm glad that you wrote to me. I'm glad I was able to bring you here.'

'We weren't brought here,' said Maggie. 'I wrote to you and said—'

'In any case, you're here. And I imagine you'd hope to stay.'

You hardly know me, Maggie thought. And then, she thought: nobody knows me at all.

'I can help,' Leah said.

'I can help myself,' said Maggie.

'Let me put it this way,' said Leah. 'We can help each other.'

Then she let go of Maggie's arm and walked on ahead, leaving Maggie standing behind, feeling bruised and angry and as if Leah had stolen something from her, though she couldn't say what.

FOURTEEN

After breakfast, with cups and plates still on the table and crumbs on the floor.

Leah brushed her sleeves, and said, 'You know, there are stories that this old house is haunted too.'

Their mother had been holding her teacup up to the light to admire the pattern. She put it down. 'Leah. We've had enough of those sorts of stories, I think.' But she leaned forward, curious.

'I'm sure, but it can't be helped. You're going to find out one way or another.'

Leah's eyes cut briefly in Maggie's direction, then away again, casting around the room as if looking for inspiration.

'They say the first inhabitants of this house were a young couple who both died one terrible winter of a sudden sickness.' She paused. Maggie could see her improvising. 'But the house was snowed in and their bodies weren't found until spring.'

Leah was a good liar, Maggie thought, but not good enough. She had the sideways cast to her eyes that Kate got when she made up stories as she went along.

'The first inhabitants?' Maggie doubted the house was more than five or six years old. 'How many inhabitants have there been?'

Leah shot her an irritable look. 'And now of course they both haunt the place together.'

Kate's eyes had gone wide. 'Both of them?'

'That's right.'

'What a terrible story,' said their mother brightly.

'Isn't it?' Leah cleared her throat. 'I can't help wondering, now the girls are here, if we might experience any disturbances. If the girls have some sort of gift, I wonder if – well, if other spirits would be drawn to them.'

Kate, who had been spooning the last drops of cream from a jug into her mouth, now had the spoon dangling forgotten in her hand.

'If the story's true, of course. And who's to say it is?' With a tilt of her head, Leah said: 'What do you think, Maggie? Are we alone here?'

Maggie clenched her teeth. She felt a terrible urge to throw her cup of water in Leah's face and walk out of the room. Her mother had turned to her expectantly. Sunlight slanted through the windows and caught the dust in the air.

Leah looked at her, waiting. Perhaps she thought that Maggie wouldn't dare.

'No.' Maggie could make up a story as well as Leah, if she had to. She thought quickly. 'I don't think we are. I didn't want to frighten you, Mother, so I didn't say anything, but last night in our bedroom I woke up and I thought I saw a figure standing at the end of the bed. I might have been dreaming—'

'I saw it too,' said Kate. 'At the end of my bed.'

'– but I felt—' Maggie glanced at Kate, who had folded her hands in her lap and sat looking delicate and anxious. 'I felt, it was like a kind of sadness, in the air, or loneliness, I don't know, it was—'

Their mother had put her hand to her mouth. In horror or delight, Maggie couldn't tell.

'How very strange,' said Leah, 'to hear you say that.

Because I've sometimes felt the same sensation, when I've been here alone. The sadness.'

Maggie sat up straighter, leaned forward. No. She had to get ahead of Leah, or Leah would lead her around like a lamb. 'No, but more than sadness,' she said, 'and we *saw* somebody. Or it could have been two people, one at the end of my bed—'

'– and one at the end of mine,' said Kate.

'– but I don't think Leah's story is right, because I don't think it was a man and his wife, I think it was' – she thought again – 'two men, actually, they might have been brothers, who lived here—'

'I think that too,' said Kate.

'– and they wanted to talk to us,' Maggie said. 'To me.'

They all fell quiet. Her mother picked up a fork, and put it down again, and looked behind her as if she thought somebody might be standing there. She was wearing the same dress she had worn yesterday, the same dress she had owned for years, her hair the same way, the same shoes.

'Your father would say,' she said, 'and your brother – they would say that this sort of talk isn't right, it isn't good for us.'

There was a small clock on the mantelpiece, and Maggie noticed its tick for the first time. And then a carriage passing by outside.

'But they aren't here,' she said.

When the breakfast things were cleared away, their mother went back to her room. The journey yesterday had exhausted her, she said, and she wanted to sleep for a few more hours. 'If I *can* sleep, without expecting to see a strange man at the end of my bed.' She gave Kate's hair an affectionate tug and went away.

Leah avoided Maggie's eyes, and began straightening cushions, and shaking out the curtains.

Leah said there had been a hired girl for a while, but she'd had to let her go. And there were hints of disorder all about the house. Dusty shelves and bedsheets not properly folded, a burned cooking pot left on the stove. Leah's daughter Lizzie had lived here with Leah for a while, but now she had gone too and the house was too large for one person.

Maggie and Kate were sharing the attic room, and their mother had a bedroom entirely to herself on the second floor. The kitchen was small but the parlor was huge, with room for Leah's piano, several seats and sofas and an impressive cherrywood table at the center.

Everything but the piano belonged to the landlady. She was a wealthy widow with whom Leah had evidently struck a good deal. Leah wanted them to be impressed by the house, Maggie thought, and so she tried not to be.

'I want to rest as well,' Maggie said, and left the room before Leah could respond. She slipped back up to her room and sat on the bed.

She slid open the bedside drawer and took out the pamphlet. Her eyes skimmed the words.

. . . that the weapons of ridicule and disbelief with which they meet these statements, and the belief which they must produce in candid minds, are the same as those used by Hume and Voltaire against the divine origin of the miracles reconciled in the New Testament . . .

That was what made it believable, wasn't it? The long words, and Hume and Voltaire. He had put Shakespeare on the front, a bit from *Macbeth*. No wonder people were impressed.

If she had run from that schoolhouse quoting *Hamlet*, or the Bible, perhaps things would have been different.

AUTHENTICATED, it said on the front, and *CONFIRMED. PUBLISHED BY E.E. LEWIS.*

She had imagined herself rushing to Amy's house with the pamphlet held high – her proof, her certificate of authenticity – *look, everybody*—

But Leah was right. It wouldn't be enough. Words on a page could never explain how it had felt, in that room, how everybody had felt when they heard those sounds. The pamphlet was a curiosity. There would have to be more.

Kate appeared in the doorway, twisting a long strand of hair around her finger. She came in and closed the door behind her, leaned against it. 'Leah's cross about something.'

'She's always cross.'

'But she says to come downstairs so we can talk about things. I don't know what things.'

Maggie opened the pamphlet somewhere in the middle, anywhere. *I live in this place. I moved from Cayuga county here, last October. I live within a few roads of the house in which these noises have been heard.* It was Mr. Duesler's statement.

'I don't know why I said that,' said Kate. 'About someone at the end of the bed. It wasn't true.' She looked out of the window. 'It's just nice. Being part of something. I like it.'

'I know.'

'Did *you* see somebody?'

Maggie ignored the question. 'Leah says there's people here, in Rochester, who've heard about us.'

'I know. She told me too. They might even want to meet us.' Kate gave an excited little shiver, and then laughed at herself.

'Do you want to?'

'Of course. Don't you?'

'They might be disappointed in us.'

'Why?'

'They'll want to see something for themselves. They'll want some sort of – encounter, for themselves. To tell their friends.'

Kate had twisted the piece of hair all the way to the top, and she let it fall back in a loose curl. 'That's alright though,' she said, without pausing, as if she'd already thought about it. 'We can just do the same as we did in Hydesville, can't we? With our toes. Do you think people would come here to see us? We could try and talk to the couple who died, or the brothers—'

'There are no brothers. I made it up. So did Leah.'

'Oh.' Kate blinked. 'Of course. But there might be others. There might be spirits she doesn't know about.'

Maggie glanced around the room, the dusty walls and empty corners. She listened for a moment, half hoping to hear raps from the floorboards, disappointed at the silence.

Leah had a piano lesson at eleven o'clock, and Maggie stayed in her room, listening to some child or other banging tunelessly at the keys. The notes had an eerie, unsettling quality, drifting up through the floorboards. Or perhaps she had managed to scare herself with her imaginary ghostly brothers.

She tried to write a note to Amy, telling her that she was back in the city, and would like to visit. It only had to be a few lines, but each time she started she lost confidence, and thought there must be a better way to say it, a way that didn't sound so desperate.

Instead, she dragged a wooden chair to the window and

sat looking out across the rooftops. A breeze had picked up, and ragged clouds drifted across the sky. The piano music stopped and started in awkward bursts. In one of the silences, she heard herself whisper, 'Is somebody there?'

When there was no answer, she cracked the middle toe of her right foot. Once, for yes.

When the lesson was over, Maggie heard Leah saying goodbye at the door, and then speaking to Kate in the kitchen. A few minutes later, the front door opened again, and she looked out to see Leah crossing the road and walking down the street to a two-story white house with a small, tidy front yard and a neat little fence. Leah knocked at the door, and a moment later she went inside, but Maggie couldn't see who had opened it. She watched for a while, to see if Leah would emerge, and when she didn't, she went downstairs to the kitchen, where she found Kate kneeling on the floor with her skirt tucked up and her feet bare, scrubbing.

'If Leah tells you to do something,' Maggie said, 'you don't have to do it. We only just arrived.'

Kate sat back on her heels and smiled, pushing her hair from her face with her forearm. 'I don't mind. I like it. It's better than school. Look.' She pointed at the bucket of water beneath the table, which was almost black. 'I don't think Leah *ever* cleans.'

'We're not here to be her hired help.'

'I wonder if a rich family would hire me. I could spy on all their secrets and look at their jewels.'

'You'd hate that.'

'I don't know.' Kate looked down at the rag that was scrunched in her hand. 'You have to do *some*thing.'

Maggie heard the front door open and close, and went to

the hall. She saw immediately on Leah's face an expression that would have looked like guilt if it had been anybody else.

'Where have you been?'

'Maggie.' Leah cleared her throat. 'I have some interesting news.' She sat down on a stool by the door and began to unlace her shoes, rubbing her stockinged feet as she dropped the shoes carelessly. 'I just called on my dear friend Eliza Adams and her husband, and we got to talking. Of course I told her my sisters were visiting.'

'Of course.'

'Eliza is one of the friends I mentioned who's read the pamphlet. I told her you were visiting and of course she and her husband would like to meet you, and Katie.'

'Leah—'

'They were especially keen when I told them we'd had our own ghostly activity here. Eliza already believes she's spoken with the spirit of her dead grandmother or some such, so I'd say she's susceptible to this sort of thing. In any case, they're coming tomorrow evening, and they're hoping for some sort of – what shall we call it? A demonstration.'

Leah wasn't looking at her. She stood again, and went by Maggie through to the parlor, where she began tidying the piano music that lay on the table. Maggie stood in the doorway, momentarily speechless, until she finally managed to choke out, 'Tomorrow?'

'That's right.'

'*Leah.*'

'So I suppose we ought to think about what we might do to entertain them.'

'Tell them no. Go back and tell them no. We can't. I won't.'

'Maggie. When you were a little girl there was nothing

you wanted more in the world than *attention*. Well, you have it. Why don't you try and *enjoy* it?'

'But what will we do? What's supposed to happen?'

'That's what I'm waiting for you to tell me. How you do it. Whatever it is, we must be able to recreate it.'

'We *don't* do it. The house was haunted.'

'Then this house will have to be haunted too.'

Kate came out of the kitchen, still barefoot, the rag in her hand. 'There are *some* things we did,' she said, and Leah turned sharply in her direction. 'We were playing some tricks to scare Father and that's when' – she hesitated – 'that's when he started talking back to us.'

'Who?'

'The peddler. And we did some tricks for the neighbors too.'

Kate's voice was quiet, but Maggie heard a trace of pride. Leah gave Maggie a satisfied look.

'No. No, Leah. It's not like you think—'

'Some tricks,' said Leah. 'How interesting.'

'It was *real*.'

'Katie, would you like to meet some of my friends, and try your tricks again? Who knows, we might stir up another spirit for you to talk to.'

Maggie was shaking her head, but Kate wasn't looking at her. 'Yes, alright,' Kate said. 'I'd like that.'

She couldn't stand it. The sparkling sensation was back in her hands. Her blood burned. She pushed past them both and ran up the stairs to their bedroom, slamming the door. She picked up a hairbrush that Kate had left lying on the bed and threw it at the wall, where something cracked, either the wall or the brush, she didn't look. And she sat down on the floor, with her back to the door, so they couldn't come in.

She needed to be by herself, without her sisters or her mother or any of them.

She clenched and unclenched her hands, until they felt normal. Leah, she thought. Leah, Leah, Leah. She should never have written to her. She had invited her into the world they had created, her and Kate, and now Leah was changing the furniture and repainting the walls. It had always been like this. Leah had ruined her own life, choosing a worthless husband who left her in disgrace, and now she was determined to ruin everybody else's, with her schemes and ideas. Controlling everything, taking everything and making it her own. Her own daughter couldn't stand her, and so Leah thought Maggie and Kate could take her place.

Did she *hate* her sister? She wondered for a moment. Yes. She thought she did. Hated her in the painful way that was mixed up with love and other things. When she was young she had looked at her with a kind of awe, and the thing they were all supposed to be ashamed of – that Leah was alone, with a baby, not even the dignity of widowhood – had impressed her. It was hard to let go of those childhood feelings, but she must. There was nothing to admire about Leah. She was awful.

There was a soft knock at the door behind her. She closed her eyes. The handle turned and the door was pushed, but Maggie wouldn't let it open. Another knock, and Kate's voice. 'It's only me, Maggie. Please let me in.'

She took two deep breaths, and opened her eyes.

'Please,' Kate whispered, almost too soft to hear. Sometimes Maggie thought Kate was talking to her from inside her own head.

She pushed herself away from the door and moved to sit against the wall next to it. She didn't open it, but a few moments later Kate gave it a tentative push, peered around the corner at Maggie, and then came in. She stood for a moment, chewing her thumbnail, and then sat down on the floor against the end of Maggie's bed, so they faced each other.

They were quiet for a while. Then Maggie said, 'Now Leah thinks we made everything up.'

'I don't care what Leah thinks.'

How Maggie wished she could feel the same. She couldn't imagine what it would be like. She cared what Leah thought. She cared what *everybody* thought. Whoever she met, whoever she spoke to: *What do they think of me?*

It was why she couldn't bear it, after the schoolhouse, that nobody believed her. She was not a liar, not insane, and they thought she was.

She knew something, she knew an extraordinary thing – that ghosts were real. And nobody believed her.

Until Hydesville.

'It doesn't matter what she thinks,' Kate said. She spoke very slowly then, as if she were the older sister. 'It doesn't – matter – what – she – thinks. Everybody who was there in Hydesville knows it was real. Even Father. Even David and Calvin, I think.'

'But she's asking us to *pretend*. She's invited her friends because she thinks it was all just a show that we can put on again. And there's no – there's no *time*, even, to think about anything. They're coming tomorrow.'

'I know. So we have to think of what to do. We've got all day, and tomorrow. You can think of something. You must have some ideas.'

'Katie. It won't be *real*.'

'It might be. We might find a way to make another spirit

speak to us.' Kate crawled up on to her knees and looked at Maggie earnestly. 'When we spoke to the peddler, I knew he was there, and I wasn't frightened. I felt like I was lit up and I was powerful.' She paused. 'I felt like I was closer to God. I want to feel that way again. Don't you?'

No, Maggie thought. I am frightened. Kate had not been there, in the schoolhouse.

But she remembered the power too. The light that had burned in her. Could it have been *God's* light? The idea was wild and beautiful.

'*Please*, Maggie. I want to.'

And Kate was her little sister again, begging her to play a game.

'But if nothing happens, we have to lie.'

Kate was shaking her head. 'If we make them believe, that's a gift to them. It doesn't matter how we do it. We're still showing them the truth.'

FIFTEEN

I am here to show people the truth.

Kate left her and went back downstairs.

Maggie looked at the blank wall, eyes burning. I have come to Rochester to show people the truth. She liked the way that sounded. All the people in the city, flowing through the streets, moving with so much purpose, making things and changing things. She was one of them. She could not be sent away again. She had to make a place for herself here. The truth.

In her trunk, which lay under the bed, was a small exercise book, and a pen. She found the book, flipped to a blank page. At the top, in her best writing, she wrote *Revealing the truth*. And underlined it.

Later, as she went downstairs, she paused at her mother's door, and pushed it gently open to look inside. Her mother was sleeping, one hand loosely clasping a book. It was strange for her to be tired so early. But she was getting old, Maggie thought. Both her parents – they were older than most parents of children her age. And they had worked hard, all their lives, worked through many brutal winters. And Maggie had caused them so much trouble.

'I'm sorry,' she whispered. And she went downstairs.

Maggie suggested the table. Back in Hydesville, their toe-cracking trick was best performed at the kitchen table, where nobody could see their feet. If her idea was to work, they would need a table.

The afternoon had grown suddenly overcast and the room was gloomy. At Maggie's instruction, Leah closed the curtains, lit a solitary candle and placed it in the middle of the table.

'By the way,' she said, as she sat down, 'I've had a note from David. He's sending Calvin to join us tomorrow.'

'Why?' Maggie was watching Kate, who was wandering around the room, picking things up and putting them down as if looking for something.

'I expect he's concerned what might happen without a man to supervise us.'

Did Calvin mind, Maggie wondered, being sent places, on errands for the family? Whatever they asked of him, he always did.

'I don't know how long he'll stay. Last I heard he'd read something somewhere about the Oregon Trail and was thinking of going out West—'

Maggie sat up straight. 'What?'

'– but he's hardly the only young man with ideas of that sort. I'm sure he'll stay a while if David's told him to. I don't know where he'll sleep.'

'He wants to leave?'

Leah spread her hands. 'Ask him,' she said. '*Kate*. Will you please sit down.'

Kate looked stung. She sloped back to the table and sat down, sharing a glance with Maggie.

'Now,' said Leah. 'Maggie. Why don't you tell us your ideas?'

Maggie had missed lunch, still waiting for her temper to cool, and not ready to face Leah again. But she had begun to scribble things, searching back in her mind to the things they had done in Hydesville. It was difficult to tease out what had been them, and what had not.

She was hungry, now, but the hunger made her light-headed in a half-pleasurable way.

'My idea,' said Maggie, 'is that people don't want to talk to any old spirit. We can make up any story we like about this house, but wouldn't they rather speak to somebody they know?'

'Yes,' said Leah. 'I'm sure that's right.'

'So we should ask them when they come, if they've lost somebody or if there's somebody they want us to – reach out to.'

'Yes,' said Leah. 'Yes, yes. Quite right.'

Maggie shot her an irritated glance. 'But to work best they should give us a few names, I think, and then we choose one to spell out.'

Leah was leaning forward. 'And after that? How do we advance the conversation? And give the right answers?'

'We have to ask very simple questions, I think. We only let the, the – spirit – answer yes or no. One rap for yes, two for no.'

'Yes,' said Leah. 'Yes. Very good. But now, girls. These raps. It's time for you to tell me—'

There was a sudden, sharp *crack* from beneath the table, that made Leah and Maggie both jump.

Kate was smiling. Leah pressed a hand to her chest.

Maggie, pleased at Leah's shock, cracked her own toes, twice.

'*Oh*,' said Leah. '*Oh*.'

'We can crack our toes,' said Kate. 'And our knuckles.'

Leah nodded, still looking startled. 'I remember.'

'There was more,' said Maggie. 'There were other things, but when you're in a room, at a table . . . Nobody seemed to understand where it came from.'

Leah was impressed. Maggie felt a stirring of pride. 'It's very simple,' she said.

'Wonderfully simple.' Leah clasped her hands together. 'Wonderful.'

'And the candle,' Maggie said. 'And if it's dark. It was easier in Hydesville, it was always dark, and the house was strange, and cold, and it made people – it made it easier to believe, I suppose. It might be more difficult here.'

'Yes. Yes. We'll have to recreate a certain mood. And practice a few more techniques. A few effects to begin the thing, to startle them. After that I think their imaginations will do a lot of the work. I read the pamphlet, all those different accounts, all of them so convinced – by the end I imagine you could have sneezed and they would have thought it was a spiritual manifestation.'

Kate folded her arms. 'It wasn't like that at all.'

But Leah wasn't listening. 'And with Eliza and Nathaniel, I'm sure it will take no effort at all: Eliza already believes all of this and Nathaniel is terribly superstitious, I'm sure of it. It won't always be so easy, there'll be others who are more resistant—'

'Which others?' said Maggie. 'Who?'

'Others, who come to meet us. If tomorrow night is a success I dare say they'll be queuing at our door. Eliza has friends all over the city. But if we take the time to prepare, to learn some details in advance, who's lost a loved one and so on—'

It came to Maggie very suddenly, and she was astonished that she hadn't realized before.

'Money,' she said. 'You want to do this for money.'

'No,' said Leah evenly. 'Not yet. Not until we know if we have something worth paying for.'

'I won't do it for money.'

'What's so wrong with money?'

'I want to be believed.'

'People are all the more likely to believe something if they've paid for it, in my experience. Mr. Lewis has made his money, hasn't he? Why shouldn't we?'

She'd been to a show, she said, just a few weeks before, outside Rochester. A kind of traveling preacher, but his religion wasn't clear, and he had stood on a stage and claimed to have given a blind man sight – right there, in front of them. Anybody could see it was nonsense, she said – the man hadn't been blind to begin with. And some of the audience had jeered and called it blasphemy, but others in the audience had shrieked and moaned and fainted, and then they had emptied their pockets into the collection tins. It was exciting, Leah said. And worth paying for.

'And not so different from Reverend Anderson at our old church, anyway,' she added. 'Standing there and promising our place in heaven. These gentlemen know how to command a crowd. That's all there is to it. They make anything seem convincing.'

'That might have been real, with the preacher,' Kate said. 'I'd have liked to see it. You don't know.'

'Quite,' said Leah. 'You don't know. And that's the secret to it. Besides, it's not wrong to deceive people if they *want* to be deceived.'

'Nobody wants to be deceived,' said Maggie.

'Visit a church. *Everybody* wants to be deceived.'

The candlewax glistened in the flickering light.

Leah cleared her throat. 'I mean to say,' she said, in a gentler tone. 'They want to be *entertained*. They want to be thrilled. And they want to believe that their dear dead Aunt Agatha is still with them.'

Maggie stared at the table, at the dancing patterns of light and dark. Then she looked back at her sisters. In the dim light Maggie could see the ways in which they all looked alike. The shape of their eyes, the angle of their chins.

'We'll see, tomorrow. That's all. We'll see what happens, and if you don't enjoy yourselves, we won't try it again. There'll be no harm done. We can go back to our *ordinary* lives, school and housework, you can go back to Wayne County. Eliza and Nathaniel are my friends. We won't be asking anybody for money. We'll only be asking for a little bit of faith.'

'I won't do it for money,' said Maggie.

'You can do it for whatever reason you choose, little sister,' Leah said. 'We all have our reasons.'

SIXTEEN

And so they practiced, that afternoon, and the next morning as well. The way they had rehearsed the little plays they had sometimes put on when they were children at Christmas.

They would sit around a table, and hold hands, so that nobody could accuse them of knocking on the table themselves. They experimented with toes and knuckles. Kate had been practicing, and could make a clicking sound with her ankle. To make their faces blank and make no visible movements, that was the way it had to be done.

Leah tried herself, but she had no skill for it. Age, Maggie thought, probably made the bones stiffer, the joints more rigid. Things cracked, but not when they were supposed to. They had this skill because they were girls. Leah was concerned with details, the kinds of questions they might ask, to gently discern the answers they needed. She told them everything she knew about Eliza and Nathaniel, their family, their money troubles, their personalities, and beliefs. She could have written a book on them, Maggie thought, wondering how Leah could store so much information.

By the time Calvin arrived, at lunchtime, the house was crackling with energy and anticipation.

Maggie saw him first, from the gable window. She saw him dismount a carriage and pay the driver. He pulled his shabby suitcase from the seat and looked up at the house. He'd tried to smarten himself up to come to the city, Maggie could tell. He'd used oil to press some of his curls down at the sides, and his shirt was new, or at least freshly starched. His coat was not new, was years old, but it still fitted him well and the fact that he had bothered to wear it on a warm spring day showed he'd tried to make an effort and had made a pretty decent one.

She waited until she heard his voice downstairs. Kate was laughing, and there was a sound of tinkling piano keys. Leah's voice was a warm murmur. Leah had always been more open with Calvin than with anybody else in the family. Their mother had said that once and Maggie had felt the truth of it, without understanding the reason.

She went downstairs.

'We haven't missed you.' She leaned in the doorway.

'Of course not,' he said. 'Why would you?'

'We've been running wild.'

'Why I'm here. Put a stop to that.'

'Gambling dens,' Maggie said. 'That sort of thing.'

'Feared as much.'

'Maggie, please,' said Leah. She was laying out the table with a glass of beer and a basket of bread.

Their mother came through the door with a jug in her hand, which she placed on the table. 'I hope this dear boy can talk some sense into all of you.' She gave him a look. 'They're talking about the spirits still.'

He raised his eyebrows. *'Really?'*

'I'm afraid so.'

'We think there's spirits here too!' said Kate brightly. 'And they'll talk to us. It's wonderful.'

'That is wonderful.'

'Never have daughters, Calvin,' their mother said, sitting down at the table. 'More trouble than they're worth.'

Maggie ignored her. She smiled at him. 'The ghosts might talk to you too, now you're here, Calvin. If you'd like to listen.'

'I don't think they'd be interested in me,' he said.

'We'll see,' said Kate, in a sing-song voice. She was sitting at the piano, and she hit a few keys, tunelessly and loud, until Leah slapped her hand away.

Maggie took Calvin to his room. She led him through the kitchen to the small room that led from it, with a mattress on the floor, newly made with clean sheets that still smelled of soap.

'It was the only room left,' she said. It looked smaller now that two people stood in it. She said apologetically, 'I think it's supposed to be the pantry.'

'I think you're right.' Calvin put down his case and rapped his knuckles against the wall. 'Nothing wrong with that. I'm lucky enough to have your company. Happy to sleep in the street if necessary.'

'You don't have to work so hard to be charming all the time, Calvin.'

'I know,' he said. 'I don't know how to stop myself.'

They both looked down at the mattress for a moment.

'Leah says she's heard of a bed we could buy. One of the neighbor's nephews just died.'

'This'll be fine,' he said.

'It'll be warm in the morning when the stove's lit.'

'I expect it will.'

'Maybe too warm.'

'Maybe.'

As they turned to go back through the kitchen, Maggie took his arm. 'Have you seen our father since we left?'

Calvin nodded. 'I was out at the new house yesterday.'

'How is he?'

'Some of the frame needed replacing. Ice got in the wood and splintered it.'

'So it's not—'

'Another month or so, I reckon, before it's finished. If the weather stays clear.'

'Have you been back to Hydesville?'

'No. They're all still talking about it, though, your father says. Neighbors still hanging around the house, listening for who knows what.'

'Really.'

'It was a good idea, you all coming out here.'

'Are you going to stay?'

He shrugged. 'If you'll have me. David thought you might want the company.'

'You shouldn't stay because David told you to.'

He blinked. 'I know that.'

'But we want you to stay,' she added quickly. 'We're glad you're here.'

He paused. 'Your father said there was a carriage overturned in town on Saturday, killed a little girl.'

'That's awful.'

'Yeah. So I'd be glad to be away from it all, if I were you.'

There were a few little girls in Hydesville. Maggie couldn't think of any of their names, but she could picture their faces. She thought of a yellow dress, a dark sky. 'I am glad,' she said.

'Calvin.' Leah came into the kitchen, smiling. 'Won't you come and join us for lunch?'

At the table, Maggie darted glances between Kate and Leah. She was conscious of the day collapsing into the

127

afternoon, and then the evening, and that they should prepare, there was still more to prepare. It was like waiting for a party, or what she imagined it would be like to wait for a party.

Calvin talked sweetly to their mother, making her laugh, until eventually Leah cleared her throat, straightened the fork that lay by her plate, and nodded at Maggie. 'Calvin,' she said. 'We have some friends visiting this evening. Some friends of mine.'

'Oh?' he said. 'Should I help with something?'

'In fact' – she paused – 'they're really coming to meet Kate and Maggie.'

That fact, said out loud, made Maggie's heart flutter with a secret pleasure.

'Is that right?' said their mother.

'They've read Mr. Lewis's pamphlet, as it happens,' said Leah.

'Oh yes?' Calvin looked amused.

'And they're interested to see – as are a number of people, in fact – if the effects that were produced in Hydesville—'

'The ghost,' said Kate.

'– might be – well, *experienced* here.'

'Oh, Leah,' their mother said softly.

Calvin was nodding. 'And do you think the effects will be?' he said, still smiling. 'Experienced?'

'There've been a number of strange occurrences since the girls arrived here, as it happens.'

'I see.'

'And we found yesterday that gathering together at this table, and truly focusing on trying to communicate, we were able to—'

'*We* were able to,' Maggie interrupted. 'Kate and I.'

Leah gave her an irritated look. 'We asked some questions,

and there were sounds which seemed to answer. We felt a presence.'

Calvin really looked as though he might laugh. Not unkindly. As if he only wanted to share on the joke they were all playing.

'*Really*,' he said.

'It's true, Calvin,' Maggie snapped. 'You wouldn't be able to explain it.'

He held up his hands. 'I'm sure.'

'Leah, no,' their mother said. 'Enough. What would your father say, encouraging the girls like this?' Before Leah could give a scornful response, she looked at Calvin. 'Calvin. Won't you talk some sense into them? This is dangerous. I'm sure this is dangerous. We can't have spirits everywhere we go.'

Calvin's eyes softened, and he took her hand. 'Don't worry, Mrs. Fox. It's not dangerous. I'm sure it isn't. It's harmless, I promise.'

Mrs. Fox looked back at him with utter confidence. Maggie saw Leah sigh impatiently. That confidence men had, that they knew best. Where did it come from? It was exasperating. Maggie would have to make fun of him later.

'Anyway.' He spoke with a teasing tone that always made their mother smile – Maggie almost groaned with how easily Calvin could charm her. 'Aren't you a little curious?'

'I know you are, Mother, so there's no point denying it,' said Leah.

'Well, as long as Calvin's here perhaps there's no harm,' she said, and Kate mimicked, under her breath, '*Oh, as long as Calvin's here*—' breaking off when Maggie hit her arm.

'Good,' said Leah. 'Then I hope you'll both join us shortly, for an experiment.'

*

Practicing on Calvin would be their rehearsal for the evening. They prepared in the upper bedroom, memorizing their questions. When they came back to the parlor, their mother was sitting on the sofa with her sewing. Calvin was leaning against the mantelpiece with a book he'd picked off the shelf, some sort of scientific text. He was riveted enough that he didn't look up, at first. When he did, he smiled, and folded the corner of his page, sliding the book back on to the shelf.

'Are you ready for us?' he said with a grin.

It was still light outside. Maggie began to close the curtains. 'You need to sit at the table,' she said.

Her mother put down her sewing and came to the table with a nervous little laugh. 'My girls. I ought to disown you all.'

She was sure to close the curtains all the way, so only a faint slash of gray came from underneath, and the parlor was all gloom and shadow.

'It needs a little patience,' Leah was saying as Maggie came back to the table, where they were all taking their seats.

'Or not,' Kate said. 'Sometimes it might hear us straightaway.'

'It?' said Calvin.

'It. They. I don't know.' Kate smiled at him.

Maggie sat down. The mood was wrong, she knew; Calvin's good humor and skepticism wouldn't help what they were trying to do. Her mother's anxiety was helpful, but something needed to change. She needed to find that mood that captured everybody in Hydesville, heightened nerves and breath caught in the throat, senses that startled at the slightest sound.

'The bell's important, I suppose?' said Calvin.

'Yesterday,' said Leah, 'it was standing on top of the piano, and it rang, all by itself.'

It was a lie, but Kate picked it up effortlessly. 'It was when we asked if anybody was there.'

'And we thought it might provide a useful means of communication,' said Leah.

'Of course,' said Calvin. 'Only sensible.'

Maggie cleared her throat. 'Let's hold hands. Like this.'

She took Kate's hand and her mother's on the other side. Calvin obediently took Kate's other hand, and Leah's.

A small pause. It was a strange sensation – even Calvin couldn't deny it was strange, to sit in the dim light like this, in a circle, together, all connected. If one of us was struck by lightning, Maggie thought, it would travel through the circle and kill us all.

Somebody in particular: that was her idea. They would want to communicate with somebody they had known.

Maggie looked at Calvin. 'Is there anybody you'd want to speak to, if you could?' she said.

'What do you mean?'

'Somebody you might know who – died.'

Calvin blinked. His face went blank. 'I can't think of anybody,' he said.

'Just pick someone,' said Kate. 'Pick somebody. It doesn't matter who.'

'Alright,' he said. 'George Washington.'

'*Calvin.*' Kate gave him an impatient look.

'George Washington,' said Calvin. 'I've always wanted to talk with George Washington. Since I was a little boy.'

'You're making fun of us,' said Maggie.

'What would George Washington say, if he was here? That's something I've asked myself, plenty of times.'

Leah cleared her throat. 'And if George Washington isn't available,' she said, 'is there anybody else?'

131

'No. Nobody but George.'

'Well, the spirit must be drawn to the presence of the people in the circle.'

'Enough talking,' said their mother suddenly, and Maggie jumped. She'd almost forgotten she was there. 'We're here to talk to the spirits, aren't we, not to each other?'

Leah looked momentarily flustered, but she said, 'Indeed. Quite so.'

'Yes, let's be quiet,' Kate said, in an oddly grown-up voice. 'Let's be quiet and wait.'

They stopped talking, and, as they had planned, Maggie let the eventual silence settle before she spoke. 'If there is anybody listening, from another realm,' she said, 'we want to open the pathways of communication.' She thought Calvin might laugh at her, but he didn't.

Silence, Leah had told them. *The longer the silence lasts, the more sensitive they will be to sound.*

So she let it last. Let it take root. Let it pass through a stage of awkwardness into something else. Until it seemed a shame, almost, to break it. When had she ever done this? Sat quietly in a room with people that she loved, just breathing?

She forced her thoughts back to the moment. 'I feel something,' she whispered suddenly and urgently, sending a tingle down her own spine even as she knew this was what they had planned. She felt a sudden surge of hope, that there would be a response. A yearning for the thrill and mystery of it.

'Is somebody there?' Kate said, and then they let the moments after that build in silence, and then – and it seemed impossible, even knowing how it was done, it seemed impossible and startling – the bell rang.

Both Calvin and their mother jolted in surprise, and then

Calvin laughed, but only in that shocked, helpless way that people sometimes laughed.

'Is somebody there?' Kate said again, and the candle – the same height as her mouth and closer to her than anybody else – flickered slightly. Maggie cracked her toes, and saw her mother's eyes go wide, saw Calvin flick a startled, confused glance around the room and back to Kate.

'Are you a spirit?' said Maggie. 'Ring the bell once for yes, if you can.'

A long pause, and then Maggie said, 'Spirit—' and the bell rang.

The bell was too much; they had wondered if it would be. The initial shock worked well, but the noise of it would eventually break the mood. They needed something softer.

She caught Kate's eye, and Leah's, and gave a tiny nod. The signal that they should switch to taps; Maggie to speak and Kate to answer. It was important, anyway, to see how well it worked around this table, if it was obvious where the sounds came from. And they had more than cracking toes at their disposal, now.

'Is there somebody in the room who you want to communicate with?' Maggie said softly. A pause, and then, 'Can you tap once for yes?'

A single tap.

'Is it Calvin?'

A single tap.

Across the table, she could see something shift in Calvin's expression, a hint of tension around his eyes.

What came next would have to be Kate's decision. They had all casually assumed he would want to communicate with his parents. A flurry of uncertain conversation as to the names of his parents, before they decided they could simply spell out *mother* or *father*. Even simpler, they could simply ask, *Are you his mother?* They hadn't planned anything else.

Are you his mother? That's what she was supposed to ask now.

Maggie suddenly saw the cruelty of it. His mother.

They hadn't rehearsed a *stop* signal. She wanted to stop. It wasn't fair to him.

Perhaps she could ask, *Are you George Washington?*

Leah was looking at her.

'Are you—' Maggie hesitated. 'Will you tell us your name, if I spell out the letters?'

A tap. The table shook slightly. Only Leah, nudging the table leg that she knew was uneven. She was frowning.

Kate looked calm, as if she already knew the name she would spell.

'A,' said Maggie. There was silence. 'B, C, D, E—'

A single tap, and then a flurry, as if the spirit – Kate – was excited. It was effective, Maggie thought. Stopped the thing from being too predictable.

'Your name begins with an *E*?

Tap.

In the corner of her eye, Maggie thought she saw a shadow pass across the wall. She blinked a few times. Black dots sometimes floated across her vision when she was about to get a headache. They had practiced too long and it had exhausted them.

She began spelling again. Calvin and her mother were both leaning in, curious. Maggie could feel her mother's hand tightening.

Maggie shared their suspense. *E?*

There was another tap when she got to *T*. Another for *H*, then *A* and *N*.

'It's Ethan, Calvin,' Kate said. 'He wants to talk to you.'

Maggie felt Leah's uncertainty, the way the power in the circle had shifted to Kate. Kate, whose delicate feet could find the end of the thread that was tied to the bell, that ran under the tablecloth and down the table leg. Kate, with the curved piece of wood beneath her foot, a warped fragment of an old picture frame that they had made into a lever.

Maggie saw, with relief, that the tension had passed from Calvin's face; he was only confused.

'Ethan?' he said.

'Do you know an Ethan?' said Leah hopefully.

'No.'

'Perhaps there's some mistake.' Leah shot Kate an impatient look, but Kate's expression was serene.

'Unless—' Now he looked amused. 'Ethan who used to run the general store on the corner of our street?'

There was silence. Maggie said helplessly, 'Ethan who used to run the general store on the corner of Calvin's street?'

There was silence, and then, abruptly, two hard taps.

Maggie was lost. She scoured her imagination for another question. A smell seemed to have crept into the room, like grass.

The bell rang, and then, without warning, a small silver picture frame that had been standing on top of the piano fell, hit the surface so hard that they all heard the piano strings vibrate, below. They all jumped so suddenly that the circle broke apart – her mother's hands flew to her chest, and Calvin pulled away and twisted around in his chair, toward the door, which stood slightly ajar. Maggie couldn't remember if it had been closed or not.

'Somebody touched my neck,' he said, amazed. 'Something.'

'That's enough,' said their mother. 'I've had enough of this.'

'No,' Kate said. 'We can't stop now—'

But the mood had already broken; the grass smell had gone.

'That's enough, Leah,' their mother said. Leah nodded and got to her feet, went to draw back the curtains, and they blinked in the light, looked at each other.

Calvin was smiling. 'Excellent,' he said. 'Have to say. That was excellent. The final bit, especially. I'm disappointed that George didn't appear, but—'

'Did something really touch your neck?' Maggie said.

'Felt like it. I don't know how you did that.'

'We didn't.'

'Of course. I'm sorry.' Still smiling. 'It was Ethan.'

'How could we have done it, Calvin?' said Leah. 'Honestly?'

'I have no idea.' He held up his hands. 'You're quite right. It was a spirit.'

Their mother had stood and was walking around the room, looking at the walls and the ceiling as if they'd give up the answers.

'Really,' said Calvin. 'It was excellent. I'd pay good money for that, if I had any.'

'What did it feel like?' said Maggie. 'On your neck?'

'It felt like – I don't know. A hand, could have been. It was cold. A breeze, I suppose. Like with the candle.'

'A cold hand?'

'Well, we're glad you enjoyed it,' said Leah briskly. 'You might tell people, in fact. That the Fox sisters have brought their talents to Rochester.'

'If I had anybody to tell,' he said, 'I'd tell them. You can be sure of that.'

*

A small, unarranged gathering in the kitchen, speaking in whispers.

'*Ethan?*' Leah said to Kate. 'Who in heaven's name is Ethan?'

Kate shook her head. 'I don't know. I didn't know I would spell that, it just happened – and I didn't know what his mother was called, I couldn't—'

'If you're going to make up names, Katie, at least let's decide them in advance,' said Leah. 'Have *you* even met an Ethan?'

Kate looked confused, still shaking her head.

'Who did the picture?' said Maggie. 'That wasn't me.'

'It wasn't me either,' said Kate.

'The piano lid must be uneven,' said Leah. 'Or the weight of the frame simply – I don't know. It was just good luck.'

'Perhaps there's some way . . . we could make it fall again,' said Maggie. 'It was just—'

'Yes, yes,' said Leah. 'Yes, you're right. It was perfect.'

'And something touching Calvin's neck?' said Maggie.

'That wasn't me,' said Kate.

'*Obviously,*' said Maggie. 'But who—'

'Don't you see?' said Leah. 'I told you as much. Give people a few cues and they do it all themselves. Even a cynic like Calvin – give them a darkened room, a few ghostly sounds, and their imagination will do the rest.'

Maggie shook her head. 'But he didn't believe it was real.'

'It hardly matters, does it?' Leah looked at her sisters with bright eyes. 'Either way, it's a thrill. And with somebody who wants to believe to begin with—'

Maggie thought of the stories that had sprung up like weeds all around Hydesville once word of the strange sounds had gotten around. When people wanted to believe, they did most of the work themselves.

The evening ahead burned with possibility, enough excitement that she forgot her disappointment that no real spirit had answered them.

Somehow, that evening, through some muddle of questions, letters, raps and knocks and a falling candlestick, Nathaniel Adams came to believe that his Uncle Zachary had come back from the dead to resolve the matter of the family will. Maggie felt they had scarcely done anything; darkness and nerves had carried them. She had thought, for one moment, that she had seen a dark figure standing in front of the fireplace, and had leaped back in fright, startling everybody. But then she saw it was only the shadow of the potted fern by the window. It didn't matter; fright was contagious. Soon they were all seeing shadows.

And by the end, Eliza Adams was wide-eyed and delighted; Nathaniel Adams was pale, silent, half stunned.

Kate seemed disappointed, but then Eliza hugged and kissed her and called her a miraculous girl, and Kate flushed with pleasure, not used to anybody paying her so much attention.

Mr. Adams grasped Maggie's hand as they left, said, 'Well, girls,' and then he didn't seem to know what to say next.

When Leah closed the door behind them, they stood in the hall for a moment, looking at each other. Leah was glowing, and Kate looked wild and exhausted.

Already, Maggie could imagine them going back out into the world, Mr. and Mrs. Adams, telling everybody what had happened. Whispers sweeping through the city like a storm.

Laughter rose up in her chest; she pressed her hand over her mouth, but it escaped – a silly, childish laughter that made Kate laugh as well, and then Leah, and when Calvin came down the stairs they were too breathless and giddy to explain anything to him.

Eventually, Maggie stopped laughing and wiped her eyes. 'I want to see Amy and Isaac,' she said. 'Tomorrow.'

'Oh, me too,' said Kate.

'I'm going to send them a note in the morning.'

Leah was nodding; Maggie imagined she could see ideas spinning behind her eyes. 'Yes,' Leah said. 'Yes, let's do that. Let's send them a note.'

SEVENTEEN

Maggie sent her note first thing in the morning, and the same boy came back with a reply an hour later. *Of course*, Amy wrote. *Please come this afternoon.*

The afternoon: another headache lurked. Was it something she ate, she thought sometimes, that gave her these headaches, or some perfume in the air, something her body couldn't tolerate? Kate had them too, but nobody else seemed to, so it must be something they got from some distant relative or something, passed on to them, some kind of weakness. She'd feel it coming like a cavalry of horses over the hill, hooves pounding in the distance.

Not today. She couldn't let it. She drank a glass of water. She had a task.

She took the pamphlet. She placed it inside a book of Leah's to keep it flat, and carried it in a small basket with a ginger cake that she had made that morning as a gift.

It was only her and Leah. Their mother said it wasn't polite for all of them to go at once – four guests, or even five if Calvin came, it was too many – so Kate cried and then got left behind. And Maggie said she was sorry but was secretly glad, because it was complicated with Amy, and even more complicated with everybody there. If she had her way Leah would have stayed at home too.

Rain showers drifted over in the morning but had cleared

140

by the afternoon, and the air was fresh and warm, grass snapping up straight and puddles drying. Maggie wore her spring dress from last year, but it pinched below the arms and she wondered if she should pass it on to Kate. It was torn as well, but the tear was hidden within the folds of the skirt and she thought nobody would notice.

Maggie rehearsed her greeting in her mind – the expression she would wear, how she would smile, grown-up and calm and intelligent.

As they approached she saw that Amy was not alone.

The Posts had a narrow porch built by Isaac, with a long wooden bench, and Amy was sitting on it. Next to her, a black man in a shirt and waistcoat sat with his hands loosely clasped in front of him. He looked Calvin's age or maybe David's. And Elizabeth Reid was standing in front of them, holding a piece of paper.

'Let them have their meeting,' the man was saying. He rubbed his eyes as if he was tired of their conversation. 'It doesn't matter.'

'It doesn't matter to *you*,' said Elizabeth.

He sighed and dropped his head back.

'It's a convention on the rights of *women*.' Elizabeth waved the sheet of paper. 'And I see my *white* sisters are very well represented among the speakers. And I see a Mr. Davies here, and a Mr. Schiff, and I don't know who they are but they do *not* sound like women. And what I don't see—'

'I'll appeal on your behalf,' said Amy.

'I'd like to appeal on my own behalf.'

Leah and Maggie had stopped at the gate, and when Amy turned her head she saw them, finally, and stood. It took her a moment to smile. 'Leah,' she said. 'Maggie. Of course. I forgot the time. *Welcome*.' She turned to Elizabeth.

'You remember Maggie Fox, Elizabeth? And this is her sister Leah. Our dear friends.'

Elizabeth gave them a distracted smile, and the man stood, raising a curious eyebrow, and said, 'Fox? The Fox family? Are you the girls from Hydesville?'

'That's right, Mr. Garret,' said Amy, before Maggie had a chance to ask how he knew. 'And it's wonderful to see them both. I was so glad to receive your note, Maggie.' She hesitated for a moment, and then held out a hand to Maggie. 'Come in. Our girl has laid out a lovely spread.'

She had. The table was laid with sandwiches and fruit and pieces of chicken, and there was a rich smell of stewing meat.

'Isaac has found a new building for his apothecary,' she said. 'A double storefront, and they're selling all sorts along with the remedies and prescriptions, and with all these endless new arrivals to the city – well. We're very blessed.'

The man was introduced as Will Garret. He was Elizabeth's husband. Maggie looked at Elizabeth, impressed by this fact, that she had gotten married in the time since Maggie had last seen her. She was only a few years older than Maggie, and marriage cast a new light of elegance and maturity over her.

'We'll be leaving,' Elizabeth said. She put a hand on Mr. Garret's arm. Her gaze lingered on Maggie for a while, curious, as they stood around the table. 'Before Will delivers his lecture on the Revolutionary War.'

'I'm writing a history,' he said, with a half-smile and a nod. 'On the black soldiers of the American Revolution. I'm told I talk too much about it.'

'I didn't know there were black soldiers of the American Revolution,' said Leah.

'Then I hope you'll buy my book, when it's done. I'll be happy to sign it.'

Elizabeth laughed, and he placed a hand on her back and they shared a look that made Maggie feel lonely, that she didn't know anybody who looked at her like that. Mr. Garret was handsome. And writing a book.

Maggie placed her basket carefully on the table. She was thinking of her torn dress, and wondering if the tear could be noticed after all. The kitchen fell quiet. It was too warm, with the stove and the low sun outside. The fruit would soften and brown if they didn't eat it.

Maggie tried not to think of the last time she was here. The sound of Mr. Crane pounding on the front door, ready to accuse her. Things were different now.

'You found us in the midst of a debate,' said Amy. 'There's some conflict between the organizers of our convention this summer.'

'On women's rights,' said Maggie, finally remembering how to speak, remembering the work Amy had been doing last fall.

Amy nodded. 'Indeed. Their rights in marriage, their rights to vote – and Elizabeth would like to speak, and *I* would like her to speak, but there's some disagreement among the organizers—'

'We're all sisters, of course,' Elizabeth cut in. 'But no black women must be heard, at any meeting, ever. It's very dangerous. We mustn't speak on abolition, in case we distract from the cause with women's issues, and we mustn't speak on women's issues, in case we distract from the cause with issues of race.'

'So you find our movement at odds with itself, as it often is,' Amy said. 'But I hope these are the struggles we learn from. Let me pour some coffee.'

143

Maggie watched Elizabeth, thinking of the time she had seen her argue with James Crane. Did she know about Mr. Crane's accusations? Surely everybody did. But Elizabeth paid little attention to Maggie, and why should she. Maggie's problems were not hers.

'I'd like to read your book too, Mr. Garret, when it's written,' Maggie said.

He looked pleased. 'It'd be my pleasure to send you a copy,' he said. 'And did I hear right that you're the girls from Wayne County who're involved in this thing, this thing with knockings?'

She saw Leah turn the full beam of her attention to him and begin to speak, but Maggie interrupted: 'We're not from there, really, we were just staying there for a while, we were in Rochester before then, but – but yes, that was us.' She watched Amy from the corner of her eye. 'Some things happened that no one could explain.'

'I'd like to hear about it,' said Will. 'I have an interest in things of that nature.'

'Oh,' said Maggie, and suddenly wished she had two copies of the pamphlet. 'Then – in fact, there's more than that. It's happened here too, just last night, actually—' Amy was still moving things on the table, Will listening to her, curious and attentive. But Elizabeth was turning toward the door.

'We can't stay any longer, Will,' she said. 'They're expecting us at the church.'

Will nodded, reaching for his hat which lay on a table by the kitchen door, still looking at Maggie.

'Mr. Garret,' Leah said, as Will and Elizabeth said their goodbyes, 'before you go, since you're interested, let me tell you a little more—'

And she followed them out toward the door, their voices fading once they reached the porch.

Maggie was left alone with Amy, who sat down, finally, and looked up at Maggie.

'You look well,' she said.

'I am, I think.'

'You're recovered.'

It was a trap, that question, and Maggie did not answer. Instead, she said, 'My sister told me that Mr. Crane has gone to New York City for the spring.'

'He has. They have family there. He plans to return in summer for the antislavery fair, I believe.'

Maggie nodded, and brushed her hands against the handle of the basket she had brought. She took out the cake. 'I made this for you.'

'Oh,' said Amy. 'Maggie. How thoughtful.' Amy gave her a long look, and then reached out, and she touched Maggie's hand. 'Thank you.' She gestured to a chair.

Maggie sat down, clasping her hands between her knees. She took a deep breath, but it made her light-headed. 'I caused you some trouble, before we left.'

A faint smile passed over Amy's face. 'Maggie, I'm used to trouble,' she said.

Maggie nodded. She swallowed. 'But I know that Mr. Crane was – is – your friend.'

There was a long silence. Maggie felt a stab of sympathy for Mr. Garret and Elizabeth. Leah had clearly trapped them.

Amy said, 'All kinds of people work together here. We aren't all friends. I know Mr. Crane, of course. I was happy to work with him toward a common goal. I prayed for all of you.'

145

Maggie tried to pick apart those words to see what they meant. Outside on the road she heard Leah's bright laughter.

What had she had planned to say next? She looked at a newspaper that was lying on the table, but she couldn't make out any of the words. 'There's been a pamphlet written about us,' Maggie said. 'And what happened in Hydesville. I thought you might like to read it.'

All the pamphlets that Amy used to lend to her, all the important subjects. Perhaps she should feel ashamed to have brought her this one, full of village gossip and murder accusations.

'I've read it,' said Amy. 'Isaac picked up a copy in the little bookstore east of the river. The owner ordered some in at our request.'

'Oh,' she said. 'Oh.' Then, she couldn't help herself, 'I think that I might – that spirits might be drawn to me, somehow.'

She felt herself blush the moment she said it, a rush of heat that stung her cheeks. 'I know that might sound' – she tried to think of the word – 'absurd, but it was very strange, what happened. And real. Mr. Lewis took statements, from everybody.'

'Yes. I read them. It's a remarkable set of accounts.'

'And since then we've had more – events. Just last night, with some of Leah's friends, we tried to reach out to the, to the – spirit world, and we heard answers.' Something changed in Amy's expression, but Maggie couldn't make sense of it. 'We're going to try again. We might even be able to show you, if you're interested.'

Amy was silent for a moment. 'Would you like to show me?'

'Yes.' Blood rushed in her veins. Her too-tight dress

pinched her arms as she leaned forward. 'I would, yes. And Isaac. I think you'll be interested. I do.'

'Last November, Maggie. I'm sorry that I didn't see that you were so sick. The things you were saying, I should have known—'

Maggie began to shake her head.

'— and as you say, Mr. Crane was a friend of sorts, and his dear wife before she died, and we were caught between—'

'No.'

'— caught between your family and his.'

My family? Maggie thought, and almost laughed. As if her family had stood with her.

'No,' she said. 'No. I wasn't sick. Not like they said.'

'Maggie.'

'You'll see. You're going to see. We can show you.'

Another chance gone, to be forgiven, to simply say, *yes, yes I was sick and I didn't know what I was saying*, but she couldn't do it, it was the lie she couldn't bring herself to tell. She had to make Amy see. She had to make her know.

Leah came back into the room, beaming. 'Well, Mr. Garret is *very* interested in all of it, so I thought we could organize a little supper together tonight and see if we experience any more disturbances.' She took a seat at the table and picked up a piece of fruit. 'What do you think, Maggie? Amy, perhaps you could join us?'

Maggie held her breath.

'Tonight.' Amy stood and went to the window, looked out for a moment, and then came back with a plate for Maggie's ginger cake. 'It sounds very interesting, but we have a speaker visiting from Boston. We raised the funds for his travels—'

'Yes, yes,' said Leah, 'they told me, so I suggested afterward.'

'It's Everett Turner,' she said. 'You might have heard of him. He escaped slavery in the South and so naturally he speaks more powerfully to the abolition question than we ever could.'

'I'm sure,' said Leah. 'So, afterward?'

'I'd like to hear him,' said Maggie.

A small silence.

'Of course,' said Amy. 'You should. You must. He's only here for one night, passing through, and they say he has to be heard.' She looked to Leah. 'I would be happy to host a supper afterward, for all of you. And of course, we'd be interested to see your' – Maggie saw her stumble for the word – 'disturbances. Mr. Garret takes an interest in all kinds of things of that nature. He has a boundless curiosity. So does Isaac, as a matter of fact. I'm sure he'll be delighted to try it.'

'I don't know if anything will happen,' Maggie said. 'We can't really – we don't control it.'

'Not as such,' said Leah, 'but—'

'That's no matter,' said Amy. 'I shall have no expectations. Your company is pleasure enough.'

Wilson Hall was owned by the Presbyterians, Amy said, but they would hire it out for general use, and the money was easily raised when there was a speaker from out of town. Maggie walked there with Amy and Isaac. Leah had gone home to fetch Kate and bring her to the supper, afterward. Kate would sulk, most likely, at not being invited to the lecture, but they had all agreed she was too young.

The hall was already crowded. As they approached, Maggie saw Elizabeth Reid standing outside. The way she leaned against the wall, alone and composed, stirred something, some kind of admiration or envy. Elizabeth raised a hand in greeting, and then turned her attention to Mr. Garret, who had just arrived. 'You're late,' Elizabeth said to all of them as they assembled. 'Every seat's taken.'

It was a mixed crowd, black and white all mingling, which Amy always said was a good thing, though Maggie knew not everybody agreed, not even all of the antislavery people.

Inside the hall, they all stood, even Amy and Isaac, though several people anxiously tried to offer them their seats. The hall was hot, with maybe a hundred people, their collective breath making the air damp. Men loosened their shirts and women dabbed at their brows with handkerchiefs. Somebody propped open the door with a stone, which let in a gentle breeze but also the sound of people passing on the street, talking too loudly, and Maggie, standing near the back, found it hard to concentrate on the first speaker, a white, red-haired man whose weak voice was absorbed by a dead wall of humidity from all the bodies in the room.

'What's he saying?' she whispered to Elizabeth, who was standing next to her, crushed tightly so their ribs almost touched.

'I can't hear,' she said, without lowering her voice very much. 'It's Adam Feeney, so I expect he's mainly celebrating his own contributions to the cause.'

Somebody shushed her, and she shot them an irritated look.

Finally, Adam Feeney came to the end of his speech. He stopped, cleared his throat, and there was a ripple of polite applause. 'And now,' he said, 'I have great pleasure in welcoming Mr. Everett Turner to our humble city—'

The applause rose and drowned out the rest of his

introduction. Everett Turner crossed the stage. Maggie craned her neck to see him better. He wore a black waistcoat and a cream shirt, his shirtsleeves rolled up to his elbows, and when he spoke, his voice was deep and warm.

'My friends,' he said, 'I'm grateful for your invitation and for the opportunity to address you this evening.'

In front of them, a man turned to murmur something to his friend, and this time Elizabeth was the one to *ssh* them angrily. He turned and looked at her, flicked his eyes up and down, and turned back.

'I am grateful for the support of our friends in the North,' Mr. Turner said, 'and the risks you undertake through your participation in this struggle against slavery.'

A few people nodded.

'My mother was born into slavery in South Carolina, as was I,' Everett Turner was saying. 'My father was a white man whose name I do not care to speak.'

More people had now crowded into the hall and Maggie was shorter than most of them, and was distracted by the uncomfortable closeness of so many bodies. She wished she'd worn a lighter dress.

'I was born into slavery,' he said again, his voice hardened. Then there was a pause. He turned a sheet of paper on the lectern, and then turned it back again. He looked up at the audience. There was something in the pause. The powerful and awful thing that lay just underneath the fine words.

'We are grateful for the support of our friends in the North. But who knows, as you all sit here this evening, that the clothes on your backs are not made from cotton that I picked? That my mother picked? My brothers and sisters?'

Out on the street, somebody laughed. Somewhere else, a

door slammed. The hall seemed to be breathing itself, its walls expanding and contracting. Maggie wondered if she would faint. She tried to concentrate.

'– time to ask yourselves,' he was saying, 'if the sugar in your tea is blood sugar – your tobacco, your grain – the commodities on which you are dependent here in this great city of Rochester—'

Somebody coughed. There were shadows, Maggie noticed, thrown against the walls and moving, hard to understand who or what was casting them.

'– I mean to say that while the institution of slavery may seem distant to some of you here, it is not. Slavery is woven through the fabric of our country, from north to south, and we must acknowledge this before we can move forward.'

Some people were not listening. She could tell, from the way they shifted and looked around the room. She was briefly distracted by her own anger at them, and then realized she wasn't listening herself.

She listened.

'But I wish to talk this evening about religion,' he said.

There was an uncertain murmur in the hall.

'It is time,' he said, 'to call upon our religious leaders, those who are silent, to *end* their silence. It is time to question the leaders who say that because slavery is the law of the land, it must also be the law of God. It is time to challenge those ministers who say it is our moral duty to obey our government, to go quietly and peacefully about our business without causing any disturbance.'

He stopped, and cleared this throat.

'What is religion *for*, if not to disturb the powerful? To lift up the oppressed and bring light to those who live in darkness? What is religion *for*? *Who* is it for? Is it for me? For you?' He looked out across the room. Maggie shivered, despite the heat. 'This is a decisive moment in our country's history,' he said. 'And it is time for us all to decide whose rules we will follow.'

EIGHTEEN

Kate had been fetched, and was waiting for them on the porch of Amy's house with Leah. She was pouting, and gave Maggie a look of betrayal.

'Forgive us lurking outside your house like thieves,' said Leah. 'We were enjoying this lovely mild evening.'

Another couple who had been at the lecture, Susan and Alexander Grady, had taken an interest in Maggie, and joined them. They all exchanged lively introductions on the porch. Then Leah asked for a few moments alone with her sisters, and the others went inside.

'I don't want to do it,' Kate said.

'Katie, we have to.' Maggie gave her an urgent look. 'They're all expecting something.'

'You can just sit there if you want,' said Leah. 'Maggie can take care of the raps. You just sit there and look as if you're in a trance, which half the time you do in any case.'

Kate's mouth pulled down at the edges as if she would cry. She was tired, that was all. It was late. Kate would usually be in bed by now. Their mother probably ought to have kept Kate home, but Leah always got her own way.

'Who knows, Katie, a real spirit might answer us, if we call them,' said Maggie. She tried to send her thoughts right into Kate's mind, how important it was, to show Amy what they could do. 'Please. For me.'

Leah was muttering to herself, 'I certainly *hope* a real

spirit decides to join us – it isn't as if we've prepared anything. All we've got is your toe-cracking, a bit of improvisation—'

Kate sniffed again and shrugged. It would have to do.

Amy and Isaac's parlor was plain, purposeful. The windows had blinds instead of curtains, which after supper Isaac fastened shut. There were no mirrors. The mantelpiece was lined with books, and a framed miniature of a little girl, Matilda, Amy and Isaac's daughter, who had died before Maggie knew them.

Amy carried an oil lamp across the room and placed it at the center of the table.

'Friends,' she said. 'Shall we sit?'

Elizabeth and Mr. Garret were still sitting on the sofa, discussing the lecture with the Gradys. Maggie didn't know the Gradys. They were Quakers too, but they had moved from Ohio not long ago. She had tried to decide why they were here, couldn't work out if they might disapprove.

They all stood then, and began to take their seats at the parlor table.

Leah was right: they had nothing prepared. What they could do would only be simple. A few raps, perhaps a shake of the table. But if the lamp was turned out, they would have complete darkness, and that did a lot.

Maggie felt that part of her mind was still back in the hall, straining to hear Everett Turner speak. A man had stood and told them all that their clothes were made from cotton picked by slaves, and now here they were, simply moving on to the next part of the evening as if that fact changed nothing.

Leah put her hand on Maggie's back and steered her gently toward the table.

'What do you call this?' asked Susan Grady. 'Does it have a name, what you do?'

'This is still a new revelation to us,' said Leah. 'We've only held a few gatherings. But there is a word: *séance*—'

'Yes,' said Amy. 'Very appropriate. A sitting. A coming together.'

The room was cooler than Leah's parlor, but not drafty. The air was still and dry, like an empty church.

Mr. Garret sat opposite Maggie, his expression alert and curious. But Elizabeth had risen again, crossed the room to pour a cup of water from the jug on the corner table.

'Elizabeth,' said Amy. 'Will you join us?'

It wasn't clear that she would. Her body was angled toward the door, her eyes lit with doubt, irritation. She sipped her water. 'I don't know,' she said.

'Liz.' Mr. Garret turned to her. 'Let's,' he said.

In Hydesville it would have seemed strange, white and black people mixing like this, socially. There would be people in Rochester too who wouldn't approve. Maggie wouldn't have thought too much of it, except that Everett Turner's speech had made her feel ashamed, and she found herself wondering that Mr. Garret and Elizabeth didn't simply hate them all. Perhaps they did.

But they were Northerners too, of course. They all wore the same clothes.

Elizabeth came, finally, and took the last empty chair.

There was a smell in the room of dried flowers, though Maggie couldn't see any.

'Now,' said Amy. 'We don't gather here with expectations. We'll sit here peacefully, together. We're grateful to be together in the company of friends.'

A murmur of agreement, and then Maggie felt the drift of their attention shift toward her.

All these people, waiting for her.

'Shall we hold hands?' said Leah gently, looking at Maggie.

'Yes.' Maggie straightened her back, made herself look at each of the group in turn, with an expression on her face that she hoped was serene, and strong. 'We'll hold hands. With our hands on the table, like this.'

Alexander Grady had reservations about taking instructions from a girl, Maggie could tell, but with a sigh he took Elizabeth's hand, and Isaac's, who sat on his other side.

Maggie took Leah's hand, and Susan Grady's. Kate took Leah's, and Isaac's.

'And now,' said Maggie, 'we'll close our eyes.'

She kept her own eyes open until she saw that they had all done as she asked. Then Leah slipped her hand from Maggie's and reached to turn down the oil lamp, all the way until it was extinguished and the room was perfectly dark. Leah took her hand again and squeezed it.

The silence gathered and became heavy. All the noise of the evening, the heat and light and conversation, fell away; its sudden absence made the silence deeper and more powerful.

They all felt it. She was sure.

And she waited.

There was a movement at the table, someone shifting in their seat, a heavy exhalation. A little murmur of uncertainty, excitement. Maggie could feel Elizabeth's impatience, *I have better things to do*, and it stirred something inside her, an impatience of her own.

But she waited.

The darkness was a gift. Any of them could have opened their eyes and it wouldn't make a difference – Maggie still had her eyes open, but the darkness offered up only the vaguest shapes and shadows, any of which could have been in her own mind. It changed everything. All the certainties of light, all the things you had to be able to see in order to know.

And then, waiting, what you thought was silence started to reveal itself as something else. Creaks in the floor, a soft tap that could have been a moth against the window, and the tiny sounds that humans made, skirts against petticoats, feet shifting against the rug. Somebody's breath had a damp sound, a rattle. Illness. Had they even noticed until now?

She waited. Your mind could turn to anything when it was like this, all of your thoughts worked differently, and trickery was unnecessary.

Something was coming. It was moving up toward them. Her mind reached for it. Oh, she thought, with a fierce hope, edged with fear. This is real.

They would all have somebody in mind, a loved one who had died. Even Elizabeth. How could anybody resist? Even if you had no faith. You'd think of the things you would say. Of what it would mean to know that they weren't gone.

The rap on the table may as well have been gunfire for the shock it sent around the circle, the sudden gasps and the jerk of hands, tightening around their neighbors.

Leah, no longer holding Maggie's hand, had rapped her knuckles against the table. When she took her hand again she squeezed it, as if to remind her what they were supposed to be doing. *There's no need*, Maggie wanted to tell her, *something real is here*, but the sound had broken her thoughts and she was no longer sure. And everybody was waiting.

'Is there—' she swallowed, and took a breath. Her mouth was dry. 'Is there somebody there who would like to talk to us?'

Without waiting for Kate, she cracked a bone in her toe. In this room, the sound was soft enough that it could be ignored, if not for the timing, and the darkness, and the rapt attention of the guests.

'Are you known to somebody at the table?'

She cracked the same toe. *Yes.* The table sparkled now, nerves lit like flames. She took a breath. She felt a rush of confidence. And then a name came to her. It seemed to burn in the dark before her eyes. *Libby.* Her heart pounded. She had a name. 'If my sister calls out the letters, will you tell us your name?'

Yes.

She had meant Kate, but Leah said immediately, 'A.' And stopped. Silence. 'B.' Leah was good at it, she had found a soft, even tone that cast its own spell. *C, D*, all the way to *L* when Maggie cracked her toe, and they began again.

With the final letter, *Libby*, Maggie heard Mr. Garret take a sharp breath.

Her pulse was racing. 'Is there a Libby known to somebody here?'

A moment of silence, and then he whispered: 'My sister.'

His sister. Not a cousin or an aunt or a neighbor. A *sister.* Maggie thought she might weep with delight. The room was theirs now, they had the guests in their thrall, and all it took was a name.

The rest was less successful. She tried to spell out *All is well* but she got lost, forgot which letter they were on, and Leah grew impatient. But it didn't matter. *Libby* was all they had needed.

Afterward, when the lamp was lit and they looked at each other again, the room was all nerves and delight and surprise. Leah was beaming, but Mr. Garret's expression was raw. He remained seated as the others began to disperse. Elizabeth stood behind him, with a hand lingering on his shoulder, and he looked at Maggie. 'This isn't a game of some kind?' he said thickly.

Maggie tried to meet his eye. 'No, Mr. Garret.'

'She died only a year ago. Libby. She'd been sick but – she was only nineteen.'

'I'm sorry.'

'I think I see her sometimes.'

Elizabeth was watching Maggie, with a strange expression that Maggie turned away from. 'I'm sorry,' she said again. 'I hope you don't – I hope this helped, somehow.'

She wasn't used to men looking at her with such emotion. She shifted in her seat, and tugged at her sleeve.

'Yes,' he said. 'Somehow, yes.'

It was late. As the guests began to leave, Mrs. Grady took Maggie's hand, and said, 'I hope you'll let us come again,' as if it was Maggie's house they had visited. And Mr. Garret looked at her for a long time, then shook her hand and thanked her. 'I'd like to come again too,' he said.

Amy sat quietly at the table, watching.

When the others had gone, Amy settled on to one of the long chairs beneath the window, and gestured toward Maggie. 'Come and sit with me.'

Leah and Isaac and Kate had seen the guests to the door and were now talking softly in the kitchen.

Maggie had stayed at the table. Standing up, she felt how much it gave her strength. Without it her body was small and awkward. She crossed the room, sat next to Amy.

'We're grateful for your time,' she said. 'Thank you, Maggie.'

Maggie looked at the wallpaper. A burnt orange with no pattern. It merged with the candlelight to make the room glow.

'That was very interesting,' said Amy.

In the kitchen, she heard Leah laugh.

'I don't know—' Maggie hesitated. 'I don't know what it is, exactly. But what happened at the schoolhouse – it's all related, somehow. There are spirits, and I think they can sort of – they can interact with us, with me, they can—'

She broke off and risked a look at Amy, whose expression was unreadable. *Just say it. Say you believe me.* Amy was silent.

'Maybe you think it's wrong,' Maggie said. 'Doing this.'

'What would be wrong about it?'

'If it's evil or something, blasphemous. That it shouldn't be our place to talk to the dead.'

'It seems more as if the dead are talking to you.'

Maggie blinked. Her eyes felt gritty, blurry, from the candle smoke. She forced herself: 'Do you believe in it, then?'

Amy's eyes drifted to the picture of her daughter on the mantelpiece, and then back to Maggie. 'I've always believed in the possibility that the spirits of our loved ones are still among us. We each have an inner light, Maggie, and I don't believe that light is extinguished by something as simple as death.'

'Because I know it's not really, not really what the church says. There's meant to be heaven and hell but not this other thing. I know that maybe ministers wouldn't like it.'

Immediately, Amy snorted. 'Of course not. Most churches

in this country have decided precisely how everything is ordered and the precise ways we should serve God and that way of thinking isn't very accommodating of new ideas. But Americans oughtn't only to take guidance from ministers. Particularly those who seem to be silent on the most urgent of moral issues in our country.'

'Like slavery.'

'Indeed. Better, I think, to take guidance from our own hearts, and reflect on what our own experiences reveal to us.' She paused, and gave Maggie a look as if she was realizing something new. 'Then I suppose you might say, why not from the spirits? In these turbulent times perhaps it's only natural that they should reach out to us. What do you think, Maggie? Why do you think this is happening to you?'

Before she could respond, Leah burst back into the room announcing that Kate was exhausted, and they really ought to leave. So the question hung in Maggie's mind, unanswered. *Why do you think this is happening to you?*

A cool evening breeze was coming in off the river as they walked home, and Maggie shivered, felt the burn of it in her lungs. Leah and Isaac were ahead, deep in conversation. Kate walked beside her.

Her head was beginning to pound. The day was all mixed up in her brain, hot and bright and muddled: Everett Turner, and Will Garret; Amy's bright eyes and Susan Grady's warm hands.

And a name, *Libby*. Burning in her mind as if written in fire.

NINETEEN

The light was thin, the sun risen but not yet warm. From the kitchen, Maggie could hear Leah making up the fire for the stove, humming to herself. Calvin was bent lacing his boots. He looked up when Maggie came into the parlor.

'Morning,' he said.

Maggie reached for a cup of water that sat on the table. 'Where are you going?'

'It's a while since I was here longer than a day or two,' he said. 'Thought I should go and visit my parents.'

At Maggie's expression, he said, 'Their graves, I mean.'

'Oh.'

'It's been a while. Haven't had the time when I've been here.' He finished his laces, straightened up. 'Haven't *made* the time, I suppose I should say.'

'I didn't know—' Maggie hesitated. 'I didn't know they were – here.'

'Sure. They were both born here, so.'

'Oh.'

'Yeah.'

'I should have known that,' she said. 'I'm sorry.'

He waved the apology away. 'Suppose I should take some flowers or something. What you're supposed to do, isn't it?'

'You could pick some on the way.'

He nodded. 'I could pick some on the way.'

'Where is it?'

162

'The cemetery?'

'Yes.'

'It's the old one east of the river.'

'I don't know it.'

'I heard they might stop taking bodies soon,' he said. 'I think it's nearly full.'

'Oh.' Maggie cast for something to say. 'Will you walk?'

'Of course.' He looked at her. 'Do you want to come?'

They picked a few wild flowers on the way. Yellow irises and Queen Anne's Lace, and a few that Maggie couldn't name. She'd had a book once, with the names of flowers, but she had forgotten most of them. Anyway, they were nice, although Calvin didn't seem especially interested. He was talking about other things. Whether he ought to look for work here or if he would be needed back on the farm, if their father would need help with the house, if Kate should be back in school now they were in the city, and whether he should arrange it, whether their father was hoping he would arrange it.

After a while, Maggie stopped listening. It was farther than she had expected, and her legs were beginning to ache. They'd left the heart of the city, and the trees were growing dense again, pushing up against the road, and the houses were more scattered. The time of year meant everything was bright green and surging with new life.

Not so long ago this whole city had been a wilderness. This whole country, people liked to say, although her history books had told her this on one page and then told her about the Seneca, Mohawk and Oneida on another, as if both could be true, that the country was a wilderness and also full of people, as if all those people were somehow supposed to be *part* of the wilderness and ought, eventually, to disappear along with it. Except they had refused, and were still here. She was taught history that buckled and fell apart if you looked too closely at it. What was a wilderness, anyway?

'We're here,' Calvin said eventually, as the road curved past a small stonemason's, and revealed a fenced-off cemetery circled with trees and spread out much further than the burial ground of a church, wide and flat and crowded with graves.

It was huge: nothing like the graveyard in Hydesville, or the one behind the Rochester schoolhouse. A path cut through it, and it was lined with the grander monuments – stone angels and crypts with the names of entire families. Out toward the edges of the ground the headstones grew smaller, closer together, some of them crooked. Calvin walked carefully through the graves toward a small stone, the same as all the ones that surrounded it. Maggie followed. They stood in front of it.

'Here they are,' said Calvin. Wind fluttered through the trees, gently shook the grass around them. He reached for the flowers Maggie was holding, and crouched to lay them against the stone. It only had their names. Mary Brown and Alexander Brown. Maggie tried to think of something to say, something thoughtful.

'I'd like to have had the dates,' Calvin said.

'Why didn't you?'

'They charged by the letter. I sold my father's watch just to get the names.' He paused. 'Thought I'd have gotten more for it but I was too young to know how to bargain.'

They stood still for a moment.

'I didn't know what year my mother was born, anyway. My father had some documents, family records and so on.

But she didn't have anything. She always just said she was twenty-five. Every year, if she'd have a birthday, she was always twenty-five.'

On the other side of the cemetery, amidst the statues and grander headstones, Maggie saw a small carriage come to a stop. A group of mourners were following on foot. They were too far to see their expressions. But she saw the cut of the ladies' dresses, and the men's coats. They were wealthy.

'Amy told me that Quakers don't have lots of words on their headstones. Or statues or anything. Because everybody's supposed to be equal, even in death.'

'That's nice. Let's pretend we were Quakers instead of poor.'

'Didn't you want to bury them in a churchyard?'

He made a face. 'No point. They never went. If I'd asked the minister, he'd have said there was no more space. I might have gotten them in with the Baptists but I don't think they'd have liked that.'

The sun was getting higher and the clean half-shadow that covered the cemetery was retreating.

'This is better, anyway,' he said. 'I think it is. It's nicer. Newer.'

Newness didn't seem like what you'd look for when you were burying your family. It seemed like you'd want something old and permanent-seeming. She'd always thought that God seemed more present in old places.

'It's nice. It's peaceful,' she said.

'Yeah,' Calvin said. 'And anyway, they don't know any better.'

She looked at him.

'All of this.' He gestured vaguely at the ground around them. 'The dead don't care where they're buried.'

'Do you really think that?'

'Yes. I sometimes think I should've just saved the money, not bothered with the headstone. I could've done with the money back then. They wouldn't have minded. My mother would've probably told me to do that, if she could. She hated to waste money.'

'You couldn't do that,' she said. 'Calvin. You couldn't. People have to be buried properly. It's important.'

'Why?'

'So they're – at peace. Their souls.' I don't know why, she thought, but she still knew it to be true – she knew better than anybody that once a grave was made it should not be disturbed.

'Not a lot of peace they're getting with you and your sister summoning them up for conversation every evening,' he said.

She looked back at the headstone, felt a flush on her cheeks. 'It's not like that.'

'What's it like?'

'They come to us.'

Maggie heard his intake of breath, preparing to explain to her why she was wrong. 'Last night, Leah called the letters and I spelled out a name with raps, *Libby*, and it was the name of Mr. Garret's sister. His *dead* sister. I couldn't have known that, Calvin.'

He paused. 'You spelled it out?'

'Yes,' she said, and then realized what she had confessed. 'No. The spirit, Calvin. *No*. That's not what I mean.'

'Maggie, it's alright. I already know. I know Katie made that bell ring, I know you're doing something under the table, with your toes, or something, I don't know what. I don't mind.'

'*No*. That isn't it. That's only part of it. What happened in

Hydesville wasn't us, and what happened last night – yes, I spelled it out, Calvin, but that was because I *knew* the name. She was *there*. Libby.'

'Libby.'

'Yes. It's not such a common name, not like Mary or Sarah, I couldn't have guessed it—'

'It's short for Elizabeth.' He looked thoughtful. 'And Elizabeth Reid was there. Perhaps that's what made you think of it.'

'It was his sister's name.'

'Yeah, that was lucky. Maggie—'

'It wasn't *luck*, Calvin. It wasn't.'

'– it's not as if I'm mad at you. I *like* it. I think it's interesting, what you're doing, the things that happened. The different ways people react and the things they believe – I like it. It's the kind of thing you could study and write a book about. And Maggie, it's harmless – better than harmless, it'll help people, they'll like it. They comfort people, these ideas. There's nothing wrong with that. I'll even help you if you like, if you want to carry on.'

'It isn't harmless. Spirits are real, and they aren't harmless. Mr. Bell was accused of murder.'

'I'm sure he's fine.'

'Hannah Crane was thrown down the steps and broke her arms.'

Calvin put his hands in his pockets and kicked at a stone on the ground.

'I didn't do that, Calvin. I couldn't.'

'I know. She probably slipped. Her father should never have accused you like that.'

'She didn't slip.'

He took a deep, long breath, and then took his hands out

167

of his pockets again and rubbed his eyes. 'She either slipped, or you pushed her, and I know you wouldn't do that, so she slipped. It was raining. Those steps are steep.'

Her voice was beginning to shake. 'I know what I saw. Mr. Crane and his friends disturbed the graves behind the schoolhouse for the new building, and it stirred up the spirits of the people buried there, and they were angry.'

Calvin was quiet for a while, and then he said, 'You know, they're discovering all kinds of new things, every day. All kinds of things about the brain, and electricity, and medicine.'

It was like three separate things thrown out without connection, *the brain*, *electricity*, *medicine*.

'Sound,' he continued. 'Light.'

'I know that.'

'The things that seem unexplainable now, somebody somewhere in a few years might be able to explain it, with science.'

'With science.'

'That's right.'

'And what if it *is* science? What if the explanation is that our souls can stay on earth after we die, that there's a way for the spirit to communicate—'

Calvin was shaking his head. 'There's no such thing as the soul.'

'Calvin—'

'It's just the brain, and the body, and that's it. They're all one thing.'

'So when we die—'

'So when we die, nothing.'

'You can't really believe that.'

'You know what I think?' he said. 'I think you should go back to the schoolhouse. Now you're back in Rochester, go

168

and visit it. They must have finished that new building by now. Walk around it. You'll see it's just a place, like any other. You were sick last time, you had a fever, and you saw a horrible accident, and it's distorted your memory, the shock of it. Go back there and see. It'll help you.'

No. She would not. The idea turned her stomach, brought cold sweat to her palms. It was the first time she had ever felt that she was hated, that day at the schoolhouse. The sunken-faced man staring at her. He knew that she had seen him and so he poured out all of his hatred in her direction, and it had stuck to her; she still felt it sometimes on her skin.

Calvin looked into the distance, past the boundary of the cemetery to where it gave way to forest. Caught on the wind, from the group of mourners on the other side, Maggie could hear the murmur of voices and a sound like crying.

'You're wrong,' she said. 'About all of this.'

He was becoming impatient. 'It doesn't even make sense, Maggie, what you're saying – why would some spirits appear and throw children down steps, and some knock on floorboards?'

'People are different, aren't they? Spirits must be too. They want different things. They have different powers.'

A terrible shriek carried on the wind from the other group of mourners, but it was quickly stifled. Maggie glanced at them, and then looked away.

Calvin took a deep breath and bent down to straighten the flowers he'd laid. When he stood back up he said, 'You *were* sick, when you left Rochester. And before Christmas, when I came to see you.'

'You can't explain what happened in Hydesville by saying that I was sick. All those people heard it, they gave their statements. *You* told me you felt something in that house.

A man was murdered there and his soul or his spirit was trapped—'

'Maggie.' Calvin raised his voice. 'There's no such *thing*. The brain and the body are all one thing. The soul isn't a piece you can separate and have it go on by itself. It doesn't make any sense. Nobody wants to admit it but it doesn't make any sense. We're born, we die.' He looked down at the small headstones. 'We go in the ground.'

He was wrong. Never mind about spirits: she felt it inside of herself. The inner light, Amy called it. Something that she would call a soul. Something more than bones and blood. Something that was awakened by the sound of music, that recognized beauty. A light inside her, that pulled toward faith, toward her fragmented ideas of God. She knew there was something more, something larger than her own life, a moral architecture to the world: she felt herself part of it. She felt that she had a soul. And it was stronger than her body.

She felt it in Calvin too, her sisters, people in the street sometimes, Everett Turner, Amy, Elizabeth. This thing that lit them from within. How could Calvin not recognize it in himself?

Impossible to believe that the soul could simply burn away like morning mist when the body died. It was so much more powerful than that.

TWENTY

They were quiet as they walked home, but as they got closer Calvin began to talk again – idle, meaningless conversation. He was talking himself back into the day, into his usual, cheerful self. It was soothing. Maggie made herself forgive his skepticism. Perhaps he *could* help them, all the same. And sooner or later, she would make him believe.

'Maggie, Calvin,' Leah said, as they came through the door. Her face was flushed and she was beaming. She grasped Maggie's arm. 'I have wonderful news.'

'What's that?' said Calvin, bending to remove his boots before they trailed mud through the house.

'You've heard of Andrew McIlwraith.'

'Oh, of course,' said Calvin.

'You've heard of him?'

'No.'

'Maggie?'

'No.'

'Andrew McIlwraith,' she said, 'is the proprietor of the *Rochester Herald* and one of the most influential men in New York State.'

'That *is* wonderful news,' said Calvin. 'For him more than me, I suppose.'

Leah ignored him. 'And this afternoon, this very afternoon, I've received a note from Mr. Andrew McIlwraith asking to meet us.'

'Us?' said Calvin.

Leah gave him an impatient look. 'No, not you.'

'No. Of course not.'

'*Us*, Maggie.' Her smile returned. 'You and Kate, and me. He wants to meet with us and asks if we might hold a private session with him—'

'A private session?' said Calvin, eyebrows raised.

'– because he's terribly interested in all of it – a believer in the spirit world, evidently – and he's heard all about us. You. Us. He wants to sit with us and see if the spirits will talk.'

'And no doubt they will,' said Calvin. 'Once they hear that it's Andrew McIlwraith.'

'Your wit is the talk of the town, Calvin,' said Leah. 'But might I confer with my sister?'

He grinned and held up his hands. 'Sorry.'

Maggie was pulling off her gloves, trying to understand. 'How did he know how to find us?'

'Oh, he'll have asked around. I expect he has friends to discover these things for him. The point is, little sister, we have to begin preparing right away. He'll be here at seven.'

'He's coming *today*?'

'Today!' Leah clapped her hands. 'Can you believe how wonderfully this has all come together? How quickly?' She looked between both of them. 'Of course I thought there might be some interest, but this – already. It's more than I hoped. If Mr. McIlwraith is pleased then he'll write about us in his paper, and if he writes about us in his paper, there'll be hundreds of people, hundreds, who'll want to try it.'

'And out of the generosity of your spirit, you'll entertain them?' said Calvin.

'That's right.' Leah folded her arms. 'And out of the

generosity of their spirits, perhaps they'll pay a few dollars. A happy situation for everybody.'

'*Today?*' Maggie said again, her mind blank with sudden anxiety, so she couldn't even chastise Leah for talking about money. 'Leah – we can't—'

'Of course we can.' She gave Maggie a meaningful look. 'This could be the beginning of something very important.'

Maggie looked down. There was cemetery dirt on the hem of her skirt, and her shoes were worn. She felt she had caught the sun on her face, and her nose and cheeks were reddened. She had to press a cool flannel to her face, and change her clothes, and gather herself. *Something very important.*

'But what if—'

'I don't have time for *what if*,' said Leah. She cut a quick glance to Calvin, and then back. 'We'll *prepare*.'

There wasn't enough time to prepare. She shouldn't have gone to the cemetery, shouldn't have stood there all that time making Calvin think she was a fool. *Andrew McIlwraith.* It was a name with weight. An important name. And he was coming to see *her*.

Maggie looked over Leah's shoulder toward the stairs, twisting her gloves in her hands.

'Where's Kate?' she said.

'Lying about as if she's the lady of the house. Fetch her, Maggie. We've a lot to discuss.'

She found Kate in their bedroom, sitting up in bed with an expression on her face as if she had just been talking to somebody.

'When we finish it,' Kate said, 'I think we ought to have a sign or a word, to say to the spirits that we're finished. We should say *goodbye* at the end, so they know to go. Otherwise they'll stay. Or others might come. It's as if there's a door open.'

A headache was beginning. Maggie needed cool water on her face. She thought of the creek behind the house in Hydesville, felt a sudden longing for it.

'Don't you think?' said Kate.

'You mean – with Mr. McIlwraith?'

'With anybody.'

'Katie.' She shook her head, and flinched as the movement sent a bright, painful light across her eyes. 'Katie, Katie—' She caught her breath. She had to gather herself. 'Yes,' she said. 'That sounds fine. We have to go downstairs. Leah's waiting in the parlor, so we can prepare.'

Kate nodded, as if expecting this. 'Yes,' she said. 'And I have another idea too. About the bell.'

'You can tell us about it—'

'Do you think I'm right, about saying goodbye, how if we don't say goodbye it's like leaving the door open?'

Maggie grabbed her sister's hand and felt a bright, warm energy pass through her, pushing her headache away again. She felt strong. 'Yes, Katie, I think you're right,' she said, and Kate looked pleased. Perhaps she *was* right. She thought of all the doors they had left open already.

They gathered in Leah's bedroom to prepare. Leah had new ideas. She had pencils and paper, with the notion that they could write out messages as well as spelling out words. 'You'll have to appear to enter a kind of trance, Maggie,' she said. 'As if the spirits are guiding your hand. Kate's writing isn't good enough so it'll have to be you.'

'I think the spirits *will* guide your hand,' said Kate firmly.

'Yes, yes,' said Leah. 'Of course.'

She had investigated, asked neighbors and looked back

through some old newspapers to try and find some information they could use about Andrew McIlwraith, but she didn't have anything useful. 'We'll just have to be guided by what he tells us. I'm sure he's already a believer. He'll guide us in the right direction without even knowing it.'

'Perhaps he's not a believer,' said Maggie. 'Perhaps he's a businessman, and he thinks this is an opportunity.'

'Either way,' Leah said, 'we ought to put on a good show, don't you think?'

The door creaked, and Maggie looked to see their mother standing in the doorway, watching them. 'Girls,' she said. 'Won't you come downstairs for some lunch?'

'We will, Mother,' said Leah. 'I'll come and prepare something. We just need a few minutes. We've a lot to consider before our guest comes this evening.'

Mrs. Fox nodded. 'I suppose there's no point in me telling you that you ought to stop this.'

'Not very much point, no,' Leah said.

'I'm sorry, Mother,' Maggie said. She got to her feet and went to take her mother's hands. 'We don't want to upset you. But it's really alright. Ask Calvin, he thinks it's alright. You can join us if you like, this evening, you might—'

She shook her head. 'I can't take part in any more of this. Your father and brother will be furious with me, for letting you carry on like this.'

'They'll be furious with *me*, Mother,' said Leah. 'They won't blame you.'

This was true, Maggie thought, though she felt insulted on her mother's behalf, that she was considered powerless in these matters.

'I'll visit Mr. and Mrs. Post this evening. I don't want to ruin your evening with my nerves, but inviting this strange man to your home, Leah, for something like this, with the girls—' She broke off, and looked at Maggie. 'What if there's more trouble, Maggie?' she said softly.

'No.' Maggie tried to look kind, and confident. 'I know what I'm doing now, really. We all do. We have a gift, just like your grandmother did. You might even have it too. We're learning how to use it. It's a good thing, Mother. Even Calvin thinks so, and he doesn't believe in it. Ask him.'

'Yes, I'm sure he'll be reassuring as always, Margaretta,' she said. 'And I won't try to argue with any of you. But don't ask me to come with you.' She squeezed Maggie's hands, and stepped back. 'I can't.'

Their mother left at six. Calvin accompanied her on the short walk to the Posts' house. When he returned, he leaned in the kitchen doorway and smiled. 'So,' he said. 'Where would you like *me* to be for this evening's activities?'

'Out of our way, preferably,' Leah said, but Maggie looked at him.

'Do you want to help?' she said.

He shrugged. 'That's what I'm here for.'

'Why doesn't he stay upstairs, Leah? In Mother's bedroom. We'll pretend that there's nobody else here, but when it's quiet, he could tap on the crooked floorboard up there, or drop something in the hearth. That would be unsettling. Wouldn't it? For the atmosphere, before we start?'

The simplicity of it appealed to her. It reminded her of Hydesville.

'And can we trust him to do as he's told?' Leah said lightly.

'I think so. It's all a science experiment for you, isn't it, Calvin?'

'That's right.' He was still smiling. 'And I'd be very honored to take part.'

Andrew McIlwraith was an elegant man, with thoughtful, deep eyes. Younger than Maggie had expected, with sharply parted hair that turned to curls at the ends. He spoke in a refined way, as if he might have gone to a fine college and traveled in Europe, though he told them he had mainly only traveled in New York State. He had inherited the newspaper business, he said, but he wanted to make a go of it and to print things that he thought might be edifying to the public. And he was an abolitionist, he told them, though he was ashamed of having come late to the cause.

They assembled in the parlor. Leah poured him some wine.

'I didn't know if I should bring anything to help you,' he said. 'But I have this.' And he took out a family daguerreotype in a small case, a somber picture of four small children, their parents, and an older woman. 'It's my brother's family,' he said. 'From Boston. But I won't say any more.'

Maggie took the picture and studied it for a while. Kate stood behind her, and did the same. Mr. McIlwraith watched them. Maggie had always found pictures like these strange, something faintly disturbing about the frozen expressions.

The lamps had already been lowered before he had arrived at the door, and it would have been hard for him to notice how precariously the picture frame stood on the piano, or the fact that beneath her long skirt Kate's feet were bare. He didn't know that Calvin was upstairs.

The small servant-bell was in the center of the table. As they sat down, Leah explained. 'The bell will only ring if an unknown spirit enters. A spirit we don't want. When we begin we will give these instructions, that if the spirit of someone who is known to us is present, they should answer only in raps.'

It was Kate's idea. Leah took to it immediately. The bell had been too loud before, it had disrupted the mood, but to have it standing silently on the table created a kind of tense expectation all on its own.

'And at the end of the séance,' Leah continued, 'we must be sure to each say *goodbye*, to ensure that the door to the spirit world is closed.'

Mr. McIlwraith nodded. Maggie found herself trying to interpret every hint of expression that crossed his face, every muscle twitch or frown.

The daguerreotype was laid in the middle of the table. The candles were extinguished, and they began.

Leah gave her instructions, in the low, steady voice which she had practiced. They held hands, but Maggie sat between Kate and Leah so she could free her hands and take up the pen and paper, if necessary. And so that Leah could slip her hand from Maggie's grasp and knock on the table, or move an object – the picture, or a candlestick. When the instructions were finished, Maggie waited a moment, and said, 'Spirit, are you there? Please rap once if you are.'

And then waited again.

Finally, from beneath the table where Kate sat, though Mr. McIlwraith would hardly have been able to tell, there came a shuffling sound, and then one sharp rap.

An intake of breath.

'Spirit, we welcome you,' Maggie said. 'Is one of our party known to you?'

A rap.

'There is a picture on the table. Can you tell us how many people are in it?'

A pause, and then seven, slow raps.

Maggie thought. She couldn't sense Mr. McIlwraith's reaction. He was making no movements. 'Can you tell us – are all of the people in the picture still living?'

That he had chosen to bring the picture at all gave the answer, and she trusted that Kate would know this.

Two raps, and then Mr. McIlwraith spoke. 'Can you tell us how many of the people in the picture are still living?' he said. Leah's hand tightened on hers. They really ought not to speak themselves, the guests, until they were instructed.

The silence was long, and Maggie couldn't think how she could help Kate, she would simply have to guess – it went on *too* long, and Maggie was about to suggest a change of course, when he said, softly: 'That's right. They are all gone.'

A rap.

They let the session go on for longer than the others they had held. They answered his questions – wrongly, most of them, but when they gave a right answer all the wrong answers were forgotten.

The mood shifted from somber to playful and back again. Maggie scrawled messages which could not be read until a candle was lit – little fragments, *dear brother, the children are here, the children are playing, dear brother, we are well, be true to yourself.* Calvin walked across the floorboards and opened and closed the door at the top of the stairs. The picture frame fell. They carried on into the night, past Kate's bedtime, as if they were playing a parlor game it was simply too much fun to stop.

They heard their mother come home and pause at the door, and then continue up to her own bedroom in silence.

They drew out the story slowly – the whole family had contracted cholera within months of each other, died within a year – and never quite settled on which spirit was speaking, so it seemed as if it might have been all of them. When they finally finished—'Goodbye,' Kate whispered. 'Goodbye, goodbye goodbye' – they all looked at each other and laughed, as if they had shared some strange dream.

'Ladies,' Mr. McIlwraith said, as he finally began to gather his coat and things. 'You have an exceptional talent. I should be very grateful if you would let me assist you in bringing your work to a wider audience.'

They were standing in the hall now, close to the door. Leah was radiant, hands clasped together. Kate's excitement crackled like a newly lit fire and if Maggie touched her she felt she would be set alight. He was so charming. So attentive, and so impressed with them.

'We'd be delighted,' said Leah. 'We're from a modest background, Mr. McIlwraith, we're the daughters of a blacksmith, but I've felt from the beginning that these gifts ought to be shared with the world.'

'I quite agree.'

Maggie opened the door for him, and stepped aside to let him pass. She could see his mind was still turning. 'A parlor is the right setting for your work, of course,' he said. 'But on occasion you might want to perform on a larger scale.'

'If the opportunity arose—' Leah began. He had stepped outside and stood looking back at them, with the night behind him and his driver waiting.

'In fact,' he said, and then stopped. 'No. I couldn't impose.'

'You can,' said Leah. 'Please do.'

'In fact,' he said, 'I already know of a small circle of people who would be interested. Some of them are due at my house tomorrow evening, for dinner. I wonder—'

'Yes?' said Leah.

'Well.' His eyes passed over each of them in turn. 'Well, I wonder if you might join us,' he said.

The faces in his daguerreotype had fixed themselves in her mind. Maggie drank some of the wine that Leah had poured, which gave her a warm, blurred sensation and brought color to her cheeks, and she tried to forget them – to put those four somber dead children in a vault in her mind, and to lock it. Even Kate drank some wine, and then she tried to play the piano, and Leah and Calvin danced until they were laughing too much, and their mother came downstairs to complain. But they told her what had happened and Calvin, as always, managed to reassure her that it would all be alright, and so she drank some wine as well. It was past midnight when their good moods finally carried them to bed.

Kate was asleep immediately, but in the dark those children rose in Maggie's mind again. *I'm so sorry*, she thought. *I'm so sorry we've used you like this.* Then she whispered it aloud, just in case.

She was drifting to sleep. Beginning to dream, she thought she heard Calvin say *the brain, electricity, medicine*, and then the soft sound of a bell ringing in the parlor.

TWENTY-ONE

It began to rain the next day, so Mr. McIlwraith arranged for a carriage to collect them and bring them to his door. It was a cold, unexpected rain, slanted sideways, and you felt it could turn to ice, more like winter than spring. Mud sprayed from beneath the carriage wheels, and although it was only five o'clock when they left their house, the sky was low and gray and had turned very dark. The streets had emptied.

They were quiet, in the carriage, shivering, and nervous. Calvin had come with them and Maggie was glad. Leah was convinced he would make jokes and embarrass them but he'd sworn not to – hadn't he helped them, last night? – and it reassured their mother that they weren't going alone.

Mr. McIlwraith lived east of the river, well out of the city, in a house set far back from any road and surrounded by dense elms with low branches that partly hid the roof. It seemed grand, from a distance, the sharp angles of the roof looming dark against the sky, and small, flickering points of light in the lower windows. But as the carriage came to a stop outside, Maggie began to see signs of decay. Rotted wood around the door, a tangle of ivy that needed to be cut back. It was spring, but there were dead plants amongst the wild, dark greens that grew up around the sides of the house. The rain had begun to turn to mist around the foundations.

As they climbed down from the carriage, the front door was flung open, a rectangle of warm, orange light in front of which Andrew McIlwraith formed a dark silhouette. 'The Fox sisters,' he called out. 'Emerging from the storm. Welcome!'

The house was cold. Mr. McIlwraith apologized. 'I inherited the place,' he said. 'I ought to have some work done on it. Never seem to find the time. But you come to appreciate its charms.' They were gathered in the hall where a servant held up a lamp and another took their coats and shawls. Calvin had held his coat over their heads as they'd crossed over from the carriage to the front door, and now his hair was damp, and the collar of his shirt.

A wide, red-carpeted spiral staircase behind them appeared to circle up into darkness. There were no lamps lit on the floors above. 'I never saw the point in lighting a room you weren't using,' he said, when he saw Maggie looking up. 'Save the oil, I say. I know people laugh at me.' He smiled. 'Grace can make you some tea, if you'd like to warm up. Or we can go through to the parlor. Our guests will be here soon. There's wine, or a little beer if you'd like it, Mr.—' He looked at Calvin.

'Brown.' Calvin stuck out his hand. 'Calvin Brown. I hope you don't mind that I accompany the ladies this evening.'

'Calvin is a dear friend to us,' said Leah. 'A kind of brother, and he sometimes helps us with our work. I'm sure you don't mind.'

'Of course not.' Mr. McIlwraith looked at them all. 'Delighted.'

'Mr. McIlwraith,' said Leah. 'Before we go any further, and before the other guests arrive, I wonder if we might have a few moments alone to look at the parlor?' She spoke very evenly, meeting his gaze. 'It's better we have a certain familiarity with a room, before we start. I'm sure you understand.'

'No, of course,' he said. 'Grace will show you through. I'll go down to the cellar and look for that wine, I think. Make yourselves comfortable. Whatever you need.'

The parlor was cold too. 'How can he live like this?' Leah murmured, as soon as Grace had left them alone. 'With all his money.'

There were grand things in the room, expensive things, candlesticks and rugs and mirrors, that showed he was rich. But the effect of all of them together was less than it should have been.

The daguerreotype of his dead family was propped on the mantelpiece, above a fire which had almost died down to embers. There was a framed edition of his newspaper, the *Herald*, with a headline – *Slavery question comes to Rochester* – that perhaps he had written. Or perhaps he didn't write things, only paid people to write them. Maggie wasn't quite sure what a proprietor did.

The curtains were open; a large bay window overlooked the back of the house, a garden of some kind, but it was now so dark outside it was hard to see anything. Dark shapes outside that might have been trees, blurred by the rain, and their own reflections in the glass. Leah put down the small trunk she had brought from the house. Mr. McIlwraith had looked at it but hadn't asked. 'He'll understand that we need a few of our own things,' she said. 'It's only reasonable.' She opened it and took out a dark green tablecloth from their kitchen, shook it out and laid it over the large oak table in the center of the room. 'Perfect,' she said. It draped down to the floor. 'Katie, come here. Sit down.'

Kate obediently went and sat at one of the chairs that surrounded the table, and Leah crouched down, peering beneath the table and pulling the tablecloth to adjust it.

'You look ridiculous, Leah,' Maggie told her, and heard a muffled reply: 'We'll all look ridiculous if nothing happens this evening.'

Calvin had been sent to stand outside the door and stop anybody coming in, and Maggie was fascinated to know how he planned to do this, in somebody else's house.

'Here,' Leah said, as Maggie came over to join her. 'This is lucky. There's a crooked leg, here. A bit of pressure on this and the whole table will shake. Kate, try nudging it with your foot. Take off your shoes if you need to.'

There was chatter outside the door – Calvin, improvising, 'These door handles, are they imported?' – and Leah stood up and swept past Maggie and stepped outside. 'If you'll just give us a moment, Mr. McIlwraith,' Maggie heard her say. 'My sisters are very young, as you know, and they need a little time to collect themselves before any guests arrive.'

She saw Kate frown, and went over to sit with her at the table. 'How do you feel?' Maggie said.

'I feel fine. I like this house.'

Maggie blinked, and looked over at the daguerreotype again. She brushed her fingertips against the table, hoping to feel some kind of energy or magnetism, an intent to communicate. She shivered. Her hands were cold, and she pressed them between her knees and the folds of her skirt.

Kate gave the table a little shake and nodded, satisfied.

They were only telling lies in service of the truth.

Leah came back into the room. 'Quickly,' she said. 'We have to practice.'

The plan: they would circulate among the guests, as drinks were served, and try to pick up whatever little details they could. Things that would help them. The names of children,

185

a profession, an address. They would be unobtrusive, listening when it appeared that they were not.

The conversation was lively. The guests were excited. There was a lot of talk of politics, and Maggie was sure that some of these people would know of the Posts, or James Crane. With more bodies in the room, the temperature began to rise, and Maggie's dress – her best – began to feel hot and constrictive.

'You're not an abolitionist, then?' one man was saying to another.

'I'm no supporter of slavery,' he said. 'But in my view the institution will wither in time, without our intervention. My fear is that the issue will drive our country to war.' He took a sip of his drink. 'I've already lost a daughter. I won't see my sons slaughtered over a Southern issue.'

A lost daughter. She lodged this in her memory.

She went to stand with Leah, who was surveying the room. 'There's a rather cynical woman over there, who I don't care for,' said Leah, in a low voice. 'But I'm sure the rest of them will be converts before the night is over.'

Mr. McIlwraith came toward them. 'Miss Fox.' He smiled at Maggie, and pressed a glass into her hand. 'Please.'

She tried to hold the glass between her fingers delicately, and took a sip. White wine. It sparkled on her lips. Leah watched her carefully, a warning in her eyes. Maggie tried to smile. 'Thank you. For all your hospitality.'

'Thank *you*,' he said. 'Last night was a revelation. I knew I had to share it.' He looked at Leah, and back at Maggie, then at the corner where Kate was gazing up at a bookshelf. 'I've always found something compelling about sisters.'

Leah laughed hesitantly, and then saw that he was serious, and stopped.

186

'I'm traveling to the city in the morning,' he said. 'I have a few business interests there. I dare say I'll be recounting whatever happens tonight.'

'Well, we certainly hope so,' said Leah.

'I'm very keen to support the development of the character of this country,' he said. 'Things that are new, and interesting. To bring them to a wider audience. Parts of our society are very rigid in their ways.'

'I quite agree,' said Leah.

Maggie looked over his shoulder, at the table, waiting for them. Some of the guests had added things to the center. Mr. McIlwraith must have instructed them. She could see a locket. A handkerchief. A coral bracelet. She ought to look at them more closely, when nobody was watching.

'If this goes well,' he said, 'this – with a larger audience, I mean – then I see a very bright future for your enterprise, ladies. And not only in Rochester. Across the state. I could assist in finding venues, if you want to—'

Maggie turned to him. 'We want to help people,' she said.

'And you will.' He seemed to be sincere. 'I don't doubt it.'

There was a distant sound of thunder as they took their seats. The storm was building in strength.

'Providence favors our undertakings,' said Mr. McIlwraith, with a smile, and there was a round of uncertain laughter. Once the empty glasses had been taken away, and the lamps had been lowered, a different mood came over the group. They sat at the table quietly, and a crack of thunder made them all jump. The steady beat of rain against the windows had a strange, hypnotic effect.

They had the maids take away the final lamps, leaving only a candle in the center of the table, and a few fading embers on the fire. They began, as usual, with silence. It surprised Maggie how familiar this all felt, already, how practiced. How strange that this was so easy. As if it was what they had always been meant to do.

The curtains were still tied back, and the large, dark window watched over them. How must their group look from outside, she wondered, gathered around the tiny, flickering candle.

She was holding Leah's hand, which was cool and dry. There were small rustles of movement around the table, people shifting in their seats, breathing, waiting. You had to wait until the silence became unnerving, and then frightening, and then wait a little longer. Eventually, Katie would blow out the candle – quickly, scarcely moving, it wouldn't be clear who had done it – and then, in the dark, Leah would let go of Maggie's hand and tug at the tablecloth, just in the place where she had created a fold beneath the candlestick – and it would fall. She had practiced this for hours that afternoon.

And then Maggie would say, 'If there are any spirits here tonight, we are listening.'

There were eight guests in total, and it meant that almost any name they spelled elicited a response, a gasp of recognition. *Yes, John, my father. Mary, my cousin. Yes.* The simplest, most ordinary of names, but people were so easily convinced that a name was special only to them. They were so eager to be chosen. There was something sad about it, Maggie thought, something that gave her a lonely feeling. *Emily, yes, my sister.* Everybody carried so much grief inside them, so many deaths, so much loss, that it was ordinary and hardly to be spoken of, but it was always there beneath the surface, and the simplest gesture – a name, a message, *I am at peace* – could bring about tears, even in the men.

With each question, each call to the spirits, Maggie

waited, as did Kate, hoping for raps from the walls, from the floor, signs that there was something real here, someone real. Nothing came. But the guests knew no better.

And Maggie was collecting her strength. The faith in the room gave it to her. Strength of mind and concentration. She would call a spirit, any spirit. There must be one, listening. If they had found her before they would find her again. *I am here*, she thought. *Come and find me.* She reached with her mind, searching out dark pathways that had been lit before.

Then she felt it, a heightening of energy, a brush across her skin, light as silk, all the hairs on her arms standing up.

She freed her hands and reached forward to touch the objects on the table, one by one. Each guest sat up a little straighter as their object was touched.

She touched the handkerchief last, and then picked it up, and let it lie loose across her palm. She put it down again, and picked up the bracelet. 'Is the owner of this bracelet here?' she tried.

A hush. She felt Leah grow tense.

There was no answer.

'Is the owner—'

Two soft taps from beneath the table.

Maggie swallowed. It had to be Kate. Two taps, which meant *no*.

'Then who—' She faltered; she couldn't think of the next question. 'Is somebody else here?'

A single tap came from the walls.

'*Maggie,*' she heard Kate whisper, in a tiny voice.

A murmur around the table.

'I'd like to—' Maggie stopped, swallowed again. Her mouth was very dry. 'I'd like to talk to the owner of the bracelet. Is she here as well?'

She cracked her own toes twice, but the sound was lost to a single pound on the door that almost shook the table. A gasp. A crackle of fear.

'Please—' said Maggie. 'Can I talk to—'

The table shook. It could have been Leah. But it seemed to be exerting a pressure, as well, beneath her hands, as if it was trying to rise. 'If you have something to tell us—' Maggie whispered, 'then please—'

There was a rattle of footsteps behind the door, a rattle of the handle as if the door were locked, and then a dragging sound which Maggie realized, seconds later, was her own chair being dragged backward from the table. She tried to shriek but no sound came out. She told herself she was dreaming. Thunder, like the fall of huge rocks, or the shaking of a sheet of steel, sounded in the distance, and Maggie stumbled to her feet. She fell toward the table and grasped it, the edges pressing into her palms. '*No,*' she whispered, and the table was shaking again, rocking back and forth on its heavy legs, so that the guests began to push themselves away in fear – and the rattle of footsteps went away, across the hall – and the front door slammed.

Sick, Maggie spun to face the huge window, and felt that she must cover it, pull shut the curtains, nail a board over the glass, but of course there was no time. The circle had broken apart: some guests sat rigid in their chairs, but others had risen, hands clasped over their mouths. Somebody was saying something, but Maggie could not understand the words.

A flicker of silent lightning. In an instant of bright white illumination, Maggie saw the whole of the garden, its ragged weeds and windswept hedges, and a man standing at the far end, a man in a black hat, with an untidy black beard, looking toward them. In the hair's-breadth of a second before the light was gone, she saw him begin to lope toward the window.

When the lightning flickered again he was in the room—

– leaning in the corner with a hand in his pocket, but she couldn't see his face. There was a smell of flame and alcohol, and something older, wet and earthy and hungry—

Something struck her. Her head snapped backward and her hair whipped across her face. She staggered but did not fall. Someone screamed, and she heard a chair knocked over, felt arms around her, but she shook them away.

'No,' she said, her voice a wrenched, raw thing, it was not her own. 'Not you. *I do not want you.'* She stumbled back to the table, which was in disarray, wine spilled and pictures scattered, and grabbed for something, a weapon, she didn't know, but there was nothing she could use—

– and a cold wind rushed through the room, opening and slamming the door and causing more of them to scream. The wind caught the dying embers of the fire and it burst into life, too big and bright to look at, spraying sparks and ash across the room—

She was dying. A heart couldn't pound like this and not explode; she could picture it in her chest, a splatter of blood against her ribs, like a smashed, red fruit. And then she was no longer in the room. She was staggering down a hallway, looking for a door; she was staggering through trees, wet ground giving way beneath her; she was staggering down an empty road, and there was a wolf behind her. The walls were narrowing and the road was endless, and branches were breaking all around her. She had the sense that somebody, distantly, was calling her name. Blood roared in her ears. She fell to the ground; cold mud beneath her hands, stone, dirt. Water.

Water. Someone had thrown water in her face. Her face was wet, her neck, her hair. She reached a hand to her mouth and then stared bewildered at her fingers. Someone was calling her name. She was on the ground. The carpet. She could scarcely hear over her pounding blood, but she looked up and saw faces floating like moons, shocked, mouths hanging open, huge, red, frightened eyes. Chairs lay on the ground. Somebody was crying.

The disorder of the room began to resolve itself, piece by piece – there was light, a lamp had been lit, and there was Calvin, horrified and confused, there was Leah, kneeling in front of her and clutching an empty glass – but she couldn't form words, couldn't ask what had happened. She gulped air; pain was blooming on one side of her face.

Her brain slowly attached itself to a sound, a steady, repetitive sound that she couldn't make sense of, until she finally turned and saw Andrew McIlwraith standing by an upturned chair, a wide smile on his face, shaking his head in delight and wonderment. His broad shoulders were moving back and forth. His hands. Finally, tasting blood on her lip, she understood the sound.

It was applause.

TWENTY-TWO

In the carriage, the road rocked beneath them and the rain beat against the roof. Maggie pressed a handkerchief to her cut lip. Kate sat opposite, staring, mouth hanging open. Calvin was leaning forward, elbows on his knees and his face gray with worry.

'– some effect of electricity from the storm,' he was murmuring, '– a collective fever of some kind—'

Leah was silent, but her hand rested on Maggie's knee. Rain clouds obscured the moon and Maggie could make out nothing beyond the carriage. She did not know where they were. Her lip stung and her head pounded, and she wanted to laugh, or to hug her sisters, or to climb on to the carriage roof and scream.

'Do you see?' she heard herself say, taking the handkerchief away and smiling dizzily, so the skin on her lip was stretched and split again. She tasted blood. Kate's expression was horrified. Maggie wondered if she looked deranged. 'Do you see what they can do?'

Leah squeezed her knee, as if wanting her to stop, so Maggie turned to her. 'You *see*? They can hurt people, if they're angry enough, they can move things and—'

'Maggie, you're shocked, you're hurt—'

'Yes. Yes. You see? The schoolhouse, Leah. I think it was the *same man*. I didn't mean to, but I called him. He heard me reaching out to their world and he came back—'

'Could McIlwraith have *hired* someone?' Calvin said, still talking to himself. Maggie wanted to laugh at him. Poor Calvin. Trying so hard to make the world smaller and more ordinary than it was.

A part of Maggie had exited her body and was looking at her from above. *You ought to be afraid*, it was saying. *Why are you smiling?*

The fear hovered just to her side, waiting to be let back in. but for now she felt only wild and powerful. The *same man*. He had found her again, or she had found him. 'I couldn't control it,' she said, 'but perhaps I can with practice. There might be other things I could do, so it isn't dangerous.'

But the danger was part of the reason for her racing heart, her smile. This was a *gift*. The fear pressed at her, traced its fingers on her arm, but she would not look at it.

'Was it really him?' Kate whispered.

'I don't know.' His face was shadowed in her memory, his movements too quick and jagged to follow. 'I don't know. Yes. Yes. I think it was. He recognized me.'

'You need to rest,' Leah said. 'We need to rest.' She paused and took a shaking breath, looked at Calvin. 'What will I say to our *mother*?' she whispered.

The following afternoon, two invitations arrived, guests from the previous night, asking if the sisters would please visit them for a private reception; of course they would be glad to pay for their time, please advise them of the rates.

And a note from Mr. McIlwraith, thanking them. *I have already written to my associates in New York City*, it said. *I want more Americans to see this for themselves.*

'No,' said their mother. 'No. You mustn't. You're disturbing something that doesn't want to be disturbed.'

They were all gathered in the upstairs bedroom, where Maggie was sitting in bed, although she felt fine, stronger than ever. Leah, Kate and their mother sat on Kate's bed, and Calvin leaned by the door, arms folded, studying the floor as if the problem he was trying to solve was written there. It was a cloudy afternoon, drifts of light rain still blowing through the city, and the room was dark.

Maggie looked at her mother. 'You believe me now, don't you? You know that I didn't hurt Hannah? It was a spirit. A man. A body from the cemetery.'

Mrs. Fox's mouth shook as if she might cry, but she pressed her lips together and didn't seem able to speak.

'No,' said Calvin, raising his head. 'No, we can't all, no – No. Hannah fell, or – I don't know what happened to Hannah, of course Maggie didn't – but she fell or tripped. And last night—'

'Everybody saw it,' said Maggie.

'*You* saw it, Calvin,' said Kate.

'I don't know what I saw. There are things we can't explain in this world, but they're still *part* of this world. There are collective behaviors, and the storm affected us. It's strange but it isn't—' He broke off, and looked at their mother. 'Mrs. Fox, it isn't supernatural. I promise you.'

Calvin's voice had a raw, scratched sound. He had caught a cold.

'Whatever it is, it isn't safe,' their mother said softly, but she was still looking at Calvin so her concern seemed directed at him.

'We'll be more careful,' Maggie said. Because something shook inside her and it was a feeling that lit her up, and she could tell Kate felt the same, as if the opportunity to try again couldn't come soon enough. Like finding gold in the river and you had to go deeper, you knew there could be more. Half the country was rushing to California to find gold. They had found it here.

Leah looked as shaken as anybody, but she was holding the letters. 'We'll have to reply, at least.' She added hesitantly, 'They say they'll pay. And the rent is due.'

At the end of the following week, Mr. McIlwraith received a reply from his associates: an invitation for the Fox sisters to travel to New York City. Would they be interested in performing their work in a hotel there? The letter was full of praise, and promises of luxuries that would all be paid for.

'But it's not safe,' their mother said, as she had most days, but she never said it with complete conviction. And she looked at the letter over and over, before asking if she could keep it, to put on the mantelpiece.

She was right, Maggie thought, it was not safe. Not entirely. The ones who'd been wronged, they were the ones who made trouble. Maybe the only ones who had the strength to rap on walls and move tables and push children. The peddler had been murdered. The man from the schoolhouse had been disturbed from his rest, his grave dug up, his family's graves, the headstones tossed aside.

They were desperate to be heard, these spirits. It might not be safe, but somebody ought to listen.

PART THREE

TWENTY-THREE
NEW YORK CITY
JUNE 1848

They were at Barnum's Hotel, corner of Broadway and Maiden Lane, and they were to perform three receptions each day: 10 a.m.-12 p.m., 3-5 p.m. and 8-10 p.m. Three dollars admission, and a private reception would be five dollars, which was a lot, even Leah thought so, but Matthew Barnum said in his letter that people would be willing to pay.

'Five dollars ought to keep the rabble away, at least,' Leah said, examining the proposal he had set out. 'And we have to think of our safety.'

The day they arrived – a Friday in late May, blue sky and summer warmth beginning to gather in the air – a notice had been placed in a New York City newspaper. Leah read it to them, as Maggie and Kate ran back and forth between their adjoining bedrooms.

'*Announcing the arrival of the Rochester Fox Sisters*,' Leah read, then paused and gave a satisfied smile. 'Girls, we've been *announced*.'

They had their *own* bedrooms, their own beds, with crisp new sheets and crimson quilts. Each room had a tall, ornate standing mirror in one corner, and a window with a cushioned window seat, looking out over a noisy, bustling street. There were fresh flowers in all their rooms on arrival – white lilies in Kate's, purple irises in Maggie's. The quilt had been perfumed, she was sure of it – she gathered the soft material to her face and breathed deeply. Yes: it had been scattered with lavender oil. Just for her. She buried her face for a moment, to stop herself shrieking with pleasure and excitement.

The carpet was thick, and deadened the sound of their voices. Beyond the room was a narrow corridor with dark red walls and whale-oil lamps on recessed ledges. Their bedroom doors were oak, and heavy.

All paid for, all theirs.

Calvin was with them. As their guardian. It was more decent to travel with a man – their brother, they called him for simplicity's sake – and Maggie knew it was some kind of comfort to their mother that he was there. She said she was too old to accompany them and too frightened of what might happen, although as she had waved goodbye Maggie was sure she was a little envious.

Calvin had his own room next to Leah's, a little further down the hall. He joined them after unpacking his bag, sat on the chair in the corner of Maggie's room. He was pale, shadows under his eyes, and he coughed into his sleeve as he sat down. He hadn't shaken the cold he caught at Andrew McIlwraith's that night. 'No flowers in my room,' he said, when he caught his breath. 'I'm insulted.' Then he held something out. 'They sent a note, to my room. I believe they think I'm your manager.'

Maggie snatched it from his hand, and read. 'Please join Mr. Barnum, the proprietor, and friends, at six p.m. in the public parlor, to discuss your work at the hotel and how we can make you welcome.'

Kate was brushing her fingers over a small jewelry box on the dresser in Maggie's room. 'Are they all old men?' she said.

'Almost certainly.' Leah looked up from the newspaper.

'Old men who are providing these rooms, so please be charming.'

'What should we wear?' Maggie caught sight of herself in the mirror. Still untidy from the journey, and wearing a dress her mother had made two summers ago. 'We should have new clothes.'

'At five dollars for a private reception, I expect we soon will.' Leah looked back at the paper, a small, satisfied smile on her face.

At six o'clock, the same boy who had carried up their things when they arrived led them to the public parlor.

They passed by the dining hall, which was half grand – elegant furnishing and polished silverware, large windows with freshly painted sills – and half unfinished. Unpainted walls, and a screen thrown up to ineffectively cover a corner where building materials lay, and a ladder was propped against a wall.

'Thank you,' Maggie said to the boy, as they followed him. 'I don't know your name.'

He grinned at her. 'I'm Sam, Miss Fox.' He was tall and lanky, with dark hair that curled around his collar, and green eyes. She wondered if they were supposed to give him money, but she had none, so she said, 'Do you live here?'

'Sometimes, if I'm working late at night.' He tilted his head as he opened the door to the parlor and gestured them in. 'I'm always around, in any case,' he said, and winked at her. She met his gaze and smiled again. She felt herself blush. A sensation like bubbles rising in her chest.

Then she turned and more men were looking at her attentively. Four of them, mostly old, but one who was perhaps only twenty-two or twenty-three, and had sharp cheekbones and a soft curve to his lips. Maggie caught his eye, still blushing, and tucked a loose piece of hair behind her ear.

They were led to a curtained-off section of the room, where soft chairs were casually arranged, and bottles of wine and champagne were laid out on a small table, and the men introduced themselves. Businessmen and investors in the hotel. The man with cheekbones was Mr. Barnum's son Elijah.

Kate had become nervous. She pressed against Maggie's side, clutching at her hand. But Maggie felt she was flying, her feet light as air, and right away she heard herself talking and laughing as if all of this was perfectly ordinary to her. She pulled away from Kate, and when a glass of champagne was pressed into her hand, she took it. The first sip tasted strange, but the second was like drinking stars. She saw Calvin looking at her with a faint frown, so she turned away from him, toward Elijah Barnum. She said, 'Do you know Mr. McIlwraith in Rochester? Have you heard about the events at his house?'

'I've heard a few details, but I'd be delighted to hear it from you personally, Miss Fox.' A flash of white teeth as he smiled. She hardly knew anybody with such straight white teeth.

Then Leah put an arm around her, and squeezed her shoulder tightly. 'That evening was a terrible strain on my sister,' she said. 'What we do can be very draining.'

'I'm sure,' said Elijah Barnum.

'But rewarding. To help those who have been bereaved—'

'And to hear the voices of those who have been wronged,' Maggie said. 'Sinned against. That's also—'

'I'm sure you have somebody, a friend or a relative, who

202

you would wish to share just a few more words with, Mr. Barnum.' Leah was trying to make her voice solemn, but Maggie could hear that she was also lit up by the champagne and company.

'Doesn't everybody?' he said.

Elijah's father spoke to Calvin for a while, in lowered voices, a man's conversation, but gradually they turned their attention to Leah and Maggie, coming to stand with them. Kate had sat down on one of the low chairs. She was fiddling with a bracelet that Leah had let her borrow.

'Ladies.' Mr. Barnum senior put down his glass and dabbed at his brow with a handkerchief. The enclosed space was warm, the air already thick with the tang of alcohol. He was blurred, his voice soft. Maggie clasped her hands together. She could imagine shadows dancing around all of them, spirits waiting to be called, their mothers and fathers and cousins and friends. It softened her feelings toward men, she realized, to think of them bereaved, as everybody was.

'Ladies. Perhaps it's time to speak candidly, now that we've welcomed you to our establishment. I don't want to be indelicate. But perhaps you can reassure us. The spirits. Are they . . . reliable?'

No, Maggie thought. They were random and chaotic and confusing. They could not be explained. He would never really understand. Even her private thoughts thrilled her. The things she had experienced that these men had not.

'We can't have anyone asking for their money back,' he continued. 'We expect all the guests to be satisfied, in some form.'

'Mr. Barnum—' Leah began, but Maggie interrupted.

'They will be. They will be satisfied, all of them. I won't

be called a liar, Mr. Barnum, I refuse. I'll make sure they all experience things they can't explain.'

'Good.' He nodded. 'And I'm a believer myself,' he added politely, but then rubbed his jaw and said, 'But if I can provide you with any support – a few men to assist you, or a few . . . *tools*, to ensure the spirits are punctual, then you will tell me.'

They were all silent for a moment. From beyond the curtain, the sound of voices and laughter rose, other guests entering the parlor.

Calvin was standing in a corner with a glass of untouched wine, but Maggie saw that there was a sheen to his face and his eyes were dull. He put the glass down and turned, trying to stifle a cough with his hand.

Leah straightened her shoulders, and smiled. 'Of course. Your support would be greatly appreciated in matters of that sort. Perhaps we could arrange to meet in the morning, and discuss a few details.'

'Good, then!' said Mr. Barnum. 'Tomorrow. But now.' He clapped his hands. 'It's time to show you the room we've set aside just for you.'

They were led back through the public parlor, guests glancing at them curiously as they passed, and out into the hall, where the lamps had not yet been lit and the light was fading, evening shadows cutting across the walls. The group went further down the hall until they reached a closed door that Mr. Barnum opened with a flourish.

Inside, a long oak table that could have seated twenty people. There was no carpet, only a dark patterned rug spread beneath the table, and a single large window over which the curtains had already been drawn. Lamps hung at odd intervals along the wall, as if whoever had begun placing them had not yet finished. In the center of the table was a candelabra of burnished silver, and a pitcher of water. An empty sideboard stood next to a grand fireplace.

'We can add more furniture or remove it, as you like,' said Mr. Barnum. 'Say the word.' When nobody responded, he said, 'Perhaps we'll give you ladies a few moments to inspect the room yourselves. Then if you'll care to join us, some food will be served in the dining hall.' A murmur of agreement, and the men left.

It was almost grand, Maggie thought, but there was something oppressive about it all the same. The walls were bare, not a mirror or picture, nothing but hooks for the lamps. Calvin, still coughing, went to the window and opened the curtains a little, letting a slash of fading sunlight into the room. She saw him push at the window but it did not open.

'Well.' Leah crossed the room and traced a finger across the sideboard, examining it for dust. 'What do you think?'

Leah did not look sure. Kate had folded her arms tight across her chest and was frowning. Maggie couldn't see Calvin's expression. His back was turned as he peered out of the window.

She was still holding a glass of champagne. Her second. It had loosened her mind, made all kinds of things seem possible. She could hear whistling beyond the door. Perhaps it was Sam. Life hummed all around them. 'I like it,' she said. 'I think it's perfect.'

Kate twisted her mouth. 'I don't know.'

'We'll have to make it work,' said Leah.

'What if we can't?' said Kate. 'That man will be angry with us.'

'He won't,' Calvin said, turning around, catching his

205

breath. 'If he is, we leave. They haven't *bought* you, Kate. Don't worry about them. You don't owe anybody anything.'

'Yes, don't, Katie,' said Maggie. 'When people come to see us . . .' She paused, trying to think how to remind her of the point of all of it. 'They bring their own ghosts with them. If there are spirits who want to communicate, they will. That's out of our control. If they *don't* want to communicate, we can perform. You told me yourself, whatever happens, we're only helping them to see the truth. Here,' Maggie said, handing her the rest of her champagne. 'You can finish this.' She saw Calvin glance at Leah, an eyebrow raised.

Kate took it, and looked at the surface cautiously before taking a sip.

'Don't drink that, Katie,' said Leah. 'You're too young.'

'If I'm old enough to be here, I'm old enough to drink champagne,' Kate said, and Leah didn't seem to have a response.

'There's a shipping office over there,' said Calvin, turning back to the window. 'And another hotel, and a coffee house, and some sort of clerk's office. And an apothecary.' He sounded distant. 'Wonder if any of them are looking for help. I should ask.'

'No, Calvin, you can't do that,' Leah said lightly. 'We need your complete attention at all times, or who knows what might happen to us.'

He turned back, grinning, a little of the usual light back in his eyes. 'Of course. And this is where the real money is, after all.'

Maggie was still looking around the room – *theirs* – and thinking of what they would do here. She wanted to start, right away, fetch Sam and Elijah Barnum and anybody who was out there, and see what would happen, what they could do. Yes, there was no doubt they would have to perform, crack their toes and find other tricks, but something more would happen, it had to. The wild fear that night at Mr. McIlwraith's, the creeping dread of the house in Hydesville, even the horror of the sight of Hannah Crane falling through the air – it was as if she had touched lightning. As if she had begun to live life as intensely and forcefully as it ought to be lived. And they were here now, and she could not let that go.

They spent a few days planning. Devising tricks and becoming accustomed to the room, its possibilities and its crooked floorboards. They replaced most of the lamps with candles, positioned on surfaces around the room. Calvin, still sick, was nevertheless full of ideas, making little sketches and crouching beneath the table to make some small adjustment to the legs, so that it could be made to rock without much effort.

And the hotel advanced them some money, so that they could have new dresses. They wore them on the first night they were to perform. Burgundy and black, made from a material that shimmered darkly in the candlelight. Leah brushed a little color on to their lips, and twisted their hair into complex rolls and waves.

Calvin was wearing a suit, though it was loose on him, as if he had lost weight. He waited for them at the foot of the stairs. He would lead the guests to their seats when it was time. Before they began, drinks were served in the public parlor, and introductions made. Maggie found her hands were shaking, and took a glass of wine gratefully when it was offered. There were two businessmen, more investors in the hotel, who had wanted to be the first to see them. There was a young man named Daniel Renner, who was nineteen and rich, and had read the Hydesville pamphlet and was curious. His cousin Alice, who was desperately nervous and made everybody else nervous too. And a Dutch couple, the Jansens.

Mrs. Jansen's sister had died on the journey to New York. One of the investors was a widow. Alice Renner's mother had recently died. When they had purchased their tickets, they had been given a sheet of questions to complete, which Leah and Calvin had devised. Maggie had thought this might ruin everything, reveal their deceptions, but Calvin had a theory that people loved to be asked about themselves, and given the opportunity to share their private griefs and losses, they would look favorably on whoever had bothered to ask. And so they were given the answers, and had carefully memorized them. A sister, Elin. A wife, Cora. A mother, Mary. Their names whirled in Maggie's mind, as she stood, wine glass trembling in her hand, smiling at the small group in a way she hoped was mysterious.

The guests, for the most part, began their evening with laughter and good humor. But the séance terrified them. Moments after Maggie called out, *Is there a spirit here?* a small framed mirror fell from the mantelpiece in the corner, and shattered.

The mirror was Leah's. The thread that connected it all the way to Kate's chair was invisible, in the dark room. The sound was so unexpected that the guests were instantly altered, sensitized and ready to believe. When Maggie cracked her toes to spell out *Cora*, the man gasped and made a strange sound like a sob. It was the sound of a man who did not really know how to cry. Grief was so *raw*, Maggie thought, so easily found, and people were so desperate for comfort.

When it was finished and the lamps were lit, the mood was more solemn than Maggie had expected. All the laughter had vanished. Alice Renner was dabbing at her eyes. The shattered glass still lay on the floor, and in the middle of the table a piece of paper on which Kate had scrawled a few sentences, *I am happy and peaceful, we are together*. The man who had lost his wife stared at Maggie for a long time, creases lining his mouth, a crumpled look to his face.

'Thank you,' he said softly. 'I don't know what to make of it.'

'We're only messengers,' Leah said. 'Mediums between one world and another. It's mysterious to us, as well.'

He nodded, murmured, 'Yes, yes,' and appeared to try and gather himself. Then he filed to the door with the other guests, leaving Maggie, Kate and Leah alone.

They looked between each other. For once, Leah seemed to have nothing to say. Finally, Kate said softly, 'Do you think that's what Mr. Barnum hoped for?'

'They won't ask for their money back, will they?' said Maggie. 'Not after that. Not after his wife spoke to us. *Cora.* That was her name. I heard him gasp. I knew the letters, I *felt* them—'

'Maggie.' Leah gave her a complicated look. 'We *knew* her name.'

Candle smoke stung her eyes. She was breathless, tingling. 'I know that,' she said, though she had entirely forgotten.

TWENTY-FOUR

In the morning, a driver was hired to give them a tour of the city. He took them everywhere, showing them all the different neighborhoods, the churches and storefronts and shipping yards, the halls and coffee houses, the rich people, the poor people, the banks and taverns. New buildings, several stories high, leaned up against old farmhouses that had once stood surrounded by fields. Maggie couldn't wait to get back to the hotel, just so she could write letters to her family, telling all about it. She thought of writing the neighbors in Hydesville, to Stephen Whitaker in the post office. *Imagine where I am.*

Calvin was too tired to join them on the tour. But he met them in their private parlor in the afternoon as they began to prepare their evening reception, and brought the answers the guests had provided when they bought their tickets.

He dropped the papers on the table and then sank into a corner chair. 'Quite a crowd,' he said. 'There's a doctor, and a man who lectures in philosophy, and a journalist. I wonder if we can join them for dinner, afterward. I'd like to talk—'

'A journalist?' Leah reached for the top sheet of paper and started to read. 'A reputable one?'

'How can you tell?' Calvin rubbed his eyes. 'He can spell, at least, and write his own name—'

'I wonder if he plans to write about us.' Leah pursed her lips. 'There's not much else here to work with. Never married. Both his parents are alive.'

'Well, he answered those questions last week,' Calvin said. 'One of them might've expired since then.'

'Let's hope so!' said Leah brightly. 'These are exactly the sort of men we must impress.'

But that evening – still warm outside, with pale stars beginning to appear in the sky, and a clinking sound of glasses that Maggie already found soothing – she began to feel the men were trying to impress *her*. The journalist was very young, practically a boy. He introduced himself as Patrick Connell, and proceeded to tell Maggie all of his achievements, waving his glass nervously in the air and trying to be charming. She was beginning to lose the sense of who was attractive and who wasn't, because they *all* were, everyone in this city. They were all new and different and interesting. She made herself perfectly composed, and listened as if all the articles he had published did not really impress her, when in fact they did.

'I've written on the issue of women's rights too,' he told her. 'All men should be concerned with it.'

The doctor's wife had joined them. Mrs. Grace. She gave Patrick Connell a brief, indulgent smile, and then looked more seriously at Maggie. 'Miss Fox has come from Rochester, where a great deal of organizing on women's issues has taken place.'

'Yes,' said Maggie. 'That's right. Some of our close friends are very involved in that kind of work. I learned a lot from them.' She searched her mind for something to say, something from one of Amy's pamphlets. 'We ought not to be compelled to submit to laws when we had no voice in their formation.'

Patrick Connell nodded fervently, and Mrs. Grace gave her a look that Maggie was sure was admiration.

When they gathered at the table, Leah went to each corner of the room and snuffed out the candles, leaving only the one standing on the table. The oak door was shut against the noise from the hall, and this time the porter locked it from the outside. They had thought the heavy click of the lock would heighten the nerves, and Maggie saw immediately that they were right.

Their things on the table. The bell. Paper and pencil. Little pieces of card with words and letters. They had placed a Bible there this evening, to try and make things look decent.

Maggie sat between Kate and Leah. 'First,' she said, 'we will all sit and hold hands.'

'If an unknown or unwanted spirit arrives in the room, the bell will ring,' said Kate, and that caused its usual little shiver around the group.

'We expect the spirits to communicate with raps,' said Leah, in her soft, low voice. 'But if they are so inclined they may will us to take up this pencil and write for them.'

'If anything unexpected should happen,' said Maggie, 'don't be afraid.'

The Bible, of course, had a tiny hook fixed to the cover, like the clasp of a thin chain necklace, with a tiny thread that ran over the tablecloth down to the floor where it formed a loop that Kate could hook with her toe, making it move across the table.

They waited, and waited, and then Kate suddenly blew out the candle, and the darkness was complete. And they began.

Two pieces appeared in the papers by the end of the week. Leah came to Maggie's room early in the morning, holding them up triumphantly. 'According to this, the Fox sisters of Rochester are *uncommonly gifted*, Maggie. We're *extraordinary* and *worthy of attention and respect.*'

Maggie grabbed for one of the papers and tried to find the page. 'Mr. Connell wrote about us?'

'Mr. Connell and a man I've never heard of, who hasn't even visited us, he only interviewed some of our guests. It's barely an article. It's an advertisement.'

Maggie had been sitting in bed, trying to read a book of poems that a guest had given to her as a gift. She was pleased by it, the idea that he thought she might read poetry, although her eyes kept closing as she tried to read. She wasn't sure *how* you were supposed to read poetry.

'I've spoken to Mr. Barnum, and he says they've had twelve enquiries this morning about booking tickets. He plans to print a new sign for the hall downstairs, using quotations from these articles. And there are three dinner invitations.'

Maggie found the article. '*The Fox sisters have unlocked a hunger for the new and coupled it with a desire for the old,*' she read, and looked up at Leah. 'I'm not even sure what that means.'

'It means we're wonderful. Exceptional. Sought after. That sort of thing.' She sat down on the chair in the corner of the room. '*Respectable,*' she added. 'At last.'

Maggie swung her feet from the bed to the floor, sinking her toes into the thick carpet. 'We should send copies to Mother, and Maria and David, and—' She tried to think who else would care. Amy and Isaac, although she wasn't sure they would approve. 'Mr. Lewis? We could thank him.'

'He ought to be thanking *us*. He's made his name and his money from that pamphlet, and it was all down to us.'

'You weren't even there, Leah. Not in Hydesville.'

Leah was hardly listening. 'I *will* send copies. I'll ask at reception now, if they can have more copies sent to my room. I don't know what our father will make of it, but Mother will want to put these in a frame, I'm sure.'

'I'll go to reception, if you like,' Maggie said. 'I'll ask for the papers.'

Leah looked up. 'Of course you will. Your friend is usually there on Friday mornings, isn't he? What's his name?'

Maggie flushed. 'Sam. He isn't my friend. I only know him.'

'You know, if you're beginning to think of that sort of thing—'

'Leah.'

'– there are sure to be young men you could be introduced to, all kinds of men, with money and prospects and education. Don't give your affections to the first charming boy who smiles at you, Maggie. You'll regret it. Believe me.'

'I haven't given him anything, and I'm not beginning to *think* of anything, either. I'm offering to ask for the papers.'

Leah's attention had drifted back to the article. '*Uncommonly gifted*,' she murmured to herself again.

Maggie dressed quickly and went to the hall, where Sam leaned against the desk and grinned as soon as he saw her. 'It's the *extraordinary* Miss Fox,' he said. 'Will you still talk to me, now that you're famous?'

The hall in the morning was flooded with light, and busy. A couple argued loudly in French, and a smell of food drifted from the dining hall.

Sam *had* education, Maggie thought. She didn't know what kind, but she could tell. He was sharp and spoke nicely and knew things, it was obvious. And he had prospects too. He was young, and worked hard. He would not be a hotel porter forever, and even if he was, she thought, what did it matter, if she was going to be rich?

'I'll consider it,' she said, leaning against the desk herself, and meeting his eyes, which were framed by long lashes, as clear and bright as gems.

TWENTY-FIVE

At the end of the month, Mr. Barnum asked if they would renew their contract for another three, and they did. Spring had given way to a humid summer, the air wet and heavy, a yellow haze hanging low over the streets and sickness everywhere. Their father sent his first letter, a short, terse note enquiring if they were going to church, and if Kate was having lessons of any kind.

There was a small Methodist church a few blocks from the hotel, and they had gone a few times, to a service on Sunday. But by Sundays Maggie was so exhausted she could barely listen to the words. *Yes, Father*, she wrote back. *We are going to church.*

There was no time. Mornings collapsed into afternoons, into evenings and nights, with so many new faces each day that Maggie could scarcely tell the difference, even though there were all kinds of people, young and old and black and white and Irish and English and laughing and crying. By the end of July she began to cry herself sometimes, unexpectedly, for no reason other than that her nerves were shredded.

And that Calvin was sick. His cold had worsened, during June, and suddenly he had coughing fits that left him weak and gasping. He had fevers that came and went, and began to sleep all day. Doctors visited, and prescribed things, but they didn't seem to help, or only helped for a little while. 'It'll pass,' he kept saying. 'I'll be better tomorrow.'

She had begun to have nightmares. She was trapped in a

fire, her father watching her beyond the flames. She was drowning, James Crane holding her head beneath water. Men furious with her. Once she woke up standing at the window, rattling the frame as if she was trying to escape. Once she woke up kneeling on the floor, breathless, sick with an unnameable dread.

'It's the heat,' Leah told her, when she tried to explain the dreams, the sleepwalking. 'It gives us all bad dreams. And you used to sleepwalk as a child. You mustn't worry.'

Stop. Maggie heard her mother's voice in her mind sometimes – her mother, who was back on David and Maria's farm in Arcadia, it felt a thousand miles away. A single word: *stop.* But she couldn't. There were three receptions each day, and the guests already had their tickets.

Friday, a half hour until their final reception of the day. The public parlor in the hotel was crowded, their own guests and another lot, who had come for a lecture in the dining hall. All of them, the lecture crowd and their own, shot them fascinated looks as Maggie and Kate sat together at a corner table. The evening manager put down a bottle of wine and three glasses. 'From Mr. Cary,' he said, as if they should know who that was. He poured a glass, which Kate took.

The hotel had a huge wine cellar, like nothing they had ever seen, and the bottles that came out of it were endless. The previous night, their guests had demanded that Maggie and Leah stay up with them after the final reception, and poured endless glasses of a heavy, sticky red wine that Maggie didn't really like, and they had talked about politics and religion and asked all kinds of questions of her that eventually she could no longer answer, because her eyes were falling shut and their faces had begun to spin. She couldn't remember going to bed, and today she was cold and dizzy and sick, and longed to lie down in a dark room.

Kate sipped the wine – it was a clear and very light yellow, almost like champagne. She made a face, but took another sip.

'That's not for you,' Maggie said. 'Mr. Cary doesn't know how old you are.'

Kate shrugged. 'There are three glasses.'

Her thirteenth birthday had been celebrated last week with a cake made in the hotel kitchen, covered in sugar and dark red cherries, and there were jars of rock candy which they all ate until they felt unwell, and then there was a pile of gifts to open. 'From admirers,' the porter had said, as he carried them in. A colored shawl, a silk scarf, a silver pocket mirror, an embroidered needle-case – they laughed at that, when did Kate ever sew, now? – and a book of poems with an inscription inside: *To Kate on your birthday, a small gift in exchange for the gift you have given us. Adam and Mary Milton.*

The Miltons had lost a child. They had come to six receptions so far. They always went away joyful. And Kate was their favorite. There were other guests like this, who came once a week or more, who couldn't seem to stop themselves, no matter how much it cost.

Maggie saw Leah cutting her way through the crowd, stopping on her way to shake hands and smile, gesturing toward her sisters apologetically. Her dark blue dress had a fine pattern of gold thread on the sleeves which caught the light and glittered as she moved.

She arrived at the table, and took the wine from Kate's hands, taking a sip herself and putting it down. 'This crowd will believe anything,' she said. 'So we can enjoy ourselves this evening. I do like Fridays.'

Maggie took the wine glass herself, and finished it. Perhaps it would help.

'Where's Calvin?' she said.

Leah blinked. 'He's upstairs.'

'He's not coming down?'

'Not tonight.'

'He isn't well enough?'

'You know he isn't, Maggie.'

Of course she did. Leah took out a small notebook which she had tucked at her waist. 'A few facts about our guests,' she said. 'Abigail Tully is back again, and Daniel Renner. I think he likes you, Maggie.'

'I think – I need some air, before we start,' she said. She stood up, and pushed past Leah, out of the dining room and toward the door, ignoring the murmurs as she walked by.

On the steps outside, she stopped, and took a deep breath. The light was warm and hazy and the evening beckoned, promising twinkling laughter and attention and the usual shimmering thrill of the séance. But her stomach was turning, and her palms were damp with sweat.

She had to collect herself. Study Leah's notebook and memorize the names. She had been faltering lately. Forgetting the names she was supposed to know and spelling meaningless ones instead, names that came to her from nowhere and elicited no response from the guests. Leah would have to intervene, explaining that they could not always control the spirits who visited. Maggie hoped that was the explanation, but lately she had begun to doubt those names were spirits at all: they were simply a product of her exhausted mind. The hotel itself seemed exhausted, as if the energy was sucked from the air.

She went back inside. Kate had stood up, and her wine glass was full again.

There was a man talking to Kate, his head bent low to hear what she was saying, with a smile on his face and his hand drifting toward her shoulder. She was looking up at him placidly, a flush on her cheeks from the wine. An old man. Older than David, much older than Calvin.

She went toward them and grabbed Kate's arm. 'I'm *so* sorry,' she said to the man, with the most withering look she could manage. 'I have to talk to my sister.' And dragged her away, out into the hall, taking the wine from her hand and finding the nearest table to put it down.

'He was looking at you like a piece of meat on his plate. Don't let men touch you, Katie. People will talk about you.'

The hall was quieter, but there were still people lingering, and a porter leaned across the reception desk, trying to charm one of the maids who had just finished her day's work. She looked around for Sam, but couldn't see him. A man she didn't recognize sat in the corner, watching them intently. When she caught his eye he looked away, and pretended to read a newspaper, but when she turned back to Kate she felt his gaze burning at her again.

Somebody had propped the front door open and wedged it with a piece of wood, but the air that rolled in was hot and hardly moved. They were both running out of summer dresses – the ones they had were too small and came back from the hotel laundry tinged with gray. But Leah said they would have new ones made soon.

It could make you dizzy, the heat. It could make your eyes blur, could make strange shadows appear in corners or swirl up with the dust from the road under the streetlamps.

She looked at the clock that stood at the foot of the staircase. It was a quarter to eight.

'Come on,' she said. 'It's time to get ready.'

TWENTY-SIX

More wine was poured after the reception, more glasses pressed into Maggie's hand, and she drank it until she no longer felt the sickness from the night before. Perhaps that was how it was supposed to be done, she thought. On and on without stopping and you never had time to regret it.

Something woke her. She thought it was the distant sound of a bell, but when she opened her eyes it was gone, and must have been a dream. She couldn't remember going to bed. She was still in her clothes and lying on top of the sheets. She was in her room, and the light was orange from the gas lamps that hung outside, just below her window. The sky was purple. She sat up, rested on the edge of the bed for a moment, her head aching, and hungry. Then she stood. The water in the pitcher on the mantelpiece was warm and had a film of very fine dust on top of it. She poured some into a glass and took a sip anyway, and then went to the window.

It was hard to sleep when your mind burned with all the things that happened that day, and might happen tomorrow, even if you were so exhausted you shook.

At the other end of the long narrow hall that led to their rooms, she heard somebody coughing, an awful, racking sound. She didn't think it was Calvin. His room was too far away. Whoever it was, she hoped that there was somebody with them: that they weren't dying in their hotel room alone.

Everything had emptied out of her, all the joy and intensity that built up in their séances. Each night she wished she could hold on to those feelings a little longer, instead of just returning to her room and feeling dark and flat and lonely.

There had been half a bottle of wine still standing on the sideboard in the parlor when they left. She wondered if anybody had taken it. It shouldn't be left there, she thought. It might attract flies. She looked at the dusty water in her glass and then emptied it into the fern that stood in the corner of the room.

Perhaps there would be some food downstairs, something left over in the dining hall. She could look.

It was strange to creep down the hall alone at night. All the doors were closed. Whale-oil lamps sat on recessed ledges all along the walls, but they were turned down low, and the carpet was a dark red color that soaked up all the light.

She came to the staircase, which spiraled down to the main hall where one small light burned over the reception desk. As she came down, she saw that the night manager was asleep, his head buried in his folded arms. She realized she didn't know what time it was, but when she looked at the clock it was too dark to see. Strange: she hadn't imagined that there was ever a time when the hotel was truly silent. It must be later than she thought.

The marble floor gleamed in the dim light. Last thing at night, every night, it was swept and polished, ready for another day. She admired it for a moment, and then slipped past the desk to the grand doors of the dining hall, but she knew as she approached that they would be locked, and they were.

Then she turned right, and went further down the hall, to their own parlor, which had a sign with their names on outside.

As she came toward the door, she saw a light underneath it, and stopped for a moment, with a kind of dread.

Stop. Her mother's voice.

But she thought of the wine, the way a few sips would warm her blood and soften her thoughts and give her back some of the magic of the evening. It wouldn't hurt anybody, to take it.

She opened the door. Two of the corner lamps were lit.

A thin man in a dark suit sat at the table with his back to her.

'Oh,' she said. 'Excuse me.'

He didn't move.

'I'm sorry,' she said, though she didn't know why. 'I was here before and I forgot something.'

He turned around, although his chair didn't move, and nor did his legs that she could see. He just turned, so he was sideways on the chair, his head twisted toward her. A thin white man with a long face, eyes flat and glinting like coins.

'I thought I'd wait here,' he said.

'You can't wait here,' she said. She felt the dark expanse of the hall behind her, the sleeping man and the silent, shining floors. 'This is our room, where we work.'

She looked at the sideboard. The wine bottle was still there.

'I know that, Miss Fox. That's why I'm waiting.'

'We're finished,' said Maggie. 'We're finished for the night. And you have to buy a ticket.'

'I've got a ticket.'

'You'll have to come back tomorrow.'

'I'll still be here tomorrow.'

She felt behind her for the edge of the door and found it, the sharp corner of the latch pressed into her palm. 'Are you a guest here?' she said, although she hardly had the voice for it, and the words came out a whisper.

'I don't know about a guest,' he said. 'But I was invited.'

He was standing in front of her, and she could feel his breath on her face. He was holding the bottle.

'Here you are,' he said.

Her eyes snapped open to darkness that then became the swirls of paint on the ceiling, and a roughness beneath her that then became the carpet. She sat up, gasping. She was in her nightclothes, and they were drenched in sweat. Her windows were wide open. Her hair stuck damply to her face and her head pounded. She got to her knees, saw her bed, unmade, sheets twisted. And the dark shape of the wine bottle on the mantelpiece, empty.

TWENTY-SEVEN

The morning brought shining, rain-washed sidewalks and a soft gray sky. She had slept through a storm. She was desperately thirsty, and gulped the last drops of the stale water from the pitcher.

The wine bottle still stood on the mantelpiece. There were dark marks on her bare feet, as if smudged by the floor polish from the hall.

A fearful sense of recognition lingered in her mind.

Amy had asked her, once, how she saw the Devil. And she had drawn his picture in the corner of her writing book. A thin white man in a suit.

Her stomach turned as she looked at the bottle. She had done it in her sleep. Walked downstairs in a dream, walked into the parlor in a nightmare.

Leah had told her not to worry about sleepwalking, but she had heard of people committing murder in their sleep, or throwing themselves from windows. If she could leave her room, walk all the way downstairs—if she was dreaming of the Devil, now—

She could tell nobody. They might think she was dangerous.

She was trembling. She thought she might cry.

When she had washed and dressed, she went downstairs and saw the entrance hall restored to its usual activity: porters carrying bags and guests coming and going, the day manager supervising, whistling as he strolled the floor.

She had done a poor job with her hair, she knew, and her skin was blotched and dry. She needed to eat.

She went to the reception desk, a memory of the sleeping man last night flickering behind her eyes, and stood, waiting to be noticed by the morning man, who had his back turned and was returning room keys to their hooks. Eventually she rang the bell for his attention. Her hand was shaking.

'Oh,' he said, turning. 'Miss Fox.'

'Good morning.' She felt him casting a skeptical eye over her appearance. 'I just wanted—Are there any letters for us? Or me?'

He nodded, and then gave a sharp whistle to a boy who came instantly to his side. There was no sign of Sam. 'Get the Fox sisters' letters,' the man said, and the boy dashed away.

He continued looking at her as they waited, and then said, 'Busy day ahead?'

She couldn't even think what day it was. 'Yes. I expect so.'

He nodded again, and she tried to peer over his shoulder to the dining hall to see if her sisters were there.

Then he spoke in a lowered voice. 'My wife's into all your nonsense now. Her father passed a few months ago and you've got her thinking she can talk to him through coffee beans or whatever it is you people—It's not right, in my view. What you're doing to people.'

She blinked a few times, weak with exhaustion. She was so hungry she could hardly register the shock of his words. 'We give them comfort. And peace, and – and pleasure.'

'It's humbug.'

Her mouth was dry. 'It's up to you what you choose to believe.'

'Belief isn't a choice, in my view.'

'Your view is your own business.'

225

'That's right.'

The boy came back with a bundle of letters, and the man took them and tossed them on to the desk. 'There you are,' he said.

The talk in the dining hall was full of relief, that it had rained and was a little cooler.

She found Leah and Kate at their usual table, tucked in a far corner, beneath a window.

'Calvin?' Maggie asked, as she took her seat, dropping the letters on the table. Kate immediately reached for them and started shuffling through.

Leah gave a shake of the head.

'Is he alright?'

'He had a bad night.'

'Oh.'

'But he may come down later.'

Maggie nodded. He wouldn't.

Leah was looking at a newspaper. She had several delivered to her room each day, and always scoured the pages for mention of the Fox sisters.

It was the *Post*. Leah was frowning, studying the same page for a long time.

'Is there something about us?' she said.

'Nothing I would waste your time reading.'

'What is it?'

'Some desperate little man looking for attention.'

Maggie reached and snatched it from her, read a few lines before Leah snatched it back.

– while some suspect them of fraud, I have come to suspect them of much worse, that their 'entertainment' is not fraud but a kind of witchcraft—

'What is it?' Kate was reaching for the coffee pot. She'd begun drinking coffee, although Maggie was certain she hated the taste.

'Evidently we're all agents of the Devil sent to sow discord among the Lord's faithful masses,' said Leah. 'And what have you.'

'Oh.'

'Let me read it,' said Maggie, as Leah reached for the coffee herself.

The *Post*. Read by who knew how many thousands of people. 'Let me read it,' she said again.

'If you must.' She tossed the paper back in Maggie's direction. 'I wouldn't waste the time if I were you.'

Maggie bent over it. *These deceitful girls are engaged in a practice that this writer can only describe as an affront to our nation's decency and morality, a practice of superstition and fancy at best, and an affront to the Lord himself at worst. Ours is a country of light and reason, and since the declaration of our independence from Great Britain, we have done much to leave behind the darker chapters of human history—*

'Leah, this is terrible.'

'Don't read it, then.'

– we might observe the practice of so-called 'Spiritualism' among the abolitionists and agitators and vegetarians of Rochester and wonder if these are the people to whom we ought to surrender our nation's political future, those who take their moral guidance from Spirits and think nothing of allowing women to perform their spectacles in public without regard for propriety or decency. I have witnessed the girls myself, drinking alcohol and talking nightly with unmarried men in the insalubrious environment of a New York City hotel. It has long been known that women are possessed of a particular sensitivity, with which is associated many

virtues, but which also renders them more susceptible to the advances of the Devil—

'Leah—'

'Maggie, we have plenty to concern ourselves with this morning without also worrying about the tawdry musings of some pompous little toad in the paper.'

– the girls Catherine and Margaretta Fox, still but children, thought nothing of accusing a neighbor of the murder of a peddler in the town of Hydesville, and it has lately come to my attention that the girl Margaretta was also responsible for a vile crime against an innocent child in Rochester—

She pushed the paper away as if it had caught fire, felt heat rising in her cheeks. Leah looked at her.

'Did you read it all?' said Maggie.

'I read as much as I cared to.'

'He knows. He knows about Hannah Crane, about what happened. It says here. He thinks – the *Devil*, Leah, he thinks—'

Had he *spoken* to James Crane? This idea reared in Maggie's head – Mr. Crane was in New York City somewhere, wasn't he? That's what Amy had told her. She had hardly thought of this, the city was so big, but had he seen the first notice in the paper? Did he know that Maggie was here too?

Leah reached for the paper, studied the article again. She was quiet for a while, frowning at it. 'We'll ignore it,' she said eventually, lowering her voice. 'The Hannah Crane story is only rumor, Maggie.'

'But it's not rumor.'

'No one else knows that.'

'He thinks we're witches.'

'It doesn't matter. People love what we do, and they'll pay for it no matter what some trivial man says about us. I dare say

228

there's plenty reading this piece this morning and wondering how they might go about arranging a session with us. Notoriety can have its advantages.'

Maggie's eyes blurred. She turned to Kate. 'Don't you mind?' she said.

Kate seemed not to have been listening. 'I don't mind. All kinds of people say nice things.'

'Did you ever imagine, Maggie, you would be the subject of newspaper gossip?' Leah was becoming impatient. 'There's plenty of girls these days who dream of fame. Remember when nobody had any interest in you at all? Which would you prefer?'

The tinkle of teacups and murmur of conversation faded behind her. Maggie felt she could hear her own blood in her ears. Her appetite was gone.

'You're upset,' said Leah.

'Of course I am.'

'Well.' Leah sipped her coffee. The staff were beginning to bring out fruit and bread and butter. 'Sometimes a few tears is the cost of an interesting life, little sister.'

As it was Saturday, there was no morning reception to prepare for. Maggie forced herself to eat a few pieces of bread and some cold meat. Then she went upstairs to her room, and sat on the bed, stunned with tiredness. The room was untidy, and exhausted her to look at. She tried to keep her things neatly, unlike Kate, but she wasn't successful. The pretty ornamental fan she had been given was lying on the floor, along with a silk scarf and a small stack of books, also gifts. There had been one letter addressed to her, the rest for Leah, and she held it in her hand. She recognized Amy's handwriting.

She tore open the letter carefully and read it, once, twice.

Amy would be visiting the city in a few weeks, with a number of friends from Rochester including Will Garret and Elizabeth, to stay with somebody called Phillip Sullivan from the New York City Antislavery Society, and discuss a new alliance. He had a grand old house on the outskirts of the city, she wrote, and very much hoped they would all visit. Mr. Sullivan had said they would be welcome to stay the night, and would send a driver to collect them from the hotel. *We think of you often here*, it said, *and our friends are all eager to hear more about what you are doing in the city. A number of them have been moved to try your spirit-talking themselves, with some success, I hear.*

Her father had said something similar in a letter to Leah a little while ago, that there had been an outbreak of 'spiritual communication' around Arcadia. They had all tried to interpret his tone. Was it a rebuke, or praise? Then their mother had sent a letter saying the same thing but declaring it wonderful, and how proud she was that her daughters had begun it.

She would write back immediately, she thought, but then sat, doing nothing, without the energy for it.

I send my very warmest wishes to you, Katie, Leah and Calvin, the letter said. *I think of you very often.*

Calvin.

She got up and went to his room, knocked gently on the door. She didn't hear anything, but she turned the handle and pushed, and the door opened.

He wasn't in bed. He was sitting on the window ledge, which was deep enough that it could be strewn with cushions and blankets. He was dressed, more or less. He held his knees against his chest, his forehead pressed against the window.

'Calvin?'

He startled, then laughed. 'Maggie. You scared me.'

'I'm sorry.' She came into the room, closed the door behind her.

'Are you alright?'

'You didn't come down to breakfast.'

'I know.'

'I could bring you something. There's some bread, still, and fruit—'

'Got no appetite.' He made a face, half apologetic.

'You have to eat.'

'So I'm told.'

When somebody began to look different, over weeks or months even, when you saw them every day, you didn't always notice.

His eyes had sunk. His lips had no color and his skin was so pale that she could see blue veins at his temples.

She crossed the room and sat on the bed. 'Can I do something for you?'

'I don't think so.'

'I mean—'

'I know what you mean.'

Maggie looked past him, out of the window at the soft, gray morning. 'It's cooler today,' she said.

'I guess so.'

'What will you do?'

'Do?'

'We only have one evening reception. Maybe if you feel stronger you could come.'

'Can't,' he said. 'Not today. Wish I could. I try to stand up and I fall back down again. Besides, I think a hacking bloody cough from the corner of the room might spoil the atmosphere.'

'We could throw a sheet over you and tell them it's a spirit.'

This made him laugh properly, which inevitably turned to coughing, and it was another five minutes before he could speak.

'I might be a spirit soon enough,' he said when he had his breath.

'Calvin.' A lump rose in her throat. 'Don't say that.'

'I was thinking. I could marry Leah.'

'You could – what?'

'I could offer to marry Leah. Do you think she'd accept?'

'Have you lost your mind?'

'That way, if she had my name – it would help, wouldn't it? She'd be respectable. And if I died she'd be a widow, and people wouldn't talk so much. People respect a widow.'

'Calvin.' Maggie was shaking her head. 'No.'

'She won't want it?'

'You won't die.'

He gave her a brief smile that didn't reach his eyes. 'I don't want to,' he said. 'I'm terrified of it.'

'You won't. Not for a long time.'

'If I do—'

'I don't want to talk about this.'

'If I do—'

'Calvin. Please don't.'

'Please don't die?'

'Please don't talk about it.'

A door slammed in the corridor. Two children were laughing as they sprinted toward the stairs. Their voices grew louder as they went past Calvin's door, and then faded away again.

'Are you alright?' said Calvin. 'Your eyes are red.'

'Oh.' She rubbed them, and Calvin said, 'That'll make it worse.'

'I had bad dreams. And there was a piece in the paper about us,' she said.

Not fraud but a kind of witchcraft. She wanted to tell him all of it, so he could tell her all the reasons why it didn't matter, so he could reassure her, comfort her. Tell him about sleepwalking, about the dream, so he could promise her that it *was* a dream. Because the article had sneaked fear into her bones. – *also renders them more susceptible to the advances of the Devil—*

But she should be comforting Calvin, not the other way around. 'It wasn't very kind,' she said weakly.

'I'm sorry.'

She shook her head. 'Maybe we deserve it.'

'I doubt that,' he said. 'You're not doing anything wrong. You're not doing any harm.'

'Harm and wrong aren't the same thing.'

'They are as far as I'm concerned.'

And then he took a sharp breath, like he'd felt a spasm of pain, and the breath turned into more coughing. Maggie went to his side, but she didn't know what to do. She put a hand on his back, but she could feel the bones beneath his shirt and the raw, wet movement in his lungs, and she took it away again, in fear.

When he finally stopped his eyes were watering. He looked gray.

'Should I get someone?' Maggie whispered, but he shook his head. After a while he sat up straight again, wiped his mouth with the back of his hand and leaned his head back against the wall. There was a trace of blood on his lip.

TWENTY-EIGHT

Later that week, the gray skies began to turn yellow again, and the temperature rose; then another storm, and it continued like that into the next week: the heat rose, and broke, and it rained, and the heat rose and broke and it rained. It filled the streets with steam and mud and it seemed to make Calvin sicker.

It was ten days before Maggie wrote her reply to Amy. She wrote a few bits of nothing – the weather, Kate's birthday – and then, pen pressed hard against the paper, she put *Calvin is still not well*, and could not think what to write after that, so she started a new line. Her writing had begun to slope downwards across the page.

Thank you for your invitation to Mr. Sullivan's house. It is very kind of both of you and I think it would be wonderful. I would like to have a séance with you and any of your friends, Mr. and Mrs. Garret if they are there and Mr. Sullivan if he is interested.

When she took the letter downstairs to leave with the porter, she saw a group of people gathered around the reception desk, heads bent, looking at something.

She pushed through, and heard a couple of sharp gasps, and a man snatched up what they were reading, which looked like a sheet of newsprint. Several sheets, in fact, bound together by a piece of string through a hole in the top corner.

'What is it?' she said, aware that people were stepping back, away from her, and whispering to each other. Sam stood at the far end of the desk and was looking at Maggie with a strange, unhappy expression.

'She should see it,' somebody said, a man she half recognized from the dining hall in the mornings.

'I'd like to sign my name,' said another man, in a cloth cap, looking at her with narrowed eyes.

'What is it?' The attention was unpleasant, and there was a sour, turning mood. Maggie looked for somebody in charge and saw, finally, Mr. Barnum coming toward them.

'What's the commotion?' he said, giving Maggie a nod and turning his attention to the man who held the sheets of paper, whose eyes were blue and sharp as ice.

'Mr. Barnum,' said the man. 'How fortunate. I have something here to present to you, on behalf of myself and a number of the other residents.' He looked at Maggie. 'But it might be better to talk in your office.'

'What is it?' asked Maggie again, hoping for once that Leah might appear and help her.

Mr. Barnum took the sheets and stood studying them for a while. The group had dispersed. Some went on about their business and others retreated a little further away, to watch.

'This is an underhand attempt to interfere with my business,' said Mr. Barnum eventually, looking at the blue-eyed man. 'Which I will not stand for. Yes, we will talk in my office.'

'What is it?' said Maggie. 'What does it say?'

'I don't see why the girl shouldn't see it,' said Mr. Barnum. 'It concerns her.'

Maggie held out her hand. 'Let me see.'

The first page had been printed, like a newspaper, but beneath the printed words there were scrawled signatures, which continued on to the next page. A third and fourth page were still blank.

A PETITION IN RESPECT OF THE FOX SISTERS RESIDENCY AT THIS HOTEL

Guests of long standing and members of staff and local businesses would like to complain to the Management about the ongoing residency of 'The Fox Sisters' and their daily performances, which are beneath the dignity of this place. We contend that the sisters are not of good character and their work is blasphemous in nature.

After investigation we report that:

This petition's creator is in possession of a letter signed by MR. JOHN C. BELL of WAYNE COUNTY NEW YORK declaring that in March of 1848 Margaretta and Catherine Fox did baselessly accuse him of murder and greatly damage his reputation.

And a letter signed by MR. JAMES A. CRANE of ROCHESTER NEW YORK declaring that in November of 1847 he witnessed the older girl Margaretta Fox push or throw his daughter of six years old down a set of steep steps breaking both her arms.

The petition's creator makes no claim as to whether this wickedness is fraud or witchcraft, as others have debated, but only demands that the three unaccompanied Fox sisters are removed from the hotel and their deceptions are no longer practiced on the residents of our city.

If this demand is not heard we the undersigned will ask for the sisters and this Establishment to be investigated by both the Church and the Police.

A hush had fallen. Maggie felt tears blur her eyes, and she blinked furiously to clear them and then raised her head and held out the petition to Mr. Barnum, who took it. She looked to Sam, who turned away as if embarrassed for her, and then at the man with the blue eyes, who held her gaze.

Her letter for Amy was tucked into her skirt, and with a shaky hand she held that out to Mr. Barnum as well.

'I have a letter,' she said, her voice as steady as she could manage. It was hardly Mr. Barnum's job to collect the mail, but it was all she could think to do. 'Will you please see that it's sent today.'

Mr. Barnum nodded. 'Of course, Miss Fox,' he said, and put the letter in his pocket, and turned away from her.

TWENTY-NINE

She found Leah in Calvin's room. He was sitting up in bed, holding a pillow against his chest. His face was ashen and there was sweat on his brow, but he managed to smile when Maggie came in.

She lingered in the doorway, feeling awkward. Leah was sitting on a wooden chair by the bed, holding a Bible.

'She's making a late attempt to save my soul,' said Calvin.

'But it seems I'm not well suited to it,' said Leah. 'Maggie's always had a more religious sensibility, perhaps she can—'

'We need to – we need to talk about something,' said Maggie.

Leah put the Bible on the bedside table. 'What is it?'

She looked at Calvin, and the bruises beneath his eyes, the sharp angles of his face. 'Not now,' said Maggie. 'I could talk to you in a while.'

'What is it?' Leah said again.

'She doesn't want me to know,' said Calvin. 'In case I die of shock. Go outside if you want. I don't mind.'

Leah gave him a reproving look. 'You shouldn't talk so much.'

'Then go out, and I'll have no one to talk to.'

Leah followed her into the hall, and they closed the door. 'Well?' said Leah.

She listened as Maggie explained, and her expression remained the same. When Maggie had finished, she waited as if expecting more, and said, 'Is that it?', as if it didn't matter, but Maggie could see the tension all over her face. Her pinched mouth and the hard light in her eyes.

'*Letters*,' Maggie said again. 'From Mr. Crane and Mr. Bell. They've investigated me.'

'All of us.'

'Me, most of all.'

'The letters probably aren't real. We should ask to see them.'

Maggie shook her head. The red carpets and dark walls closed in on her. 'I don't want to see them.'

'The hotel won't put us out. We bring them far too much money. This is nothing but a few envious, ungentlemanly characters who don't like to see women gain any respect. They don't like to see women at *all*, unless they're mending their shirts.'

'We can't stay here,' Maggie whispered. 'Not now. It talks about the *police*, Leah. We can't stay here if all these people think these terrible things about us.'

'Of course we can. We can stay wherever we choose. Who are these people? How many signatures? Ten? Twenty?'

'I don't know. A lot. A page full of them.'

'People will sign anything. I expect most of them can't read.'

From behind the door, they heard Calvin cough. They both stopped, and looked at the door until he fell silent. Leah's hand drifted toward the handle.

'We can't stay here,' Maggie said again. 'They know. They know about Hannah Crane.'

'*What* do they know? You've told us a thousand times that you did nothing to that girl, so there's nothing *to* know. It's lies and slander. We should take Mr. Crane to court. All of them.' Leah's voice was rising. 'We should take all of them to court. How *dare* they—'

'Call us liars?' Maggie tried to be quiet, so Calvin wouldn't hear, and her voice came high-pitched and broken. 'We *are* liars.'

Leah's eyes went wide. She was shaking her head. 'No. No. No more than anybody else.'

'It's all lies, what we do. Cracking our toes—'

'You're the ones who *believe*. You and Katie, you both tell me endlessly that it's more than a game.' Leah took her arm, gripped so hard it was painful, it would bruise. 'Don't let them do this. They want to shake us, but we mustn't let them. We deserve to be here. We've worked harder than anybody. We do *good*.'

'We make money.'

'Money,' said Leah, in a harsh whisper, 'is good. If you don't believe me, try starving.' She let go of Maggie's arm, took a deep breath, and smoothed down the panels of her navy dress. 'Now, if you're so upset, then I'll see about it. I'll speak with the management and see that the whole wretched thing is tossed in the fire. Will that help?'

Calvin was coughing again, and Leah turned toward the door, then stopped. She gave Maggie a complicated look, as if she was trying to make her expression a gentle one, but had forgotten how. 'You stay with him for a little while,' she said. 'He'd like that. I'll go downstairs and see about this situation. Is Kate in her room?'

Pressing a hand against the door, Maggie nodded. She wanted to say more, to argue with Leah that it was time to leave, but it was too hard. And how could they? How could Calvin leave, when he could hardly stand?

'Good.' Leah turned the handle and pushed Maggie into

the room. 'Just give me a little while, and I'll fix all this, Maggie.'

She sat on the edge of Calvin's bed, and tried to smile at him, but it didn't work, her mouth didn't work properly.

'Would you like some water?' Maggie said. 'Or I could fetch you something from the dining hall.'

He shook his head. 'Has something happened?'

'No. Nothing.'

'You don't have to pretend. I'm sick but I'm not useless. I could help.'

'You couldn't,' Maggie said. 'Even if you were well.'

She reached for his hand. She could feel the thready beat of his heart through his palm. She thought of how she'd held his hand when she was a child, following him through town or walking around the farm. He would have been almost the age that she was now. She had liked him more than her own brother back then. He had paid her more attention. He had been such a novelty when he came to live with them, so fun and kind, and he was the only one in the house who was always smiling.

But his parents must have died just that year. He must have thought that he had to smile to be allowed to stay.

'It's just there are some people who are angry with us, about what we do. That's all.' She tried to smile again, to make light of it. 'They think we're witches.'

'No such thing as witches.'

'Of course you'd say that.'

'No such thing as witches, or witchcraft, or gnomes, or fairies.'

'I know. You don't believe in anything.'

'That's right.'

Was it fraud, or witchcraft?

241

She could only look at Calvin for a few seconds at a time. It hurt to look too long. He was so pale his bones gleamed through his skin.

She thought of the bone they had found in the cellar. A girl they hanged in the forest – that was the story she had made up to tell Kate. A girl they thought was possessed by the Devil.

Calvin started to cough again, but pressed a hand over his mouth to stifle it, and took short, gasping breaths, hunched forward in on himself. She held on to his hand still, and tried silently to think of a prayer.

After a while he managed to straighten his shoulders a little and lay back on the pillow, looking up at the ceiling. 'But you do still believe, don't you?' he said, still breathless. 'Apart from your tricks. You think there's something real.'

'Yes,' she said. 'I know you don't think that.'

'I don't think that you're lying.'

'I know.'

'Just that it affects you, the same way it does everybody else. A few strange sounds, and your imagination—'

'I know.'

'But you really believe there's this other place we go when we die, that our spirits carry on, somehow.'

'I don't know. You shouldn't talk so much, Calvin, it's not good for you.'

'Maggie—'

'Yes, I do believe it. Yes. You know I do.'

He was quiet for a while. 'So it's not the end?' he said. 'You believe that?'

She saw in his face then the expression she had seen on grieving fathers at the séance table. That desire, in spite of themselves, to be convinced.

And they *would* convince those grieving fathers. They would do it with tricks. And the fathers would go away believing that their lost child had spoken to them, when really it was only Katie cracking her toes, or Leah in another room. How long had it been since she had really felt that they were communicating with spirits? She could hardly remember. Their tricks came so easily it was as if she had forgotten to listen for anything else. Even the memory of the man from the schoolhouse now seemed distant and unclear: she no longer felt the residue of his hatred on her skin.

It was terrible, what they did. *I am at peace, Father*, they would have the child say. *Do not cry.*

'It's not the end,' was all she could think to say. 'That's what I believe.' Then she turned away, not wanting to see his face.

THIRTY

That night, she felt another storm in the air, and she pushed open her window trying to smell the coming rain. Sometimes she thought that rain must be good for sicknesses; it must clean the air and wash away poisons. But then she thought of the way puddles lingered in the streets and turned dark with oil and dirt, and rats came.

Calvin should be in the country. Anywhere but here. They were failing him. She would tell Leah in the morning. The journey would be hard on him but they must leave the city.

She heard a shuffle of footsteps outside her door, and turned around. The door rattled for a moment, as if somebody had leaned on it, and then she saw a shadow underneath. Something was pushed through the gap. A piece of paper. For a moment she couldn't move; it had startled her, and she froze.

Then her legs and arms came loose and she rushed to the door and flung it open, never mind that she was in her nightclothes. There was nobody in the hall, but there was the feel a place has when somebody has just left it. She thought of going out and searching, but the dark red carpet was as foreboding as ever, and pushed her back inside.

She picked up the paper.

It was the size and shape of a page torn from a book, but it was blank, with one side covered in spidery handwriting that she had to light a candle to read.

WITCHES, it said at the top, and she squinted her eyes to read.

> *"i.e. Such as by Contract or Explicit*
> *Covenant with the Devil, improve, or*
> *rather are improved by him to the doing*
> *of things strange in themselves"*

YOU ARE NOT WELCOME
IN NEW YORK CITY.
TAKE YOUR DEVILRY ELSEWHERE.

THE PUNISHMENT FOR
WITCHCRAFT IS HANGING.

The first drops of rain began to patter against the window, and the window was still open, so fine drops of rain were blown into the room, and she thought, I must close the window.

She read the words again.

I must fetch Leah, and show her, she thought.

I must complain to the hotel.

The first words had been copied from somewhere, nobody wrote like that anymore. It was not the Bible. She should show it to a scholar of some kind, who might know.

I must close the window.

The rain, she thought. It is raining.

Then she found herself touching the corner of the paper against the candle flame. It caught right away, the paper blackening and scorching and crumbling in her hand and the tiny flame growing until she felt it brush the edges of her fingers and the paper was almost gone and then she gasped and threw it to the floor, and a second later she threw the heavy quilt from her bed on top and stamped on it with her bare feet, and then grabbed her pitcher of water and threw that on top of it as well.

I have lost my mind, she thought suddenly. She stood, heart racing and breathless, astonished that she hadn't set the hotel on fire and killed everybody inside.

The carpet would be scorched, and they would have to pay, and the quilt was probably ruined, and they would have to pay. She pressed her hand to her heart, and saw that the tips of her fingers were red and would blister; but for the moment she felt no pain, only a dark, whirling confusion.

I have lost my mind.

In the morning she covered the burn with a small rug that had lain beneath the window. She folded up the quilt as small as she could, and forced it into a small space at the back of the closet. She had left the window open all night, and there was no trace of smoke in the air.

She found Leah in the dining hall and sat down in silence. Leah nodded to her, and looked back to her newspaper. Maggie wondered if her eyes were fixed firmly on it so that she didn't have to see the other guests watching them.

Maggie picked up a piece of bread. She tore off a small piece and forced herself to eat it.

'Calvin?' she said softly, eventually, and Leah gave a short shake of her head.

'No. Not today.'

She didn't know why she asked. It had been weeks since he had come to breakfast.

'Kate says she's not well, also,' said Leah, 'but I think it's only a headache, and of course she's very worried about him.'

She looked at Maggie briefly. 'It's a lot for a young girl, I suppose.' Leah was very pale, her eyes shadowed.

'Did you speak to somebody, yesterday, about—'

'Yes. Mr. Barnum apologized and says he'll see about it.'

'What does that mean?'

A faint, tired smile passed across Leah's voice. 'I really don't know.'

'Leah—'

'Yes?'

'Last night.' She looked at her sister. 'Last night—'

'Last night, what?'

If only she hadn't burned it. She wouldn't have to explain. Could she even remember the words?

What could Leah do? A piece of paper that nobody had seen, and a burned carpet. It was only trouble, that's all it was, more trouble, and if Calvin found out it would make him worse. She had nothing to show anybody but the scorch marks, and she could have simply knocked over a candle.

She *could* have knocked over a candle.

Her memory had become like a stage where the curtain rose and fell, pieces disappearing behind it. *Had* she knocked over a candle? Had she walked through the hotel in the middle of the night and met the Devil?

'Last night—'

'Maggie. I've hardly slept. If it's something—'

'No.' She shook her head and tore off another tiny piece of bread. 'No. It's nothing.'

Leah paused, as if she knew Maggie was lying. But she said, 'Good.'

THIRTY-ONE

On the Friday they were due to visit Amy and her friends, nobody wanted to go. Calvin was worse than ever and the physician had been called. Leah said she had to stay with him, and Kate said it was wrong to enjoy themselves when Calvin was so sick.

But it was too late to write and say not to send the driver. So Maggie packed some things. She was only staying one night. And she had to escape from the hotel, if only for a day. The walls pressed in on her, and the whispers of the other guests followed her everywhere.

She borrowed a small trunk from Leah, and packed, including an embroidered needle-case she had bought as a present for Amy. She took a Bible too, because it seemed the right thing to do and because she would be staying with good, godly people, and she thought they might look at her and see that New York City had ruined her somehow, that she would seem corrupted by all the things she had done that she would never have done in Rochester. She slipped into Calvin's room to say goodbye before she left, but he was asleep, so she crept back out of the room not wanting to wake him.

The house was only an hour from the city but as they drew closer the road became a dirt track, and the trees grew thicker around them. The light was strange through the trees, dappled and shifting.

The house stood some distance from other houses in the area. It was a large, stone structure with a wide oak door. Climbing down from the carriage outside, she felt the early September coolness in the air and it encouraged her for a moment. There was something reassuring about the house, its plain façade and even proportions.

The quiet of the forest and the smell of trees reminded her of Hydesville.

Mr. Sullivan came out to greet her. He was dark-haired, with a short, neat beard and wire spectacles, kind eyes smiling at her as the driver unloaded her trunk. 'Miss Fox, what an honor,' he said, as he led her inside. 'I have a daughter just your age but I'm afraid she's away at school. Your sisters aren't with you?'

She explained stumblingly about Calvin, as she looked around the dark entrance hallway. There were a few small, stern portraits on the walls, and nothing else.

'I'm sorry to hear it.' He took off his glasses and cleaned them with his sleeve. 'We have a simple supper planned for this evening, and I thought you might like to take a walk this afternoon. As you can see we have some beautiful woodland still here and the ground should be dry.' He cleared his throat. 'And then I have to confess I'm very eager to try your spirit-talking, if it's possible to have a demonstration.'

'Don't listen to him, Maggie, he's a dreadful skeptic,' said Elizabeth Reid – Elizabeth Garret, Maggie reminded herself – appearing on the stairs. She stopped on the small landing above them and leaned on the bannister.

Maggie was startled by her for a second, then felt that mixture of admiration and anxiety that Elizabeth still brought about in her.

Mr. Sullivan was shaking his head but still smiling. 'I'm a

skeptic of a kind but my curiosity is sincere, so I hope you'll indulge me. I'd be delighted to have my mind changed.'

'I hope you will,' Maggie said softly.

'So do I,' said Elizabeth. 'I was a skeptic myself but I've lately discovered the believers are much better company.'

Amy and Will Garret were in the parlor, which was large and bright with windows overlooking a wild garden. They were deep in conversation, with serious expressions, and Maggie hesitated awkwardly in the doorway, feeling young and out of place.

But there were warm greetings, and offers of coffee, and then Mr. Sullivan's house girl appeared with the things for their supper. She was a girl from Pennsylvania who had come east instead of west: Johanna, with light brown hair and green eyes. She talked with Mr. Sullivan casually, laughing a lot. When she showed Maggie to her bedroom she said, with a dimpled smile, 'Mr. Sullivan invited me to join you for the spirit-talking, if you do it. Do you mind?'

'No,' Maggie said. 'I'd like that.' It was a sweet attic bedroom and the bed was made up perfectly. She could have crawled into it right away.

'Oh.' Johanna clapped her hands together. 'I'm so glad. I'll set everything up in the parlor however you like. You just tell me.'

'Thank you.'

Johanna nodded. 'My father doesn't like this sort of thing.' She glanced back over her shoulder, then lowered her voice. 'He doesn't like Mr. Sullivan, or his friends, the people he mixes with. He says I shouldn't be waiting on people not of my own color.' She stopped as if waiting to see what Maggie thought of this, and then continued. It was as if she'd had nobody to talk to for a while. 'He says it's no wonder the antislavery folks are the same ones who think they can talk to spirits, because they all want to destroy the natural order of things. But Mr. Sullivan is paying for me to go to school, so he can't say anything to his face.' Hardly stopping for breath, she added, 'I'd actually like to try myself eventually, talking to the spirits, and with other people too. I wouldn't have thought I could do anything like that, but meeting you now, you're only my age, aren't you? So why shouldn't I?' She reached absently to straighten a chair by the door. 'There are no rules, are there? About how you do it? I know you sit at a table usually, but everyone has a table, don't they.'

'No. There are no rules.'

'I like that.'

'You should try, then,' Maggie said, but she thought: It's not only your father who won't like it.

Amy was waiting for her downstairs, in a cap and simple dress that did not trail on the floor. She wore sturdy boots, as if for farm work. They suited her. 'If you have the energy for a walk, Maggie, I think you will enjoy the woods. Our host promises me there's a path of some kind that will take us alongside the creek.'

They walked in silence for a while, until they found the path. It was too small for a carriage, but it cut cleanly through the trees and the ground was flat and dry. They could hear the creek before they saw it.

'Is Isaac well?' Maggie said, after a while.

'He is,' said Amy. 'He was sorry not to join us, but with things as they are—'

A few leaves had already fallen, and crunched beneath

251

their feet. Amy walked quickly. Maggie was almost out of breath, trying to keep pace with her. Her own shoes were new, and too tight, and her feet ached. She took a deep breath, preparing to begin to tell Amy everything, the petition and the newspaper and her strange nightmare, but Amy spoke first.

'We might all seem distracted, Maggie, and I should tell you why.' She gave Maggie a careful, appraising look. 'Perhaps you've already guessed. Since your family moved away we've used those rooms to – "harbor fugitives", as our lawmakers would have it. You know Rochester is one of the last stopping places along the underground railroad, with the border to Canada so close.'

A breeze shook the trees around them, a few pine needles drifting to the ground. Maggie thought of those bright rooms in Amy's house overlooking the road. It hadn't occurred to her to ask if anybody else used them.

There was tension in Amy's face, a pinched look to her mouth.

Harboring fugitives.

'You're helping people escape slavery,' said Maggie softly. She was glad to have been told, that Amy trusted her, and glad to have been told before she began to talk about her own stupid, selfish problems.

'We're supporting the African Methodist Church, and Mr. and Mrs. Garret. They accommodate as many people as they can, but there's only so much space and some caution is required. We had the rooms to offer.' Amy cleared her throat. 'Some of our fellow abolitionists think we've all been too open about the railroad. Perhaps they're right. The slave catchers know too much. And there's talk of the laws getting stricter, greater punishments for everyone involved. Imprisonment as well as fines, just for providing shelter. I'm sure you've heard about it.'

She knew a little of it, from overheard conversations and passing glances at newspapers. But her attention had been elsewhere, and she was sure Amy could tell. Back in Rochester Amy had tried so hard to educate her, to share books and pamphlets with her and take her to lectures, and what had Maggie done with what she had learned? Gone to New York City to drink wine and bat her eyelashes at grown men.

The injustices of the world were too large, too complicated to change, and where once she had thought she might find a way to do some good, now her mind went blank at the thought of it all.

'I wish I could help,' she said. 'I wish I knew what to do.'

Amy smiled. 'Perhaps you could wait until you have an audience of lawmakers, and then ask the spirits whether slavery is right. I'm sure they'd say no.'

Maggie was sure Amy was teasing her, but the idea snagged itself briefly in her mind. They had convinced all kinds of people of all kinds of things at the séance table. Could they have the spirits deliver moral lessons, as if their parlor was a church?

No. It was a conceited thought, and she shook it away.

A bird hopped across their path, cocking its head at them for a moment, and they both stopped. Something rustled in the trees above. The light was changing. It was dark, suddenly. It might rain.

'Well, that was what I wanted to tell you, Maggie,' Amy said. 'How is Calvin?'

A lump rose in her throat. 'He sends his best wishes,' she said, and Amy nodded, and didn't ask any more.

They followed the path around the creek and back toward

the house as the skies continued to darken and she heard the first patter of rain in the trees. As they approached the back of Mr. Sullivan's house, they saw Elizabeth leaning in the door. She waved. She had Mr Garret's coat around her shoulders, and called out, 'You'd better be quick, or you'll be soaked.'

She was right: a few moments after they came through the door, a downpour began with rain that pounded on the roof like thunder. It was dark as night.

'Heavens.' Amy had to raise her voice to be heard over the rain. 'I can't imagine where that came from. The creek will flood if this carries on.'

They all watched it for a moment, and then Amy excused herself to see if she could help with the supper arrangements.

Maggie continued to look out of the window, but she could feel Elizabeth watching her.

'I hear that you draw quite a crowd in New York City.'

Maggie pressed her forehead against the glass, and closed her eyes for a moment, soothed by the sound of the rain. 'Yes. There are a lot of people.'

She prepared, instinctively, to defend herself from whatever remark came next. But Elizabeth said, 'How old are you, Maggie?'

She opened her eyes. For a moment she couldn't remember. 'I'm fifteen. I'll be sixteen soon.'

'You seem older.'

'How old are you?'

'Nineteen.'

'You seem older.'

Elizabeth laughed. 'I wish I was, sometimes. I think, will everything be easier when I'm older? Will I understand what it is I'm doing, will people listen to me?'

Maggie stepped back from the window. She felt the cold impression of the glass on her forehead. 'People do listen to you.'

'No. I don't think so. They look at me when I'm talking, sometimes. But that isn't the same.'

'But you do so much work. So many good things.'

'I suppose. It doesn't always feel that way.'

A cold, wet wind pushed the back door open, and Elizabeth closed it again, and turned the lock. 'They listen to *you*, I suppose, and your sisters, in the city. All those people. Is it wonderful?'

Wonderful. The word knocked around in Maggie's brain for a moment, but didn't seem to mean anything. 'I don't know,' she said. 'It's not really us they listen to.' The rain was soaking the grass, and turning the pathway to mud. 'How old is Will?' she said. 'Mr. Garret, I mean.'

'Oh, he's very old. Thirty or something like that. He can hardly remember.'

'He's very handsome.'

'Isn't he?' She laughed again. 'And very talented, I think.'

'Has he finished his book?'

'Nearly.'

'Will it be published?'

'I hope so. He'd like to build a name as a journalist, but so far only the abolitionist papers will publish him. And there aren't enough of those, and he'd like to write on subjects other than slavery, sometimes.' Elizabeth smiled. 'He's interested in spirits, for instance.' Maggie wondered again if she was being teased.

'I saw you, once,' she said, suddenly feeling shy. 'You probably don't remember that I was there, but I saw you once argue with Mr. Crane, in Rochester. You were sitting at

Amy's kitchen table. And he was furious, he stormed out. I thought *that* was wonderful.'

Elizabeth gave Maggie a long, curious look. 'How strange that you remember that,' she said. 'I thought it was terrible. I cried all night. I was sick to my stomach. I don't even know why. I just felt I'd done something dreadful, I thought I'd never be forgiven. My sister Della was furious with me when she heard.' She shook her head. 'The next time I saw him, I apologized, and then I hated myself for that.'

'But you were right. What you said.'

'I expect I was. It's usually when I'm right that people are angry with me.'

The windows had begun to steam. Elizabeth pressed a thumb to the glass, and drew a wavy line. 'I never believed the things he said about you, after what happened to little Hannah. The man had lost his mind.'

Maggie's heart gave a hard thump. 'I didn't know if you knew about that.'

'Of course. Everyone did.'

Maggie closed her eyes for a moment. When she opened them, Elizabeth was still looking through the steamed glass.

'I told Amy,' Elizabeth said. 'When it happened. I said you should believe Maggie Fox over Mr. Crane, because he has an anger in him that leads him to deceive himself. When a person is determined to see the world in one way, they won't allow anybody to challenge it. I'm sure it's a kind of illness.' She looked behind her, where murmured voices drifted through the house. From the kitchen, there came a smell of cooking, beef and potatoes, some sort of stew.

'Della spoke on stage in Rochester,' Elizabeth continued. 'And now she speaks all over Europe, on abolition. But men still talk over her, and white women applaud her and then disparage her in private. She knows there are certain rules. There are games you have to play. She wouldn't speak against someone like Mr. Crane, because she knows it will get her nowhere. I admire her, but I don't have the patience for all those games. I think I have too much anger in me.' Elizabeth wiped clean the glass with her palm, and then wiped her hand on her skirt. 'I'd tell you that you should learn to play their games if you want a peaceful life,' she said. 'But I'm not sure a peaceful life is so desirable.'

THIRTY-TWO

There was a lot of laughter at supper, as if nobody could bear to talk of serious things any longer. Everybody said the food was delicious, but Maggie had no appetite, and could hardly taste it.

After Johanna had cleared the plates, they all moved to the parlor. Johanna was instructed to stack them in the kitchen, where they would keep for tomorrow, and join them. Which she did, taking off her apron and shaking out her hair, beaming.

A window was open, and a light rain was still falling, a soft patter on the leaves outside.

They began to take their seats around the parlor table, as Mr. Sullivan went to lower the lamps, leaving only a soft glow. 'I understand, Miss Fox, that you prefer the darkness, is that right?'

She would have preferred it to be even darker. 'Yes. It's better that way.'

'Of course.'

'I'm sure you have a theory for that, don't you, Phillip?' said Amy, with a fond smile.

'Naturally. But nobody wants to hear my theories.'

'I do,' said Maggie. 'I don't mind.'

'Yes, tell us,' said Elizabeth. 'If you're going to ruin the fun, you may as well do it now.'

He shook his head, and sat down at the table. 'No, no. It isn't the time.'

She hadn't decided, yet, what she would do. She would have to wait for the quiet, to see what noises the house made itself, to see if anybody spoke.

'I'd like to know your theories too, Mr. Sullivan,' said Johanna. 'If you don't mind.'

'So would I,' said Maggie. 'People say all kinds of things to us, I won't – I won't be offended.' She almost thought to tell him about Calvin's theories, but the thought of mentioning him brought a lump to her throat.

Mr. Sullivan pushed his glasses up his nose, and looked at Maggie thoughtfully. 'Well,' he said. 'There are a few ideas I'm interested in, that may relate to your work. The first is that some of us do have a strange and rare gift. An ability to move things without actually touching them, and without even knowing. So a group of people may see a book fall to the floor and the one who made it fall might be no more aware of what they have done than anybody else.'

'That's no more believable than spirits talking to us, Mr. Sullivan,' said Elizabeth.

He laughed. 'I know. But I believe there's a scientific explanation.'

'Which is?'

'Sadly, our science hasn't yet advanced far enough to fully—'

There was a groaning and laughter at the table, but Maggie was sitting straight, eyes fixed on him, trying to listen.

'– to *fully* explain it, but—'

'Who are these people, then?' said Elizabeth. 'Who has this gift? *Why* do they have it?'

'My theory is that those of us who have suffered some kind of disruption to the self are more susceptible to this phenomenon. That a trauma, for instance, might create a disturbance to the body that generates an electrical energy of some sort. And that energy travels through the air in the way a telegraphic message travels through the wires. Within an enclosed space it creates a force that can move objects, or even create sounds and visual disturbances, phantoms. But the person, the disrupted body – they aren't even aware of it.'

She was being accused of something, Maggie thought, yet another accusation to add to fraud and witchcraft, but she struggled to understand what it was. Mr. Sullivan's kind face did not make it less painful. 'A disruption to the self?' Maggie said. 'What could disrupt the self?'

'Well, a trauma, as I say. An illness. An intense emotion, anger or grief. I assume many of your guests are afflicted by grief. Or possibly a transition of some kind.' He paused. 'The passage of youth to adulthood, for instance. A girl of your age, Maggie, or your sister's—'

Maggie was shaking her head. 'No. It doesn't explain the things we've experienced. The spirits have told us things we couldn't know.'

Again, he removed his glasses, and polished them. He looked thoughtful. 'No. It's not a complete explanation. But there are other ideas, new developments in thought. The part of our mind that is unconscious, for instance. That knows things we don't *know* we know. Something we've overheard, without realizing it, or something we've been told and forgotten, that comes back to us in a moment of heightened emotion—'

'No. That isn't it.'

'– or the possibility that some of us are able to intuit the thoughts of others, simply through proximity, or physical connection. Consider the possibility that our thoughts generate electrical signals as well, electrical information, and that some of us are uniquely gifted in being able to receive these signals without a word being spoken.'

'I'd like to borrow some of your books, Mr. Sullivan,' said Mr. Garret, grinning. 'You've been reading some strange things.'

'No stranger than the Bible, I think,' said Mr. Sullivan. 'And I consider myself a good Christian.' He looked back at Maggie. 'But you see, Miss Fox, I don't believe this gift is any less wonderful than the ability to talk with the dead. It's still a rare and extraordinary thing. Science is full of miracles.'

A hush fell over the table for a moment, broken only by the sound of the rain. Mr. Sullivan was trying to be kind, but what he had described was not a miracle to her ears, or anything wonderful. It was a disordered mind that could not be trusted.

Suddenly Mr. Sullivan clapped his hands together and laughed. 'But I'm a confectioner by trade!' he said. 'Not a scientist or a philosopher. And certainly not a minister. So you are all very welcome to ignore my ideas. We can move on with the evening.'

Maggie felt they were waiting for her to speak, but she was lost. He had planted something in all of their minds: what could she say that would not make her appear disrupted, or traumatized, or some sort of half-person who could not control what she did?

Mr. Garret watched her for a moment and then said, 'It doesn't seem like nonsense, Phillip. Those are interesting ideas. But you need to see it for yourself, see these girls—'

'Of course.'

'My sister spoke to me at one of their séances. I swear she did, and she spelled out her name, something neither of the girls would have known. And it was a comfort to me.'

'Then I'm glad,' said Mr. Sullivan. 'I've no wish to deprive anyone of comfort. There's precious little of it in this life.'

The dim, feathery light was not dark enough to move objects without being seen, but it was dark enough to alter the mood and heighten the nerves. They were sat in a circle, holding hands.

Nobody had paid any money, Maggie thought. Nobody would complain if nothing happened.

But they would be disappointed. Amy might be ashamed, to have invited her.

She heard Leah's voice in her ear. *A few effects to begin, and their imaginations can do the rest.* Her feet twitched, bones ready to crack.

At Maggie's instruction, they all closed their eyes.

Maggie looked at their faces. These were such good people. Doing dangerous work that she would never have the courage to do herself.

She had begun, but she could not think what to do next. She missed Kate, very badly. Both of her sisters. She hadn't been apart from them in so long.

She heard herself say, 'If there is a spirit here, please rap once for yes.'

But she did nothing. She listened to the rain, to the soft collective murmur of their breath.

There came a soft tap from beneath the table.

Everyone's eyes remained closed. There was a ripple of acknowledgement through the circle. Maggie itched to look beneath the table, wondering suddenly if Mr. Sullivan might have planted something. Johanna, even.

Then she felt ashamed, for thinking that these good people were the same as her.

'I will call out the letters,' she said. 'And if a spirit is present, please signal with raps the letters of your name.'

She waited a while, and then began. 'A – B – C—'

She stopped at *C*. There had been the faintest sound, which might only have been an insect or a loose floorboard.

'C?' she said again, and this time there was a soft scraping sound. But Maggie was the only person with her eyes open, and she was the only one who saw the candlestick on the table make a tiny movement to the left. Then she began to spell again, but the moment she said *A*, the candlestick fell over. They all jumped, and the circle broke.

Maggie reached for the candlestick herself, and brushed her fingers against it, thinking she might feel some sort of charge. It was cool, and she could sense its weight but nothing else. Her eyes went to the open window. She wondered if the table was slanted. She glanced around the table and saw Mr. Sullivan looking at her.

There was a cool feeling in her blood. Something was very wrong.

The curtain fell in her mind, and rose again. She had a headache coming.

I pushed it myself, she thought. I pushed the candle myself.

No. She had not. She couldn't have.

'Could I – I'm sorry. Could I step out for a moment?' Maggie said. 'I need some air, I need – I need to step out.'

'Of course.' Amy looked concerned. 'Maggie, you're very pale, should I fetch you some water?'

'No.' She shook her head. 'No. No. Just some air.'

She left the table, avoiding their eyes, and went through the kitchen and down the hall to the front door. A little air. She opened it, and stood on the top step, rain misting over her face. Her heart was racing. Her head had begun to pound and she felt a terrible sense of dread that she could not place.

THIRTY-THREE

She left very early in the morning.

She hoped to sleep a little on the journey back, but couldn't, so when they arrived back at the hotel she was still exhausted, and the juddering motion of the carriage had turned her stomach.

When she stepped into the hotel, she saw one of the porters look at her strangely, then turn and hurry away, up the stairs.

She paused. The hotel was quiet and warm. Familiar smells of dust and paint, and the last traces of the breakfast service.

Something was different, though. Something was missing.

The same desk, same polished brass bell, same carpet, same staircase and bannister.

It was their sign: *Spirit Talking with the Fox Sisters of Rochester. $3/$5. Ask at desk.* For months it had been propped up on an easel at the foot of the staircase. It had been defaced once or twice, and then replaced. But now it was gone.

Another porter came in behind her, carrying a large trunk. She turned to him. 'Excuse me. Do you know what's happened – our sign? I'm Maggie Fox, and—' It sounded silly. 'We usually have a sign.' She flushed.

He was sweating. The trunk looked heavy. He dropped it at his feet, and shook out his arms. He said, in a careful, courteous voice: 'Yes, Miss Fox. We thought you'd be taking a break, for the rest of the week at least.'

'Why?'

'Well – your loss,' he said.

And then she turned and saw Leah coming down the staircase.

She thought: I will always remember this moment. The small details of it. The sweat on the porter's forehead. The smell of paint and breakfast things. Leah's terrible expression. Her swollen eyes and the downward turn of her mouth, her flat voice when she dismissed the porter: 'Thank you. I'll talk to my sister now.'

Something terrible.

Maggie took a step away from Leah. 'No,' she said.

She would turn and walk back out on to the street. Perhaps the driver would still be there, and she could pay him to take her across town, to another hotel, where she would stay, forever, and never hear what Leah was about to say to her.

I will go, she thought. I must go now, because once she has said it, it will be too late.

But Leah was already talking: '– very suddenly, a hemorrhage of the lungs.'

'I have to talk to him,' Maggie said. 'Calvin. I have to tell him about some things I learned yesterday. He'll be interested. It's about electrical energy, and the mind.'

Leah looked at her, dazed and pained. 'Maggie.' Leah reached for her, and Maggie took another step away.

'No,' she said. 'I should talk to him right away. He'll want to know. He might have been right all along.'

A frown, confusion. 'No, Maggie—'

'I'll go and talk to him now.'

265

'Come upstairs.' Leah pressed a hand to her mouth for a moment. 'Come upstairs, now,' she said. 'You can see him. He's still here.'

That was the question, wasn't it, whether he was still here or not. That was the question that defined their lives. When you are gone, where are you?

Certainly his body was here, laid out on the hotel bed, on top of fresh sheets. They had sharp corners, and smelled of soap.

But was he here?

She had never seen a body so close.

The shape of him was familiar, but small details were wrong. His skin was not his own. It was drained utterly of blood, and his lips were white. His hair was flat and brushed back from his face.

She couldn't remember asking to be alone with him, but here she was. Leah had gone. Kate must be behind a door, somewhere, sobbing. 'We have a few hours,' Leah had said, before she closed the door – but she hadn't explained. A few hours until what?

'Calvin?' Maggie said softly.

Outside in the corridor, the squeak of a trolley wheel, a rattle of cups.

He was utterly still. 'Calvin?' she said again. *Don't ignore me*, she thought. *I'm here, Calvin. Please talk to me.*

Tugging on his arm when she was a little girl, and he had just come to live with them on the old farm upstate. *Calvin, Calvin, Calvin. Please play with me.*

She would say: I'll race you to the barn. I'll race you to the woods. I'll race you to the fencepost and back. Him, sixteen or seventeen; her, a five-year-old with grazed knees. That

266

rusted old fencepost that marked the boundary of their land, the point after which it became overgrown and uncharted.

'Calvin,' she whispered.

She ought to do something. A prayer. No. He wouldn't like that. She ought to cover him with something. Keep him safe. She had a few hours.

A few hours until what? Someone would come and take him away?

They couldn't have him. He wouldn't want that. He would want to stay with them, as he always had. He had spent his whole life with them. He could have done something else, could have chosen some other road, but he had done this, chosen this, and ended up here. Twenty-eight, sick and dying in New York City, where he had followed them.

He had done this, and now he wouldn't do anything else.

His children, she thought, and his wedding day, and his old age, living out in California on his own piece of land. All gone. He had made it this far and no further.

She remembered hearing somewhere once that when somebody died you should open a window to let their soul out. So she went to the window, and shook it. The catch was stiff and sticky with paint, but she forced it open, a few inches. Imagined she might feel his soul rush past her, but there was only a warm, dirty breeze from the street, coming back into the room and lifting the lace curtain.

A coach rumbled past, wheels rocking on an uneven patch of road. The sound of a boy shouting.

'I'm sorry, Calvin,' Maggie said. Her eyes became hot with tears. She wiped her nose with the back of her hand. 'Can you hear me?' she whispered. She went back toward the bed and reached to touch him, but snatched her hand away. He was cold.

She stood up and went to the corner of the room, and closed her eyes, and then opened them, and he was still there. His body. 'Calvin?' she said.

She sat down on the floor, and brought her knees to her chest, wrapped her arms around them.

He had been frightened to die, she thought, and he had had to do it alone.

Everybody does. She imagined his voice, the shrug of his shoulders. *Everybody has to die alone.*

There would be a tomorrow, but he would not be part of it. He had made it only this far. To this hotel, to this city, to this quiet room, where the road ended.

No, she thought. It had not ended. Only she had stopped, and he had gone on ahead. He was gone on, up ahead, past the fencepost and into the tall grass where she could no longer see him.

THIRTY-FOUR

Kate stood outside the door, pressed against the wall, and when Maggie found her she screwed her eyes shut as if she didn't want to see what was in the room beyond. Her eyes were swollen and red and her face was damp with tears that she made no effort to wipe away. She gave Maggie a wild look. 'Is he in there?' she whispered. Her voice was trembling.

'Yes.' Maggie's own eyes were dry now, and her hands were cold and tingling. Her limbs felt detached from her body. The corridor was distorted, longer and narrower than it should have been.

'You weren't here,' said Kate. 'You weren't here. They wouldn't let me in, but I heard him – they wouldn't let me in. The doctor came. They wouldn't let me see.' Her face collapsed and she let out an awful, choked sob, pressing her hands over her mouth.

Maggie leaned against the wall, feeling as though she might faint.

'You weren't here.'

Maggie slid down the wall and sat on the floor, on the gritty carpet. 'I'm sorry,' she whispered. Kate sat down next to her, and curled over, resting her face against her knees.

Why was Calvin lying in that room alone? Would somebody come for him? She should go back in and tell him. *Somebody will come for you, Calvin. It will be alright.*

Kate lifted her head. Maggie tried to make sense of her

269

red, distorted face, her cracked lips. 'Should we try and contact him?' Kate said.

'What?'

'Should we try and contact him?' She wiped her eyes, and sniffed. 'He might still be here.'

'Katie—'

'I want to talk to him. We could go to the parlor. He might be waiting for us. We can say goodbye.'

'I don't want to say goodbye.'

'Then maybe he won't go, he might stay, we could talk to him—'

'Katie, Katie—' Maggie grabbed Kate's arm, and squeezed tightly because she wanted her to be quiet, to stop talking and stop saying these things. They were wrong. They were *wrong*. But she wanted it too. There were things she had to say to him. She just needed him for a little bit longer, a few hours. One more day. A minute.

She was made of pain. Her entire body was weak with it.

'Please,' said Kate. 'Please let me talk to him.'

She almost said yes. Then over Kate's shoulder she saw Leah walking toward them with a man Maggie didn't recognize, and she knew Leah wouldn't allow it. There were things to be done now, and they were real and solemn things. Not games played by little girls.

The day should not have continued, but it did. Maggie went to her room. Kate came with her and lay on the bed. A maid brought them a tray of tea and slices of cake, as if it were somebody's birthday. And the tray stayed in the corner of the room, tea going cold and the cake turning warm and dry.

Kate didn't want to go to dinner, but Leah said they should, so in the evening Maggie and Leah went together, and sat at a small table in the corner of the dining hall, with two chairs that stayed empty.

'He wants to be buried on our family plot,' Leah said. She was holding a fork over her plate, but neither of them had eaten anything yet. 'So that's what we'll do.'

Talking about this, in the way they might talk about the weather.

'He told you that?' said Maggie.

'Yes. He wrote it all down.'

'When?'

'A little while ago.'

'What about—His parents are in Rochester.'

'They've closed that cemetery. There's no more space for him there.' She paused. 'Perhaps we could have his name added to the stone. But his body—'

She stopped, and looked at her plate.

'I've written to David,' she said. 'And there's a few names Calvin gave to me. I've written to them. If they want to join us, for a service of some kind. In a few days. I've arranged for his body—'

Around them, the sound of forks scraping against plates, people eating and talking. Maggie cut a tiny piece of meat and put it in her mouth, forced herself to swallow.

'A minister is coming this evening,' Leah said. 'Before they take his body, the minister will say a few words. I'm not sure who we'll find at home – it's not a church plot, after all – so I thought, just in case. It's a little irregular, an evening service, but the – the body needs to be taken to Arcadia tonight and we can't wait. A short service, and then the burial in a few days. The hotel knows a minister. Evidently it's not their first death.' She put her fork down. 'Perhaps it's the food.'

'A minister.'

'A Methodist.'

'Calvin wouldn't like that.'

'It'll be a comfort to Mother, to know that we did it.'

'But Calvin wouldn't—'

'Calvin didn't believe in anything after death, and if he was right then he won't mind either way, will he? It's arranged. It's what we ought to do for him. It will be a comfort to Mother.'

They were quiet for a while, and then Leah put down her fork and pushed her plate away.

'I can't eat,' she said.

She wasn't sure she had ever been in a church at night. It was strange. Cold and much too large for the three of them. There was the plain coffin, waiting. She tried to pretend that it was empty.

The carriage waited outside and Maggie wanted to go back and ask if the driver would join them, just to have another person. Calvin deserved more than this. Just one more person.

They sat at the front, all in a row.

'There'll be more people at the burial,' Leah said softly, as if she knew what Maggie was thinking. 'This is just so that we can say we've done things properly.'

The minister arrived, a little late – Maggie wondered if he had been called away from his dinner – and went to the front without greeting them. He had thinning gray hair that grew long at the back, wisping around his neck, and small eyes set close together.

With no introduction, he cleared his throat and began to speak.

Maggie saw his lips move, but the words didn't seem to

come from him. They echoed from the walls. He was only a man opening and closing his mouth. It was like watching somebody talking underwater.

I am the resurrection and the life, saith the Lord—

Maggie felt a choking sob rise in her throat, but found that she did not want the minister to see her cry.

– and he that believeth in me, though he were dead, yet shall he live.

Holding back her tears built a pressure in her head that turned to pain, and a throb in her ears that meant she could barely hear the words. I must listen, she thought, I must listen, and she did, but she couldn't hear. She could only hear her own blood pulsing through her brain.

The minister accompanied them back to the hotel. There was really no need, Leah told him, but he insisted.

He came with them into the hall.

'Thank you for your words,' Leah said stiffly. 'That was – lovely. Very reassuring.'

The minister nodded. 'I hope you took some comfort. He was a Methodist, of course?'

'Oh, yes,' said Leah. 'A devout Methodist. Absolutely.'

'And he led a good life?'

'Of course.'

'Then you should rejoice that he is in heaven.'

There was a short pause, and then Leah said, 'I must take my younger sister to bed, it's very late and she—' Kate had already broken away, and went toward the stairs wiping her eyes with the back of her hand. 'Will you excuse me?' Leah said, and followed her.

Maggie stared after them, unable to move. She felt him looking at her.

273

'And you're all Methodists, yourselves?' he said.

'That's right,' Maggie said faintly. Around them, the hotel bustled as usual, the smell of cooked meat and the sound of clinking glasses, and trolleys wheeled across the carpet.

'I know about your work, of course.' He glanced around. 'This is where you perform your – activities?'

'Yes. We have our own parlor.'

'May I see it?'

She longed for Leah to return. The request was some sort of trap, she was sure, but how could she refuse a minister?

'I – yes, of course.'

She led him to the room. It was dark except for a solitary lamp hanging by the window. She wondered who had lit it. The heavy oak door swung closed behind them.

'We sit here.' She gestured at the table, not sure what else to say. The noise from the hall was muffled and her voice was too loud in the quiet room.

'Do you?'

'Yes.'

'What do they call it now? "Spiritualism?"'

'Yes. I believe so.'

He faced her. 'Do you think you have begun a religion, here?'

'No. Of course not. It's just, another part. Another part of faith, a different way of—'

'I was recently disturbed to discover that some of my own congregants have taken an interest in all of this.' He looked at her expectantly.

'I'm sorry that you were disturbed.'

'Miss Fox. You might take this moment, this loss, to reconsider your path.'

He was not speaking with the same voice he had used in

his sermon. It had hardened. His face was half in shadow. There was a smell of coffee on his breath.

Maggie saw an empty wine bottle standing on a table in the dark corner.

'Does your father know what it is you're doing here?' he continued.

'My father?'

'How his daughters are behaving?'

She took a step back, reaching behind her for the door. 'Perhaps you should speak to my sister,' she said.

He stepped closer, and took hold of her arm. She tried to jerk it away but he tightened his grip.

'Please—' she said.

'Your father,' the minister said again. 'Tell me, does he know?'

'Yes. He knows. He's a believer.'

'He is deceived.'

'He has experienced it himself.'

'He may think so, but he is wrong.'

'Sir.' Maggie swallowed. 'It's late, and I—'

'You will listen to me, if you care about your soul. Our country has seen this sort of thing before. It is not—' He broke off, raised a finger in the air, and shook it, as if he was preaching. 'It is *not* the place of women to mediate between the spiritual world and this one. It is the job of *men*. Men who have been called. Your activities threaten the moral order of our society. You have strayed from the Christian path. I'm sorry to speak harshly. But you must be told. You must be *warned*.'

She swallowed. 'We bring comfort—' she said, but he was shaking his head.

'How *dare* you?' His voice began to tremble. 'How *dare*

you? This is a type of *sickness*, and you are spreading it through the city. It is not your *place*. Sin entered the world through women, Miss Fox. You have invited the Devil in. Consider Calvin Brown's death your punishment.'

She recoiled as if he had struck her. Her eyes burned. She could think of nothing else to say.

He lowered his voice, so she could barely hear him. 'There are no spirits talking to you,' he said. 'It's the Devil, whispering in your ear. And you must renounce him.'

THIRTY-FIVE

Mr. Sullivan thought his ideas were new, but men had known for centuries that the mind could be deceived. That words could be whispered in the ear. That a person could become possessed with strange powers.

Only they did not call it science. They called the Devil what he was. And those who made a contract with him, they called witches.

Maggie went to her room after the minister had left. She sat on the edge of the bed. She felt that somebody had their hands around her throat.

Calvin would have liked Mr. Sullivan's ideas. Because Calvin was curious, and liked science, and believed the best in people. He did not believe in God, did not believe that there was a soul to be lost or saved.

He was wrong.

Mr. Sullivan, she thought, was perhaps half right. The things that had happened, they had done themselves. But there was no sickness or trauma that gave a person unearthly powers. There was no grief that made candlesticks fall or tables move.

There was only the Devil. Loping through the garden at Andrew McIlwraith's, rapping on the walls in Hydesville and pretending to be a murdered peddler. Watching her from behind the schoolhouse. Grasping her hand, and leading her here, to this sick yellow city where they sold tickets to strangers to come and see them perform, where Calvin died.

The Devil. She should have recognized him sooner, and she hadn't. That was her sin, and now she had been punished.

Waiting for her, in the parlor. Watching her, from behind the schoolhouse.

She tried to remember what had happened in the schoolhouse, but the memory was now distorted. Hannah Crane, flying through the air.

Perhaps she *had* thrown her. Perhaps the Devil had guided Maggie's hand to do his work, his mischief, and Mr. Crane had been right all along.

The Devil had found her that day in Rochester, and instead of praying for salvation she and her sister had invited him to stay.

And they had been punished for it.

THIRTY-SIX
ARCADIA
SEPTEMBER 1848

She hadn't seen David's farm in nearly a year. It was early September, and the evening light had begun to change. Cobwebs sparkled across the fencing that David and Calvin had built a few years ago. The air was clean and the sky spread out empty and blue.

Maggie and Kate held hands as they walked from the house down the gentle slope that led to the family plot: a piece of flat land, bounded by trees. A collection of small, neat headstones, and the freshly dug earth where Calvin would be buried.

A few men and women from the town had come. David, Maria, Leah, their mother and father, and the children, were already stood around the grave, waiting. Their father's shoulders were hunched and his eyes distant and watery behind his spectacles. He had hardly spoken to the girls since they arrived. It was as if he didn't recognize them.

The coffin was waiting, with ropes beneath it, ready to lift. The children clustered together clinging to each other's arms, frightened and fascinated.

Maggie found she couldn't look at the coffin, so she studied the clear sky, instead, and found that if she tilted her head back that helped to stop her tears. Kate was making soft, shuddering gasps next to her. Maggie squeezed her hand but she didn't look. The complex light of the September sky, mixed with gold, alive with insects and birds. She could smell the damp earth, the wet grass. The men – she didn't know all of them – grunted as they lifted and began to lower the coffin, and Maggie heard another, gentle sob – her mother – and then the rough thud of the coffin meeting the ground. She did not want to hear this sound, or think about it.

She looked back. The men dropped the ropes. One wiped his hands against his coat, and another made the sign of the cross. All of them stayed for a moment, looking down into the hole. And then one of them reached for a shovel.

The men took turns throwing dirt down into the grave. David's eyes were red and his mouth was twisted up. He heaved a shovelful of earth back from where it had been dug up and pitched it back down into the grave.

And then it was done. The group broke apart and began to walk back to the house. Maggie stayed where she was.

Wind rustled through the leaves and the sky darkened. In the city they would have been beginning to prepare their evening reception. That time of the evening, the turn of the light, it would cast a shiver of excitement and anticipation through their guests as they began to arrive at the hotel.

How false it all seemed. Here in the cooling air, surrounded by the whispering grass and creaking trees, the soil.

The new headstone was small, but it matched the others. She liked that. And David knew the stonemason in town, who had done the work for next to nothing, and so the stone said *Calvin Brown, beloved son and brother and dear friend*. Her father had wanted something from the Bible, but David had dissuaded him.

Maggie crouched down on the ground and placed her hand on the stone. 'We love you so much,' she said. 'I hope you were wrong about it all, so that we'll see you again.' Pain in her throat, in her eyes and head. 'We love you so much.'

A bird of some kind had begun to sing in the branches above. Maggie listened to it for a moment, and then stood up, and brushed down her skirt. They would all be waiting in the kitchen, talking, ready to eat. Her eyes stung with tears. She had to go. She had to leave him here in the ground, alone.

But she stayed for a while, as long as she could, as night began to fall around her.

THIRTY-SEVEN

In the house, the men sat in the kitchen, talking in low voices. Leah sat alone by the window, chin resting on her hand, looking out at the darkening evening.

Maggie crossed the kitchen and the hall to the small parlor at the back of the house, where she found Kate and her mother sitting in candlelight. In the middle of the table was a copper ring that Calvin used to wear sometimes, and a folded letter.

'What are you doing?' said Maggie.

They both turned as if they had been waiting for her.

Their mother looked old, Maggie thought. Her soft, kind face was drawn and tired. 'Maggie. My sweet girl. Please come and sit with us. We just want to sit for a little while, and see.'

Maggie's hands went cold. 'And see what?'

Her sad, tired eyes. Maggie saw her try to smile. 'And see if Calvin reaches out to us.'

Kate was watching her with a solemn expression. 'He might,' she said quietly. Then she bit her lip, and looked at the table.

Maggie was shaking her head. 'No. No. You shouldn't do that.'

'Maggie—' Her mother reached toward her.

'No. It's wrong. He's gone. He's at peace. It's wrong to try.'

'But—'

'No. Please don't.'

'Of course he's at peace,' her mother said. 'I only want a sign of it, just something, so I know. So I can be sure.'

'He wouldn't want you to.'

'He wouldn't mind,' Kate said. 'You know he wouldn't. Just sit with us, Maggie, for a little bit. We won't do anything, we won't make him talk. We'll just wait. I think he's still here. I can *feel* him. He's not gone yet. He might have a message for us.'

Maggie swiped at the tears on her face. 'I have to talk to you upstairs, Katie,' she said. She had to stop this. She should have known it would happen. If they had never started this, Calvin would be alive.

'No. Not now. Afterward. I just want to try—'

'It's dangerous,' Maggie said. 'Mother, please. You shouldn't – it isn't right, to do this. You don't know who might answer.'

Their mother looked confused. 'Maggie,' she said softly. 'You've talked to so many spirits. I only want to hear from Calvin one more time.'

'It won't be one more time. It never is. You'll talk to him and then you'll want to come back, again and again. You'll never let him go. That's what happens to people.' Something was stabbing at her heart. 'We have to let him go.'

'We don't,' said Kate. 'I don't want to.' Her voice broke. 'Please do it with us. We'll be stronger—'

But Maggie was backing out of the room. 'No,' she said. 'No, Katie. No. I won't. I won't.'

She fled upstairs to the attic bedroom, and turned up each of the corner lamps until the room was as bright as it could be and through the dark window she could only see her reflection. In the bedroom below, she could hear one of the children laughing. She flinched from the sound, and felt a rush of anger. They would all forget Calvin before long, she thought. He wouldn't mean any more to them than any of the other names in the family plot did to her. And they were *laughing*. She made a fist and then she hit the wall, twice, a third time, and then beat weakly at her own head, with a sob of frustration.

Footsteps on the stairs. She turned to see Leah standing in the doorway, one hand resting on the frame, dark shadows under her eyes. Maggie's own hands dropped to her sides.

'Can I come in?' Leah asked.

If she spoke, Maggie thought she would cry, or scream, so she shook her head and screwed her eyes closed for a moment. After a pause, she heard Leah come into the room. Leah sat down on the edge of Kate's bed, smoothing her skirt beneath her, and folding her hands.

A shriek from the children's room, and more laughter. 'It's like a party to them, everybody here at once,' said Leah quietly.

'Not everybody.' Maggie forced out the words.

Leah looked over Maggie's shoulder toward the window. 'No. Not everybody.'

'Do you know what's happening? Katie and Mother are trying to—' She could hardly bear to say it. Her voice did not sound like her own. 'They want to contact him. Calvin.'

'I know.'

'You know. You *know*.' Her head was spinning. 'Of course you know.'

'Why shouldn't they? If it comforts them.'

'They're taking comfort from a delusion.'

'I'm sure Kate won't try any tricks, not when it's Calvin.'

284

'It's *not* Calvin. It won't be.'

Another bright crack of laughter from the children's room, and this time Leah flinched as well. They heard David's feet thumping up the stairs to reprimand them.

Leah spoke quietly. 'You don't know that. And whatever it is, it will help them.'

'They should take comfort in God.'

'They do.'

'They should take comfort in their faith. Not this.'

'This *is* their faith,' said Leah. 'It's no different.'

Maggie swallowed, and shook her head, which sent a pulse of pain through her body. The room was close, and airless. She stood and went to the window, pushed it open and breathed the cool air, but it wasn't enough.

'You're behaving strangely, Maggie.'

She choked on a laugh. Tears blurred her eyes. 'I *am* strange,' she said. 'So are you.'

'Fine.'

David's voice through the wall, telling the children to be quiet or they would all have to go to bed, and to show some respect for their uncle Calvin.

'Maggie,' Leah said. 'Maggie.' There was a long pause, David's feet going back downstairs, some wild animal barking out in the woods. Then Leah said, 'We had a letter. Just before we left the city. Inviting us to visit Cleveland, Ohio. A tour. There's a gentleman who has already found a number of venues.'

The land rolled out dark and endless all around them. Calvin, alone out there in the dark. Who was so scared of being sent away. Calvin.

Leah's words made no sense, they churned in her mind like a wild sea. *Ohio. A letter. A gentleman.*

She turned back. Leah was looking into the fireplace, which was dark and dead. It had been too warm to make up a fire since they had arrived.

How awful that Leah would think of things like this, now. Leah had a type of sickness too, she thought. Greed. She couldn't stop herself.

'No,' she said. 'I won't go.'

Leah didn't look at her. 'Not right away. In a few weeks. I still have some business in the city I ought to attend to, in any case. And I need to visit Rochester this week.'

Maggie wiped furiously at her eyes. 'Not in a few weeks,' she said. 'Not ever. I won't go.'

Leah turned to her. 'You won't go.'

'I won't.'

'What do you mean?'

She saw Calvin outside their house in Hydesville on that bright cold morning, surrounded by fresh snow, holding his coffee. Saying: *Are you doing it, somehow?*

He had almost no time left to live.

'I don't want to do this anymore,' she said. 'I want to stop.'

As soon as it was said, she felt weak with relief. She could barely stand, but she wanted to. She wanted to stand taller than Leah. She leaned against the wall instead, hands pressed flat against it.

Leah's expression didn't change, but it was a long time before she answered. 'And what will you do instead?'

'Sleep. Rest. Help Mother, help on the farm, find work, teach – marry. I don't know.'

'You'll come to hate all of those things.'

'I don't care.'

'You have an opportunity to travel all over the country. To see places that no other girl your age—'

286

'This is an awful country and I don't want to see any more of it.'

'Ohio isn't a slave state, if that's your concern. In fact, Amy and Isaac have a number of friends there—'

'I don't care.'

'You need more time, then. A month. You'll feel differently.'

'No.'

'Our hearts are broken, Maggie,' Leah said, very quietly. 'My heart is broken too. I can hardly stand it.'

Was she crying again? She couldn't tell anymore. Her eyes stung, but it might only be exhaustion.

'But that's simply the way it is,' Leah continued. 'It will be the same here, it will be the same in Cleveland, the same in New York City. We'll miss him exactly the same way, wherever we are.'

'That isn't it.'

'We can wait a month, but not much longer. People are beginning to practice spirit-talking for themselves, and who can blame them. I've already seen advertisements for other gatherings. If we don't perform for months on end then we'll be replaced.'

'Good.'

'You don't mean that.'

'We should never have gone to New York City. Kate is too young and it made – it made Calvin sick.'

'We don't know what made Calvin sick. His parents died young. It runs in the blood. Wherever he was he might have been fated—'

'No.' Yes. She was crying. Tears made sticky tracks across her face. 'No. It's a punishment.'

'From who?'

She shook her head, couldn't answer.

'From God?' Leah said, and Maggie couldn't quite tell if her voice was scathing.

'I don't know. Maybe. Yes. I think so.'

Leah was silent for a long time. 'We'll talk when I come back from Rochester. I'm leaving in two days, and I'll be gone for a week. You'll have time to think.'

'I won't change my mind.'

'We'll see.'

'Don't you ever feel ashamed, Leah? Of what we do?'

'No.'

'We lie to people.'

'These people don't mind being lied to. Both you and Katie believe in the spirits in any case, so you can hardly call it—'

'No. I don't believe it anymore. I don't believe the spirits are who they say they are.'

'Maggie—'

'It's shameful, what we do,' Maggie said. 'And it's blasphemy. Against the holy scripture. It's—'

'*Maggie.*' Leah's voice came out harsh, scraped raw. 'Who told you that it's blasphemy?'

'They said it in the paper, in the hotel. Men of God. You know they do.'

'Men of God.' Leah was shaking her head. 'They're angry because something is slipping beyond their control, Maggie. We're offering a kind of faith that can be practiced in whatever way people choose. That can be practiced in homes, in parlors, that can be led by women. These men have stood in pulpits and preached the supernatural for hundreds of years. Why shouldn't we have a chance?'

'Leah, you do it for money.'

'You do it for money too, little sister, and why *shouldn't* we?' She stood up, color rising in her face. 'Why *shouldn't* we? It's what everybody else in this country is doing, and what we do brings more joy and comfort than selling liquor, I can assure you.' Leah lowered her voice again. 'That's what Calvin thought. He believed in human beings living the way they chose to.'

'He followed us because he wanted to help us, because he loved us, not because he wanted to be rich.'

'Nobody here is *rich*, Maggie. David has no money – I send him as much as I can but he has five children and the roof needs fixing and without Calvin he's had to hire a man – and our parents will work their hands to the bone until they drop dead unless we find a way to help them and I don't want that for them, any more than I want it for you, so *don't* suggest to me that anybody is getting rich.'

For a moment Maggie had no reply. She didn't want to think about money, whether they had it or they didn't. It didn't matter. 'I'm *afraid*, Leah. I'm afraid to carry on.'

'Afraid of what?'

She couldn't bear the conversation any longer, couldn't bear the sight of Leah's face. She looked past her, into the corner, directly at the lamplight, as long as her eyes could stand it. 'Ghosts,' she said. 'I'm afraid of ghosts.'

THIRTY-EIGHT

When she woke in the morning, it was clear to her what she should do.

She would travel to Rochester with Leah, and tell Amy the truth. That most of it had been fakery, and the rest she couldn't explain, other than to say that it was wrong, an affront to God. And she had renounced it. Wine, and attention. Gifts, and fine dresses, and jars of rock candy. All of it.

The house was quiet. The men were out working and the children playing somewhere. She went downstairs in her nightdress, and found some apples that had been brought up from the cellar.

She took one outside. Kate was sitting on the porch, also in her nightdress, but with one of David's old coats on top of it. The morning was cool, the sky golden blue.

Maggie sat down next to her.

Kate shot her a quick glance, and then looked away. 'I'm sorry,' she said. 'I'm sorry that we tried to speak to Calvin when you didn't want us to.'

Sunlight caught the edge of Kate's eyelashes, turned them gold. She was taller than she had been even two weeks ago, with her pale legs kicked out in front of her.

'But it made me feel better. Just to speak to him. So I won't promise that I won't do it again.'

'*Did* you speak to him?'

She rubbed her nose. 'I spoke. Mother spoke. He didn't answer but we still spoke to him.'

Maggie took a bite of her apple, but found she could hardly taste it. She had an empty feeling. Now that she had made her decision, she felt calm and cold and flat as a lake.

'I know about Ohio,' Kate said, not looking at her.

Maggie looked down the slope toward the graves, fresh dirt from Calvin's still visible against the morning sky.

'Leah told me, this morning,' Kate continued. 'She said you won't go.'

'I won't.'

'But I want to.'

'What's happened is a lesson. Calvin was a lesson. Telling us to stop.'

'He wasn't a lesson. He was a person.'

'And he was taken from us to show us – to teach us. That what we were doing is wrong.'

'I don't believe that.' Kate said. 'It's a gift, from God, when we hear the spirits, and when we don't it's still a gift, because it helps people.'

'It's not our place to mediate between the spiritual world and this one.'

'It is our place. It's where we are. Wherever we are is our place.'

She was talking in riddles, like a little girl. Maggie closed her eyes. 'You know in Ohio we wouldn't be talking with spirits. It'll be Leah, and her tricks. It'll be bits of string and hidden levers.'

'Those tricks were ours first. We started it. Not her.'

'That doesn't matter.' She looked at her sister, the light on her face and her round dark eyes looking into the distance like her whole future was waiting there.

'The tricks wake the spirits up,' Kate said softly. 'Like the peddler.'

Maggie put down her apple, and took Kate's hand. 'Katie, I'm going to go with Leah to Rochester.' she said. 'Tomorrow.'

Kate narrowed her eyes, suddenly suspicious. 'Why?'

'I want to see Amy.'

'I'll go too.'

'You should stay here with Mother. She needs you.'

'So should you. She needs you too.'

'I can't. I have to go. There are some things I have to do.'

More correctly, there were some things she had to un-do. And Kate would never let her, if she knew.

'It's only for a few days,' she said.

'And then what will happen?'

'I don't know.'

'Will you come back here?'

'I don't know. I suppose so.'

Kate frowned. 'There's a letter for you. From Amy. So you don't need to see her.'

'There's a letter for me?'

'Yes. David went to town early and picked up the mail. It's on the mantelpiece.'

Maggie handed her barely eaten apple to Kate, who made a face, but took it. Then she stood up, so she cast a shadow that fell across Kate's face. 'It's all going to be alright, Katie,' she said. 'I'm the big sister, so you have to trust me.'

Kate gave her a long, silent look, and took a bite of the apple.

Maggie found the letter weighted beneath a butter dish, and took it to her room to read.

Dear Maggie:

I have thought of you every day since we heard the news about dear Calvin. Since your visit in the city we have been traveling, and I am bitterly sorry not to have been at his funeral, and not to have been with your family in your grief. I know that he was a son and brother to you, and you will feel his absence greatly.

You know that many friends of ours have begun to take an interest in communication with the spiritual world. Isaac has also become fascinated with it, and has tried to reach out himself to the spirits – with some success, it would seem. Though I confess I have had my doubts, I still find myself full of hope and wonder to think that the distance between the spirit world and our own might not be so great as we once thought.

This belief is a great comfort to many, especially those overwhelmed with the pain of bereavement, as I have been in years past. And I hope it is a comfort to you at this time, to think that Calvin is still with you, and always will be.

There are those who have long found the churches in our country to be inhospitable places, and who have struggled to find ministers who can truly deepen their relationship with God. Perhaps through personal communication with spirits, they may be better able to know God on their own terms.

I have seen the critical letters in the newspapers, and heard the cruel remarks, Maggie. I thought you might have wished to talk about it when you visited us at Mr. Sullivan's house, but I didn't feel it was my place to raise the matter. But please be assured, I think you should pay very little heed to these critics. When men are so full of rage at young girls, you can be sure they know that their power is threatened.

Spirit-talking does indeed pose some challenge to the common institutions of power. But I know you will agree that there are some institutions which are sorely in need of challenge.

I do hope it will not be long before we are all together again, but knowing that you are often traveling with your sisters, I shall be patient.

Wherever you may go next, my heart and my good wishes go with you.

Your affectionate friend,
Amy Post

She read the letter three times, and then slipped it back into its envelope. She sat down by the empty fire, and brushed her thumb over her own name, written neatly on the front. She thought for a moment of throwing it into the fireplace. But of course the fire was not made up and probably wouldn't be for days. She could take it outside and light it with a candle. Or tear it up and scatter the paper across the grass. She shouldn't read it again, because she did not deserve those kind words, and it would only make it harder to tell Amy the truth.

She slipped it into her pocket. She would carry it. That was all.

THIRTY-NINE
ROCHESTER
SEPTEMBER 1848

Early the next morning, her father was sitting at the kitchen table, eating eggs that Maggie had prepared for him. They had come out well, she thought, and she watched him eating, hoping for praise. But he only nodded at her, and turned back to his plate, still treating her as if she was a stranger.

But he had loved Calvin, she knew that, and he was knotted up with grief as well. So she tried to make herself feel kindly toward him.

Her small trunk was already in the carriage, and Leah was waiting for her. So Maggie left her father to his breakfast and said goodbye to her mother, promising to return in a few days. Then David drove them to Newark, to take the Erie Canal packet-boat to Rochester. They would not arrive until the evening, but first thing the next day she would visit Amy. She would do it before she had time to doubt herself. Once Amy knew the truth, it was done with.

They barely spoke on the journey and arrived in Rochester tired and irritable. The house had a musty smell, and Leah moved from room to room, silently opening windows to the chill evening, wiping her fingers along the dusty surfaces. 'I will hire someone,' she murmured, to herself, as she passed by.

Maggie went to the room that had been hers and Kate's. The bed was not made up, and she had to search the cupboards for sheets and blankets which she threw, disordered, on to the bed. And then, although it was not so late and there was still a trace of light in the sky, she took off her clothes and crawled beneath the covers. Her mind ached at the thought of what she had to do in the morning, and she curled up, knees to her chest. In the darkness she tried to pray, but the words wouldn't come. She pulled a blanket over her head and kept it there until it became too hot and close to breathe.

I will atone, she thought, tomorrow I will start to atone.

She closed her eyes and tried again to pray.

When she woke, it was fully dark and she knew immediately that somebody was in the room.

She sat up, and saw Calvin sitting on the wooden chair by the door.

It was too dark to make him out properly, but she recognized the shape of him, and the way he sat, leaning forward, with his elbows on his knees and his hands clasped. The shadowed outline of his face.

She could hear him breathing.

He was looking at her.

She could hear him breathing, because his breath rattled, the way it had when he first became sick.

She was very cold. She sat without moving.

The window was open, though she did not remember opening it. The curtains were pulled back. It was not so dark after all. Small points of bright white light patterned the wall like stars, and Calvin—

– and Calvin.

She heard the small inhalation of breath that a person made before they spoke, though he did not move, and only silence followed.

The tiny lights turned on the walls.

'Calvin,' she whispered finally. Her voice sounded like cold broken glass. 'Calvin. It isn't you.'

The shape that could not be Calvin did not move.

And then the air smelled of grass, and coffee. She was racing toward the fencepost. She was looking at his parents' graves.

She was sitting in the dark, looking at him.

'Calvin.' Something wet on her face. She was crying, or it was snowing. 'Calvin. I'm dreaming.'

'Are you?' His voice was warm, and hoarse, as if it was early in the morning.

'Or I'm sick. Or you're the Devil.'

'No such thing.'

'There is. I've seen him.'

'You haven't. Nobody has.'

'Calvin.' She pressed her hands over her eyes, and heard a ragged, choking sob. Her own. 'I'm sorry.'

There was no reply. She couldn't move her hands. She was frightened to look. Frightened he would be gone, or still be there.

'I don't know what to believe,' she whispered into the silence. 'I don't know what I'm seeing. I can't trust myself.'

He was on the step outside the house in Hydesville, holding a cup of coffee, shielding his eyes against the bright snow. He was sick and dying in a New York hotel.

She took her hands away.

He was there. He was looking at her.

'I think you should go back to the schoolhouse,' he said. 'They must have finished that new building by now.'

It was an echo. She had heard the words before. She

searched her mind for the memory, and found it. Standing at his parents' graves, trying to persuade her that ghosts were not real and there was no such thing as a soul.

'Calvin—'

And then he looked to the side, as if he had heard somebody call his name, and then he wasn't there anymore.

A glass smashed, and Leah let out a cry of frustration that carried up the stairs into Maggie's room: Maggie sat up, sharply awake and with her heart pounding in shock. It was dawn. The light was gray and there was birdsong outside. Sheets were tangled around her legs. Out of habit, she looked for Kate, sleeping beside her, but of course Kate's bed was empty. And she looked at the wooden chair by the door, which was empty too. She was alone. She told herself that she had dreamed him.

I think you should go back to the schoolhouse.

Only a dream. But dreams could be meaningful. She could take instruction from them.

He was right. She should see it again.

She found Leah in the kitchen, on her knees sweeping broken glass into a pan, still in a nightdress. 'Leah.'

Her sister didn't look up. Her shoulders were hunched.

'Leah.'

'This is one of Mrs. Jordan's glasses. I'll have to replace it.'

'Leah, I have to ask you something.'

'Of course I've no way of knowing where it came from.'

'Leah.'

She sat back on her heels and looked up. 'Leah *what*?'

'The new school building.'

'Yes?'

'Did they finish it? Do you know?'

298

Leah closed her eyes briefly, as if summoning strength. 'I imagine so, Maggie, but I haven't kept up with every tedious morsel of news emerging from Rochester.'

'So you don't know?'

'I don't care, either.'

Maggie watched for a moment, as Leah went back to sweeping the glass. Then she turned away, walked barefoot into the parlor, where their table was covered with a white sheet, and the bookshelves were lined with dust. She went to the shelves, traced a finger along the spines of the books, which were all immaculate as if they had never been read, except for one, which jutted out, as if somebody had been reading it just a moment ago, and had placed it back carelessly, expecting to pick it up again at a later time. *Principles of Electricity and Magnetism.*

It was the book Calvin had been reading, that afternoon when they practiced on him, performed a séance and pretended to call up somebody named Ethan. He had slid it back on to the shelf, and never picked it up again.

Ethan. How unkind they had been that day, thinking they would use Calvin's dead parents to impress him with their performance. She was thankful it hadn't worked, and they had spelled out a meaningless name instead.

Nobody had touched these shelves since that day. It was a lonely thought. She took the book, and let it fall open. A corner had been folded, to mark his page. He had always done this. She remembered her father scolding him for folding the page of a Bible. She scanned the words on the page, though she knew it was not the sort of book she would ever want to read. *We must not rely only on the evidence of our senses, or that which we think we perceive in the natural world, but on a more rigorous method.*

If she closed her eyes she could see him. Smell coffee and hair oil. Hear his voice. What was that evidence of?

'What are you doing?' Leah's voice startled her. She stood in the doorway. She looked fragile in her nightdress. They were both barefoot, when there might be broken glass.

Maggie closed the book and held it against her chest. 'Leah,' she said. 'I'm going to take a walk.'

FORTY

It was six blocks east to Amy's house. It was four blocks east, to the school. What harm could it do, to go there first? She was about to atone, to confess everything to Amy: surely the Devil had no time for her anymore. She would see the schoolhouse and know that it was not haunted, and never had been. Just as Calvin had told her in April.

She had lost track of the days, and she had to think for a while to remember that it was Saturday. There were lessons at the school on Saturdays, or there used to be, but it was still early, and they wouldn't start for another hour. The streets were quiet. It was still cool, and the morning light was soft. As she approached the schoolhouse, she saw that the door was closed. The clock above it showed eight o'clock. She hadn't stopped for breakfast, and couldn't remember when she had last eaten. Hunger gnawed at her stomach.

The school was closed, of course it was. But she could walk around the side to where the cemetery had been. There had only ever been a rusty gate there, hanging from its hinges.

She averted her eyes from the schoolhouse steps as she pushed the gate and forced herself forward, treading carefully through the overgrown grass that lined the path. Dew made the edges of her skirt damp.

Then she came around the far corner to where the new building should be, and saw only dirt and the abandoned

301

foundations and four corner timber pillars, standing stark against the sky as they had been last November.

She closed her eyes, opened them again, and saw the same thing. The September sun dappled the grass with pale light. A breeze shook through the surrounding trees, and the pillars creaked faintly. Everything was quiet.

No: something was different. It was not all the same as last year. It took her a moment to find it.

A few feet away, the weathered gravestones that had been inside the schoolhouse were now laid carefully beneath the trees. Some were flat, and some propped up. They had been placed with care, at even distances.

She hesitated, then took a few steps toward the trees. She looked behind her, but saw only the back door of the schoolhouse, closed, and the empty windows.

She stopped in front of one of the stones. It was familiar. Her skin tingled, as if a hand had brushed her arm.

She crouched, tucking her skirt between her knees, and ran a hand over the weathered surface of the stone. Only fragments of the words remained. – *ry nd Eli – 17*—

'Mary?' she said quietly. She tried another, to see how it would sound. '*Elijah?*'

Her voice landed in the soft, silent air and disappeared. Stop this, she thought.

She was startled by the sound of the door swinging open behind her, and she spun around.

So much had happened since she had last seen her teacher that for a moment Maggie couldn't remember her name.

Miss Kelly. She stood framed in the doorway. She wore a dark skirt and a white blouse, a small silver pendant around her neck. Her long dark hair in a braid that hung over her shoulder and her blue eyes as sharp as ever.

The children used to be afraid to be alone with her, in case she had one of her fits and there was nobody else to help. This fear came to Maggie briefly. Unthinking, she took a step back, almost stumbling on the gravestone.

'I'm sorry.' Miss Kelly stepped out. 'I didn't mean to frighten you. I saw you from the window. I thought you were one of the children, or somebody lost.' She folded her arms over her chest, and shivered. 'Maggie. It *is* you. I wondered.'

Awkward, as if she had been caught misbehaving in a lesson, Maggie said: 'Miss Kelly, I didn't know anybody—'

'What are you doing here?'

Calvin sent me, she thought, and then tried to dismiss it. 'I'm visiting Rochester for a few days. And I thought – I wanted to see.'

'To see?'

'The new building.'

'Oh.' Miss Kelly paused for a moment, and then gestured toward the abandoned structure. 'Well, here you are. Beautiful, isn't it?'

'It isn't finished.'

'You were always observant.'

'Why not?' she said. 'What happened? All this time—'

'It won't be finished. It was abandoned in the summer. The men haven't been here in months. There were a series of misfortunes and they were frightened away.'

'Misfortunes?'

'A ladder broke and Colson Tyler was almost killed. Lightning struck one of the beams and it caught fire. Davy Whitman hammered a nail through his own hand. I'm sure there were more. So they gave it up.' She glanced up and down the pillars. 'A few weeks ago I finally found some

303

neighbors to help me move the gravestones back. They're as close to the original sites as I could remember.'

Maggie's thoughts scattered. 'Mr. Crane, the men, their money—'

'They took their money away. They'll build their new schools elsewhere. I'm sure somebody will come by to salvage the timber eventually.' Miss Kelly gave another shiver, and rubbed her arms. She paused, tilted her head, and fixed Maggie with a complicated look. And then said: 'Mr. Crane went to New York City, in any case. With Hannah.'

Maggie met her eye and had to look away. She pulled her coat close around her shoulders, and did not respond. There was no warmth in the sun and the breeze carried the chill of the coming fall. 'I know.'

Miss Kelly said: 'I hear you've been in the city as well. You and Kate.'

'Yes,' she said, but she did not offer any more information. She felt somehow that Miss Kelly was trying to provoke her.

They were both silent for a moment.

'You look very tired, Maggie. Would you like to come inside?'

She thought of the schoolhouse behind her: the dusty air, the high windows and long dark hall. Grasping a little girl's hand as she ran for the door.

She shook her head. 'I'd like to stay here for a little while. If you don't mind.'

'I'll make you some coffee, then. I usually have a cup before the first lesson. Wait here.'

She went back inside. Maggie looked down, brushing a hand absently over her skirt. She had been wearing it for days. She thought of all the lovely new clothes they had had in the city that were left behind, packed away in trunks at the hotel with the idea that they would return for them.

She would not return for them. Everything in New York City was tainted by Calvin's death.

She could hear the beat of hooves passing on the road behind, but no voices, as if a horse might be pulling an empty carriage through the quiet streets.

Around her, the turned, damp earth. A few discarded boards and abandoned stone blocks. Beneath her—

This was still a cemetery, whatever they had done with it.

She had told Calvin once that the dead should be buried properly. It was important, she said. *So they can be at peace.* It was what had always been done. You had to be careful with the dead. All religions knew it, all humans, they were born knowing it.

You could not dig up tombstones and toss them carelessly aside, or break them, and expect no consequences.

She shivered, and closed her eyes for a moment. Her mind was beginning to roam, her thoughts coming loose.

No. She must stop these thoughts. It didn't matter where the tombstones were.

The door creaked open again, and Miss Kelly stood behind her, two cups in her hands. She gave one to Maggie. It was steaming and almost too hot to hold. The smell was different from the watery coffee at the hotel. This was more like the coffee that David's wife Maria made at the farm.

Miss Kelly stood next to her, and blew over the surface of the cup. An ordinary person might have filled the quiet with polite, meaningless conversation. But Maggie felt she had forgotten how to be ordinary, and Miss Kelly had perhaps never known.

305

'The children all tell stories about you, you know. It began after Hannah was hurt.'

Maggie took a scalding sip of coffee and felt it burn her tongue, too hot to taste. Her heart began to beat faster. 'What stories? That I threw her?'

'Oh, no. They heard the story of your evil man, and they found that much more fun. Mr. Crane's version wasn't very interesting to them.' A faint smile crossed her face. 'The little ones were terrified one day and thrilled the next. They all began claiming to have seen him. I had complaints from their parents. They thought I might have been spreading those ideas. Which of course I wasn't, but they like to tell stories about me around here too.'

It was strange to be spoken to like this by Miss Kelly, almost like a friend, as if Maggie was now grown up and could be taken into confidence.

She *was* grown up, she thought, and she should act like it. She took another sip of coffee, her heart still skittering. She said the words she had rehearsed in her mind: 'They shouldn't have believed it, about the man. *I* shouldn't have believed it. I don't know what happened that day but it isn't right to go around talking about ghosts and spirits. It's' – she forced the word out – 'blasphemous. It opens the door to the Devil. Whatever I saw, I was deceived.'

But yet. She couldn't help but think it. There had been more accidents. The building had to be abandoned. As if something was angry, something was disturbed – and now the stones had been returned—

No. She felt Miss Kelly studying her. Again she tried to silence her unruly thoughts. To concentrate on real things: the scalding coffee, the damp grass.

She looked toward the darkness of the trees. A few of the

branches shook, and then stilled. A bird or some other animal moving unseen.

'Shall we sit?' Miss Kelly said, and before Maggie could respond she had turned and gone back to the door, brushing a few leaves away from the step and sitting down, her coffee in both hands held up to her chin.

Maggie hesitated for a moment – it wasn't right, was it, to sit on the ground like little children instead of grown women? – but Miss Kelly seemed to be waiting for her. And Maggie was hungry, and her legs had begun to feel weak. So she sat.

They were quiet, for a while.

'Who told you that, about the Devil?' Miss Kelly said eventually.

'It doesn't matter.'

'I have to say that you don't sound as if you really believe it, Maggie.'

Maggie put her coffee down, and brought her knees up to her chest, wrapping her arms around them. 'I don't know what I believe sometimes,' she said. The chill air had brought tears to her eyes and she wiped them with the back of her hand. Miss Kelly made a sound, neither agreement nor disagreement, and Maggie said, 'You should know. You know all of the Bible, Miss Kelly, I've heard you quote from all of it. And Shakespeare, and all of those things. You should know about the Devil.'

'I do. I know all of it. I know Mark chapter nine, verses fourteen to twenty-nine, for instance. Jesus heals a boy possessed by an impure spirit. He falls to the ground in a convulsion and Jesus drives the spirit from him.' Miss Kelly smiled briefly. 'Convulsions. I've been possessed by the same impure spirit myself, all my life. But Jesus hasn't appeared to me yet.'

Maggie thought of Miss Kelly grasping the back of a chair, her face turning white, her eyes going vacant, whispering, *'I'm sorry, it will pass.'* Or falling sideways, her body shaking. The children clutching each other's arms in fear and excitement.

Miss Kelly said: 'The Devil is a name for things we can't explain, which frighten us.'

It sounded like something Amy would say. Maggie shook her head. 'No. That isn't the same. They know it's a disease, it's a sickness, what happens to you. They know that now. A lot of people know that. They don't think—'

'A disease, yes. That's true. So it's either sickness or possession. Between the ministers and the scientists, I have been *explained*. How fortunate.' Miss Kelly gave her a sharp smile. 'If you ever begin to doubt yourself, Maggie, you never have to look far to find a man who can explain everything.'

Maggie closed her eyes. 'I *have* begun to doubt myself,' she said softly. She saw a yellow dress, a little girl's bent arms. 'Perhaps I did throw Hannah down the steps.'

Miss Kelly paused, and traced a finger around the rim of her coffee cup. Then she said, 'You know that you didn't.'

'I don't know that. How *can* I know?'

'By trusting yourself.'

'But I can't. I don't.'

Miss Kelly did not answer. Maggie opened her eyes. She ought to leave. She ought to go to Amy's. She had a task, and she was failing at it. She had dreamed about Calvin and it had muddied everything, and now Miss Kelly was making it worse.

'Maggie,' Miss Kelly said. Her voice had changed. She sat up straight. 'Perhaps I owe you an apology.'

Maggie turned toward her. 'What do you mean?'

She studied Maggie for a moment, as if she were applying some sort of test. And then she said, 'He had a dark beard, didn't he?'

The breeze died, and the air became still.

'And that hat,' Miss Kelly said. 'And his sunken cheeks. I think he might have starved to death; there were settlers who did back then. That's a bad death. I never saw the woman move but I saw her standing just beneath the trees one evening, watching me.'

Maggie did not move. She did not breathe. There was no birdsong, no scratching of animals in the trees. Only the two of them, sitting on the step. Maggie's heart pounded in her ears.

'I'm sorry,' Maggie heard herself say. 'I don't understand.'

Miss Kelly spoke as if to a small child. 'I saw him, Maggie.'

The smell of earth and grass, the coffee, the September morning: all of it had become soft and distanced. She could only see Miss Kelly. The faint shadows beneath her eyes, the redness in her cheeks, a tiny scar on her chin. Every detail was sharp.

'I saw him here,' Miss Kelly said. 'A few days after Hannah was hurt. Early one morning, I saw him stalking up and down the hall. Books were falling to the floor and the desks were shaking. Then he looked at me and I fled, I ran out into the street. And then I saw him once more, at the gate to my mother's house one day when I visited, standing there as if he was waiting for me. I think he knew he'd been seen the first time, and so he'd attached himself to me somehow, trying to be seen again. He'd followed me.' She paused. 'Did you ever see him again? Did he follow you?'

Maggie's mouth was dry. She could not breathe. She saw

the small curls of soft, new hair at Miss Kelly's forehead, the tiny lines at the edge of her eyes.

Did he follow you?

It was a simple question, and nobody had ever asked it.

Yes, he had followed her. She only saw him once, perhaps twice, but he had followed because the accusations had followed her, the shame, and the power too, the power to call spirits to her and hear them talk – *yes*, yes, he had followed her, but there had been nobody to tell her it was real, nobody to say that they saw him too, she had been alone—

'Miss Kelly—'

'You can call me Anna if you like. I'm not your teacher anymore.'

'Miss Kelly.' The coffee churned in her empty stomach but another feeling was rising in her. 'Miss Kelly.' She thought she would stand. She stood. She looked down at her teacher, who had to squint against the light as she looked up.

All those men, gathered in the study last November, to talk about her. *She is mad. She is sick. She is wicked.*

'You knew,' Maggie said. 'You knew. You knew that I was telling the truth.'

'Not at first. But later, yes.'

'You could have—' It was too much, too many thoughts and questions spun in her mind at once. Was Miss Kelly wicked too, had they *both* been seduced by the Devil? 'You could have told somebody. You could have helped me.'

'Yes. I could have told somebody – I could have told everybody. But it wouldn't have helped you. They would only have thought I was mad, as well, and I have more to lose than you, Maggie.'

'But we would both have told the same story—'

'Then they would have thought us both mad, or thought

I had corrupted you, or that we were working together like the witches of Salem. They could stop me from teaching, and I'd have no income to support myself. Or they could lock me away in a hospital, an asylum, for all I know. I won't risk that. I knew you could survive it better than I could. And you did. Look at you. From what I've heard, seeing ghosts is the best thing that ever happened to you.'

'No. No.' Maggie was shaking her head. 'No. It's the worst—' But that wasn't true, was it? That power, the way she felt something reach out to her, the way she was lit up inside as her mind reached across a border – and living out there, in the world, away from her father and the endless chores and lessons, the crushing everyday, hadn't she turned her life into a wild adventure? 'It's the worst, it's the best and the worst at the same time. I can't – I can't explain.'

'I'm sorry, then,' Miss Kelly said though she did not sound particularly sorry. 'I've become used to staying silent when I see things that I shouldn't.'

Maggie could not keep up with her own thoughts. *See things I shouldn't.* 'What do you mean? What else - *who* else have you seen?'

Miss Kelly was wearing a narrow silver bracelet which she had begun to turn absently around her wrist. She was quiet for a moment before she said: 'My cousin Mary. She came on the boat with us to New York, but she died on the way. We had to wrap up her body and throw it into the water. It was terrible. I saw her often when I was a child. I'd hear her knock on the window. I knew better than to tell anybody.' She looked sideways, and Maggie saw her in profile, long dark lashes and the curve of her mouth. 'Now here I am. Telling you all this. I hope I can trust you.'

Then she turned back and their eyes met. Yes, Maggie

thought, though she knew she did not have to say it. You can trust me. What else could they do but trust each other. They were the same. She had a sudden dizzy vision of another life where Miss Kelly was her sister too, where they all traveled the country performing séances together, a chaotic crowd of spirits trailing in their wake. She could have sisters everywhere, she thought, and never know it, because they were all too afraid to speak.

'Miss Kelly – Anna—' She tried her name but it was wrong, strange and unfamiliar on her tongue. 'Miss Kelly.' For a moment she couldn't think what to ask. There was too much. She said: 'Were you frightened?'

'Of him? Of course. He had power, didn't he? Some spirits do, I think. He died angry and he carried it with him. I wasn't scared of Mary.' Miss Kelly tilted her head and studied the trees as if expecting Mary to appear through the branches. 'Are you frightened of the spirits you talk to?'

Maggie felt cut loose, untethered, on the edge of a laughter that if it began would never end. The ground had disappeared beneath her. Wildly, she said: 'Sometimes there *are* no spirits. Most of the time, in fact. We use tricks.'

Without surprise, Miss Kelly said: 'I expect you'd have to.'

'Don't you think that's wrong?'

'Wrong?'

'We deceive people.'

'I don't know, Maggie. Do *you* think it's wrong? Why do you do it?'

For money, she could say. *For attention. To console them.* All of those were true but she said something truer: 'I want people to know. I just want them to know, that there's *more*. I don't want to be alone in knowing it.'

'Yes. It's lonely, isn't it?'

But Maggie had her sisters. Miss Kelly had no one. And she was right: nobody would have believed her either. She might even have made it worse. She might have tainted Maggie with her own strange reputation. They might both have been thought witches.

'A minister—' Maggie said. She swallowed. She had told nobody what he had said to her, and she had dragged his words around like a dead creature tied to her leg. 'A minister told me that the Devil was whispering in my ear. That I had strayed from the Christian path, I brought sin into the world.' She could still feel his hand wrapped around her arm.

'Oh, the Christian path,' Miss Kelly said. 'They love to map the Christian path for us. To be sure we don't find a path of our own. Who was this minister? It sounds as if you frightened him.'

'I doubt that.'

'Don't doubt it. Our country is a project dedicated to preserving power for a privileged few, but look closely at those few and you'll see that they're all terrified. As they should be. Their power comes from violence, not moral authority. From keeping others down. They're building a country on bones.' A flush rose in her cheeks. 'And they're terrified that the dead will rise.'

Then she shook her head as if she had said too much, and began to stand, brushing down her skirt and stretching her arms out. She picked up the coffee cups. It seemed to signal that the conversation was over, which Maggie could hardly believe, when all the doors in her mind that she had tried to close had just been flung open again.

'Miss Kelly,' she said. 'Why did we see him? Why was it only us?'

313

'Some of the children saw him as well. Some of them were telling the truth about that. And Hannah did, you know that, but of course her father didn't believe her. Children are strange. They often seen things other people don't.'

'Then why not everybody?'

'I don't know, Maggie. I believe some people call it *a gift*, don't they?' There was a tired edge to her voice, but she smiled briefly. 'Perhaps it's just that we were willing to look. I'm sure Mr. Crane would have seen it too, if he'd allowed himself. But he's already made up his mind how he wants to see the world, and he won't permit himself to see anything else.'

She left Maggie standing there in the gentle morning light, with the silent gravestones and the abandoned timber frame of the building.

Her eyes fell on the names again. – *ry nd Eli – 17—*

Soon those names would be so weathered as to disappear completely.

And surely too, eventually the stones would be moved again. The trees would be cleared. And there would be more schools, more houses, more stores, more mills, more. There was no choice. Everybody knew that. There was more country to be built and they would have to live with the consequences.

Maggie pushed up the sleeve of her coat and brushed her hand over her arm, where once she'd thought she could feel the residue of his anger clinging to her skin like ash. She felt nothing but the cool air, now, but if she stood very still she suddenly realized she could feel some kind of movement beneath the ground. It was probably water, she thought, some old forgotten creek running beneath the school, just like the one that ran beneath the house in Hydesville.

Impulsively, she fell to her knees and pressed her ear against the earth to listen. Yes, she thought. She could hear something, deep in the ground, although it didn't sound like water. It sounded more like voices.

FORTY-ONE

She walked home in a state of dizzy elation, and nothing seemed real: the ordinary, brightening morning, the busy people beginning to fill the streets, the trees with their leaves turning golden, it all seemed thin and insubstantial, as if it might dissipate any moment and reveal the strange, deep truth behind it. Hunger made her light-headed and she hardly knew where she intended to go; her feet carried her home without instruction.

When she arrived at the house there was a man sitting on the steps outside. She didn't recognize him, and wondered if she was dreaming or if her spinning mind was revealing phantoms. But there was something solid about him. He was young and fair-haired, and stood up awkwardly as she approached. He straightened his hat, and raised a hand. 'Good morning,' he said, looking uncertainly at her. Her shoes were damp from the grass, her skirt was stained with mud, and she could not imagine what expression was on her face.

She stopped in front of him, forgetting how to speak, how to be ordinary, until finally dredging up the words: 'Good morning.'

He reached into his pocket and pulled out a letter, held it out as if it were his proof of invitation, which it was.

'I'm Zachary Brown,' he said. 'Leah – Mrs. Fox – Miss – Leah, she wrote to me, about Calvin. Are you her?'

'I'm her sister.'

'Oh. Well. I guess he gave her my name, anyway. I couldn't make the burial but I wanted to visit you all and pay my respects.' When Maggie didn't answer, he said, 'I'm passing through Rochester, on my way west. She gave me this address and your place in Arcadia, so – but there's no one here, she might have gone to the market or—'

'But who are you?' said Maggie.

'I should have written that I was going to be passing through,' he said, 'and I thought I should – I wanted you to know I'd received your letter, anyway.'

'My sister wrote the letters,' Maggie said. 'I didn't even know Calvin had any family.'

'He hardly did. We're cousins, but both our parents died young and we didn't see much of each other after that.' Seeing that Maggie was not going to take it, he put the letter back in his pocket. 'I saw him a few times when we were boys. I was visiting the property where he used to live, him and his parents, so that's how the letter reached me. I wanted to come. Thought it was something his parents would have liked me to do. I was sorry, I was very sorry, to hear that he passed.' He cleared his throat. 'Lot of sickness in our family,' he added.

Maggie knew she should invite him in, and wait for Leah, and make up the stove and prepare some breakfast for him. But she couldn't think how to do any of those things. She could only stare at him.

'There's no one else?' she said.

'No one else?'

'No more family.'

'Oh. No. There's a few more of us, scattered around, but none that Calvin would have known.' He removed his hat, and turned it nervously in his hands. When Maggie didn't say anything, he carried on. 'There was a bit of a feud in the family, truth be told, and Calvin's father more or less went his own way. A row with our grandfather. Probably over money. I never heard what it was about. Meant Calvin was all on his own once his parents died. I was away in Virginia at the time.'

'Oh,' she said, and then, digging deep within herself to recover her manners, she said, 'It was good of you to come.'

He glanced doubtfully again at her shoes. 'I wanted to visit.'

'I'm Maggie,' she said again. 'Maggie Fox.'

He nodded, still turning his hat. 'So you're one of the girls who talks to the spirits,' he said.

She heard herself laugh, the first time she had laughed in weeks. 'Yes. I suppose so.'

'I read about you in one of the New York City papers. And then I got your sister's letter and I put it all together.' He shook his head. 'Not sure I believe in it myself.'

'Calvin didn't either.'

'I mean, I guess I believe in spirits, but I don't know that they would rap on tables and such. Not that it's my place to say. Suppose I'd have to see it myself. Hear it myself.' He coughed. 'Will you go back to New York City soon?'

She didn't know what to say. She looked up the road for a moment, and then sat down on the lower step, tucking her skirt beneath her.

He stood for a moment and then sat down again himself.

'I'm not sure what we're going to do,' she said. 'It's been a very strange time.'

He was quiet. 'Hard when you lose somebody. I lost a friend a while back, we were supposed to go into business

318

together, and after that I was stuck, didn't know what to do, I just kept thinking about him. Missing him.'

'What did you do?'

He put his hat down on the ground and spread his hands. 'This is it. I'm heading out west, see what'll happen. I got this letter delivered to me by mistake, this man talking about the gold in California. I sent the letter on, but I thought, that's a sign. There I was, wondering what to do, and then here's a letter, not even meant for me.' He coughed. 'I believe in signs, you see. That's what I believe in. They'd call it superstition but that's alright. When I'm at a place where I'm stuck I look for a sign. You see them when you're looking for them.'

Apparently embarrassed, he picked up the hat again, and put it on. 'I wouldn't always admit it but since you speak to the dead . . .'

'What other sorts of signs?' she said.

'Anything. You see a person, you hear a word. The weather is one way or another. I believe there's an order to the world and it reveals itself to those who pay attention. That's what to look for when you're not sure what you're doing in life.'

He reminded her of Calvin. His fair hair and the way he talked. 'When did you last see him?' she said. 'Calvin?'

He took on a distant look. 'Oh. Long time ago. Twenty years. We were boys. Then his father had this falling out, with my grandfather.'

'Your grandfather was his grandfather too?'

'That's right. Our fathers were brothers.'

'When did your grandfather die?'

'Oh. A long while back now.' He gave her a half-smile. 'It was a shame, that feud. He was a fierce old man, our grandfather, but he loved his family. Would've probably wanted to know Calvin better. He hadn't seen him since he was three or four years old.' Then his voice cracked. He cleared his throat in that way men did, sometimes, when they were scared that they had shown too much emotion. 'Anyway. He died a long while back.'

'What was his name?' said Maggie.

'Oh,' he said. He reached into his pocket, and took out a small tin of tobacco, flicked it open with his thumb. 'His name was Ethan.'

FORTY-TWO

It was possible to believe and not believe something at the same time. It was easy. They must have known, some of the guests. They must have known in their hearts that the raps and cracks were coming from beneath the table. That there was a string attached to the bell. That the Fox sisters already *knew* the name of their dead husband, because it had been written down on a piece of paper and given to the hotel.

But they could ignore that, they could put it away, because they knew as well – they felt, they were *sure* – that there was a truth at the heart of it. A revelation. A voice speaking only to them, a love that outlasted the body, or an anger.

Miss Kelly had seen the man too, and had not told Maggie. Had not told anyone. Maggie turned this over in her mind, with a feeling that shifted from anger to relief and back again. She remembered back to the awful weeks after Hannah had been hurt, but she did not remember thinking of Miss Kelly at all. Which was strange, in a way: had she never wondered whether her teacher might have seen him too? If she had seen her again after that day, would she even have thought to ask?

She had been frightened of Miss Kelly. She had laughed at her with the other children. She had not wanted to be alone with her.

If only she had thought of her as a real person, and not an object of scorn or fear or pity, perhaps she might have gone back to the school a few days later and asked. Miss Kelly was there, on that land, every day. It was such a simple question: have you seen him too?

Who could say how many people there might be, all over the country, the world, seeing strange things, and never telling anybody. Afraid to tell anybody, in case they were locked up or laughed at or cast out. It was dangerous to stray too far from the crowd. There were things that were not supposed to be spoken of. There were voices that nobody wanted to hear.

She would go to Ohio. She would tell Leah, today. She had found the thing that she knew how to do, and it was not cooking or cleaning or solitary prayer. It was not writing letters or making speeches. It was this.

She would probably not change laws, change the world, like Amy and Elizabeth, but she would cause a small disturbance, disrupt the order of things, and perhaps that was worth doing.

Miss Kelly was right. The minister had been angry with her. Maggie had stolen something that was supposed to be his.

You have strayed from the Christian path, he told her. But had she?

What was the difference, between what he did and what she did?

All those faiths, all their languages and rules and places to go, and their books, their thousands of pages of stories, the laws and sermons. When you took it all away, they had one idea, Maggie thought, all of them, just one idea, one promise:

we do not really die.

I will show you. Listen.

AFTERWORD

This story is inspired by the real lives of the Fox sisters, but it is a work of fiction. I have played around with the facts and changed timelines. I like to think that Maggie and Kate would understand, since they had a casual relationship with the truth themselves.

THESE THINGS REALLY HAPPENED:

On the evening of 31 March 1848, a crowd of people gathered at a small family home in Hydesville, a hamlet in the state of New York. It was the house of John Fox, who lived there with his wife and two youngest daughters, Maggie and Kate. The neighbors had gathered on hearing reports that the house was full of strange raps and knocks that could not be explained. In front of these guests, Kate and Maggie appeared to communicate with these sounds, calling out questions to which the answers were rapped out. These responses were pieced together to tell a story: the sounds were supposedly being made by the spirit of a peddler who had been murdered in the house several years before, and buried in the cellar. The murderer was even named – Mr. Bell.

Shortly after this night, an enterprising journalist called E. E. Lewis published an account of the events, with testimonies from many of those who had been present. All of the witnesses claimed they were astonished by what they had seen, and declared that they could not explain it.

This evening is widely considered to have been the birth of 'Spiritualism', a religious movement based on the belief that the spirits of the dead are able to communicate with the living. E. E. Lewis's pamphlet is the most detailed account available of that night, featuring nearly twenty separate testimonies.

The only voices missing are those of Kate and Maggie themselves, whose accounts are not included. But it was Kate and Maggie, with their older sister Leah, who went on to find fame as the spirit-talking Fox sisters, traveling mediums who performed public séances around the country.

Leah was much older than Kate and Maggie. She had been married at the age of fourteen, had a baby at fifteen, and her husband had left by the time she was seventeen. She was in her thirties when the Hydesville events took place, and she seems to have largely taken control of Kate and Maggie's lives, acting as a kind of tour manager as well as becoming a medium herself.

(In her own account of the events in the Hydesville house, published in Mr. Lewis's pamphlet, Kate and Maggie's mother says that Kate was 'about twelve years old', though in fact she had just turned eleven. I have made Kate twelve, here, and changed her birthday. Mrs. Fox describes Maggie as 'in her fifteenth year' – technically true, although her age was actually fourteen. I've made her fifteen here.)

A FEW MORE REAL THINGS:

Before Maggie and Kate were born, their father John Fox did spend almost a decade separated from his wife and oldest children, including Leah. He was, apparently, drinking, gambling and squandering money. But at some point he sobered up, and returned to his family as a serious and devout Methodist. Maggie and Kate were born soon after.

Calvin Brown was a real person, who was informally adopted as a teenager by the Fox family when his own parents died. He traveled with Maggie, Kate and Leah for several years, acting as a kind of guardian and protector. But he became ill while they were touring in Ohio, and never fully recovered. He died in 1853, a few years later than he does in this story.

The sisters did take up residence in Barnum's Hotel in New York (no relationship to P.T. Barnum). Their residency began in June 1850, a little later in their career than I have it here.

The strange fragment that appears in the threatening note sent to Maggie is taken from Cotton Mather's writings on witchcraft and possession in the seventeenth century. Cotton Mather (1663-1728) was a Puritan minister known for his involvement in the Salem Witch Trials.

The Fox family were close friends with Amy Post and her husband Isaac, and lived with them in Rochester before moving to Hydesville. The Posts were well-known radical Quakers who were actively involved in the abolition and women's rights movements of the time. Their home acted as a stop on the Underground Railroad – a network of safe houses maintained by abolitionist activists and sympathizers used to help men and women escaping slavery in the South to reach Canada. The conflict over slavery in the United States was reaching its peak in the 1840s and 50s – the Civil War was only a few years away.

The Posts were also among the first enthusiastic advocates of Spiritualism. In fact, a number of radical thinkers took an interest in it. A decentralized religious practice that could be performed in domestic settings, without institutional approval, and was often led by women, evidently chimed with the progressive politics of the time. Rochester, in particular, was a center for radical politics at exactly the moment that Spiritualism was beginning to thrive, home to noted activists and campaigners like Frederick Douglass and Susan B. Anthony.

As they grew older, Maggie and Kate's relationship with Leah deteriorated. Their personal lives were turbulent and they both had problems with alcohol.

In 1888, after nearly forty years as a Spiritualist medium, Maggie publicly denounced the whole thing as a fraud. She gave a lecture describing how they had used the joints of their toes to make the rapping sounds that occurred in their séances, and how they had used an apple tied to a string to make the knocking sounds first heard in Hydesville. She blamed Leah for manipulating them, controlling their lives and taking advantage of their youth.

In 1889, Maggie took back her confession. She hinted that she had been under pressure to denounce Spiritualism, possibly from members of the Catholic Church, which she had joined, and that she now regretted the 'injustice' she had done to the movement. She attempted to resume her work as a medium, but without much success. Both Kate and Maggie died in relative poverty a few years later.

Historical accounts of the Fox sisters tend to present them as either gifted mediums, or absolute frauds. A thing is true, or it isn't. Somebody lied, or they didn't. But I wonder if it might be more complicated than that—if the *total frauds* version of history is too simple. Their careers almost certainly relied on trickery, but as Fox sisters historian Barbara Weisberg writes: 'If a medium sometimes commits deception, does it mean that he or she always does?'

Where did they get the idea of communicating with spirits to begin with? Séances and Ouija boards are familiar concepts now, but they weren't at the time.

I can't help wondering if the little house in the woods seemed haunted because they were playing games, or if they were playing games because the house seemed haunted.

In 1904, the *Boston Journal* reported that human bones had been found at the Hydesville house, hidden behind a wall in the cellar.

In 1916, the entire house was disassembled and transported to the small community of Lily Dale, a center of Spiritualist belief and activity, even today. It was preserved as a sort of shrine. But in 1955, it burned to the ground in the middle of the night.

In 1960, somebody built a copy of the house on the original site in Hydesville, perhaps imagining it would be a tourist destination. Strangely, that also burned down.

Catherine Barter, 2020

BIBLIOGRAPHY

Talking to the Dead: Kate and Maggie Fox and the Rise of Spiritualism by Barbara Weisberg (HarperCollins, 2004)

Radical Friend: Amy Kirby Post and her Activist Worlds by Nancy A. Hewitt (University of North Carolina Press, 2018)

Radical Spirits: Spiritualism and Women's Rights in Nineteenth Century America (Second Edition) by Ann Braude (Beacon Press, 2001)

Ghosts of Futures Past: Spiritualism and the Cultural Politics of Nineteenth Century America by Molly McGarry (University of California Press, 2012)

The Reluctant Spiritualist: The Life of Maggie Fox by Nancy Rubin Stuart (Harcourt Books, 2005)

. . . and Leah Fox's own very long, self-aggrandizing book, *The Missing Link in Modern Spiritualism* (1885), which is full of completely implausible accounts of spiritual encounters, but does also give a lot of detail about the sisters' careers as mediums.

ACKNOWLEDGEMENTS

I'm very grateful to the historians who have bothered to take the Fox sisters seriously enough to research their stories. The books I relied on are in the bibliography, but I'm especially grateful for Barbara Weisberg's *Talking to the Dead* which brings alive the nuances and complexities of their story with humour and compassion.

Huge thanks to Chloe Sackur and Charlie Sheppard at Andersen Press for allowing me to take this weird turn, and patiently helping me to work out what story I was trying to tell.

Thanks always to my family for all the love and encouragement – I'm very lucky to have you. Thanks to my wonderful agent Laura Williams, and to my colleagues at Housmans Bookshop for being so supportive. Thanks to Fen Coles for ghostly GIFs, and to Rich for generally putting up with it all. I promise it's actually finished this time.

TROUBLE MAKERS

CATHERINE BARTER

SHORTLISTED FOR THE WATERSTONES CHILDREN'S BOOK PRIZE
NOMINATED FOR THE CARNEGIE MEDAL
LONGLISTED FOR THE BRANFORD BOASE AWARD

Fifteen-year-old Alena never really knew her political activist
mother, who died when she was a baby. She has grown up with her
older half-brother Danny and his boyfriend Nick in the east end
of London. Now the area is threatened by a bomber who has been
leaving explosive devices in supermarkets. Against this increasingly
fearful backdrop, Alena seeks to discover
more about her past, while Danny
takes a job working for a controversial
politician. As her family life implodes,
and the threat to Londoners mounts,
Alena starts getting into trouble. Then
she does something truly rebellious . . .

9781783445240